Omega's Trust
Guardian Dragons: Book 2

Aiden Bates & Jill Haven

© 2019
Disclaimer

All rights reserved. No part of this publication may be reproduced, distributed, or transmitted in any form or by any means, including photocopying, recording, or other electronic or mechanical methods, without the prior written permission of the publisher, except in the case of brief quotations embodied in critical reviews and certain other noncommercial uses permitted by copyright law.

This is a work of fiction. Names, places, characters and events are all fictitious for the reader's pleasure. Any similarities to real people, places, events, living or dead are all coincidental.

This book contains sexually explicit content that is intended for ADULTS ONLY (+18).

Contents

- Chapter 1 - Lucas 4
- Chapter 2 - Lucas 9
- Chapter 3 - Tarin 13
- Chapter 4 - Lucas 17
- Chapter 5 - Tarin 21
- Chapter 6 - Lucas 25
- Chapter 7 - Tarin 30
- Chapter 8 - Lucas 35
- Chapter 9 - Tarin 40
- Chapter 10 - Lucas 45
- Chapter 11 - Tarin 49
- Chapter 12 - Lucas 54
- Chapter 13 - Lucas 59
- Chapter 14 -Tarin 64
- Chapter 15 – Lucas.. 68
- Chapter 16 - Lucas 74
- Chapter 17 - Tarin 80
- Chapter 18 - Tarin 85
- Chapter 19 - Lucas 89
- Chapter 20 - Tarin 94
- Chapter 21 - Lucas 98
- Chapter 22 - Tarin 103
- Chapter 23 - Lucas 107
- Chapter 24 - Lucas 111
- Chapter 25 - Tarin 117
- Chapter 26 - Lucas 122
- Chapter 27 - Tarin 125
- Chapter 28 - Lucas 129
- Chapter 29 - Tarin 135
- Chapter 30 - Lucas 139
- Chapter 31 - Tarin 144
- Chapter 32 – Lucas.. 147

Chapter 33 - Tarin 152
Chapter 34 - Lucas 156
Chapter 35 - Tarin 160
Chapter 36 - Lucas 163

Chapter 1 - Lucas

I sat across the table from a grim-looking gentleman with short gray hair and a hairline that had receded far enough back that just shaving it all off was probably the dignified option at this point. He was sixty-three, according to the dossier in front of me, and worth about sixty million dollars. Maybe when you were that rich you stopped caring whether you looked desperate to keep your hair or not.

Not that there was that much more dignity in trying to decide if a potential client would look better with a shaved head, I guess. Still, with a nicely trimmed beard he'd have a kind of stern daddy look to him that, I admit, he could easily have pulled off. And the way he was looking at me, I wasn't ready to dismiss the idea that he was thinking something along the same lines.

"Mr. Kelley," my partner—well, technically, my boss—said as he flipped through the file in front of him, "I believe Camelot Legal would be a perfect fit for a case like yours. We've got over seventy years as the top rated firm in Atlanta for trademark cases, and I have to say this looks very promising. We could win this, hands down."

Mr. Kelley's eyes lingered on me just a moment longer. He blinked slowly, and turned his attention to Gregg. "That's what I've been told. I hear your firm goes all the way back."

Gregg had a great smile, the kind that put clients at ease, made them feel confident about him. I admit that I'd practiced that smile in the mirror, trying to match it. A good smile and the confidence of someone with golf balls for nuts and what some of the staff called 'big dick energy' seemed to be the key to getting ahead in the firm. "Camelot has been the firm's name for the past hundred years, but before that we were Smith, Gray, and Fine—and we were in this very town when it was Terminus. Before that, our founders came over on the first boats. Yes, sir."

"Made in America, as it were," Kelley said.

Truth was, Camelot was even older. The founding partners had been pilgrims from Scotland, where at the time it had been a lot less formal but they'd practiced law there as well. To hear the promotional materials tell it, the firm had been around since about the time the profession was invented. I didn't think that was true, but clients did love the story.

"I'm gonna give you a number," Gregg said, flipping pages to find a blank one so that he could take out his golden pen and scribble the retainer fee down, "and I want you to keep in mind that once the trademark dispute is settled you'll be awarded damages and Camelot will go for the throat. We always do."

"Ironic, isn't it?" Kelley murmured.

Gregg ripped the paper out of the legal pad, folded it, and passed it to the man. "Sure is."

Gregg also had a certain tone that most clients didn't get a chance to learn—the tone he used when he was full of shit. He had no idea what was ironic about what he'd said. I did, because these things honestly always got just a little under my skin. Camelot of legend was a kingdom led by a just king, with a round table of knights to keep the peace and see to it that all were treated fairly, right?

Camelot Legal was… not that.

What they were, to me at least, was a significant stepping stone that I was lucky to be precariously balanced on for the moment.

Kelley opened the paper, glanced at the number, and gave a nod. "Seems reasonable, and doable."

"You can't have made a better decision," Gregg assured him, flashing those white teeth again. He leaned over to pull the standard paperwork from his briefcase. "Let me just get a few technicalities out of the way, and then maybe you can let me treat you to a drink so we can discuss the details of the case in a more relaxing environment. Offices are stuffy, don't you think? If I don't miss my mark, I'd take you for a whiskey man. That right?"

"Bourbon," Kelley corrected. His eyes were on me again. They were a nice shade of brown, light, almost amber. "And, if I may make a request?"

"Shoot," Gregg said as he pushed a stack of papers already marked with little tabs where the signatures would go over to Kelley. "Nothing's too good for our clients at Camelot."

Kelley pointed at me. "I'd like young Mr. Lucas here to represent my company in the dispute."

My heart thudded against my chest, trying to flee the room without me.

Gregg had frozen, his smile plastered on. He blinked once. "Lucas will certainly assist me, he'll be part of my team. He's amazing, full of insight, and *fresh* out of law school so he's hungry. Definitely."

Kelley had the kind of smile that probably made small animals start looking for a place to hide. "I think I wasn't clear," he said. "I'd like Lucas here in the courtroom, pleading our case, doing the work. Assuming you'd like Templar Industries as a client."

I tried not to look at Gregg. Out of the corner of my eye, the vein on his neck seemed to swell a little. I wasn't even a junior partner. I was *part* of a few teams, but mostly I'd been relegated to research and fetching stuff. Honestly? I didn't even know why I was in this room, except that Gregg's usual go-to was on vacation.

He steepled his fingers. "Mr. Kelley," he said, still smiling like a champ, "believe me when I say that Lucas here"—he clapped a hand on my shoulder that squeezed just a bit too tight—"is a valuable asset to any legal team. But he's never been in a courtroom."

"I have," I corrected. "Twice."

"Twice, he's been in a courtroom," Gregg ground out, chuckling as his thumb dug into my shoulder. "For something like this, you really want a more experienced, savvy *partner* doing battle for you. I can assure you, Lucas will be—"

"Mr. Staucher," Kelley interrupted, "it's been my experience that the cleverest people speak the least, and comport themselves with grace, clarity, and dignity when possible. I've been in this room for two hours, and while I'm sure you're quite skilled, it's important to Templar Industries and myself personally that we select the right representation for our cases. This and others. Lucas here has the right… 'vibe' you might say, that seems more in line with Templar's values. He'll represent us. And that's my final word on the matter."

I desperately wished I could disappear into thin air, and wipe everyone's memory of this meeting. No such luck, however hard I tried.

Gregg bobbed his head slowly, too many times before he turned that smile—now vicious—on me. "Well, Lucas?" he asked, strained. "What do you say? Ready to step up to the big leagues? That would make you just about the youngest, fastest-moving little lawyer in the south, I'd say."

Kelley was watching me, waiting expectantly for my agreement. If I said yes, Gregg would probably find a way to have me dropped from the firm. Hell, he might have me killed—it was hard to say what he was capable of, I'd mostly managed to go unnoticed at the firm so far. If I said no, I might lose us a corporate client and that would definitely get me fired.

I erred on the side of money for the executives. After all, at the end of the day they were ones signing paychecks. "I'd be happy to," I said. I almost flashed my own version of 'big dick energy smile' at Kelly but thought better of it and gave him a somber nod instead. "Thank you very much for your confidence, Mr. Kelley. I will do my utmost."

Kelley pushed the paperwork back to Gregg. "See to it that this arrangement is in the contracts. I'll have my people swing by this evening to sign everything."

He stood, and buttoned his gray suit coat over his vest and shirt. All hands exchanged brief, firm shakes, and with that he left. It was just me and Gregg in the room.

"What the fuck was that about?" Gregg demanded as soon as Kelley was out of sight. He rounded on me and jabbed a finger at my chest. "Who the fuck do you think you are?"

"I didn't do anything," I countered, waving at the door Kelley had left through. "He just… I don't know what he's thinking. You're right, I've barely got any experience in the courtroom, you're the better choice."

"*I have,*" Gregg parroted. "*Twice.* Don't fucking contradict me in front of a client, you fucking maggot. Especially one worth that much money. You know how huge Templar Industries is? They've got fucking politicians in their pockets. If you think you're gonna side-swipe me on this, motherfucker, let me tell you something—I'll have your fucking balls on toothpicks and made up like Swedish meatballs to watch you eat them, you fucking get me?"

It wasn't that Camelot didn't *have* an HR department, it was just that they answered to the senior partners. And while Gregg was not technically a *senior* partner, his father was.

"I'll convince him it's better to have you representing him," I promised. "Really, Gregg, I will. That's way too much pressure for me, I'm already about to shit my pants over it, so… it's cool, all right? I'll figure it out."

He slammed his briefcase closed and snatched it off the table to storm out of the room. "See that you fucking do. Fucking prick…"

The door was on a hydraulic hinge to keep it from closing too loudly, but he nearly pulled the handle off trying to before he let it go and stalked away. Brenda, a paralegal with a cubicle just outside the conference room, grimaced on my behalf through the window, rolled her eyes, and mimed jerking off.

I grinned back at her. It was something, anyway; a small dose of comradery in an otherwise desolate environment. I gathered my briefcase, and left the conference room when I was sure Gregg was far enough away to be either out for a drink or back in his office to no doubt plot his bloody revenge against me… existing, I guess.

"That was insane," Brenda whispered as I passed her cubicle. "What the fuck?"

I winced. "Could you actually hear him?"

She nodded. "Something about Swedish balls?"

"Something like that," I agreed. "I can't really discuss the details. Confidential and all that. You wanna grab a cocktail after work?"

"I want so many cocktails." She winked.

Truth was, I would tell Brenda everything. I always did.

For the moment, though, gossip was out of the question. And I had more research to do. Just in case Kelley didn't change his mind.

I flopped down at my own cubicle, because I did not rate an office just yet, and pulled up Templar Industries to see what I could find out about them that wasn't in my dossier. Gregg wasn't going to share his, and I wasn't going to ask.

Two years I'd languished at Camelot Legal. Well, languish probably would be a strong word. I started at the bottom like any young lawyer freshly past the bar, mostly dealing with paperwork, contract law, and things that didn't avoid the courtroom. I'd taken two civil suits only because no one else would and because shit rolls downhill.

Frankly, if I could survive Gregg, something like this could be huge. Though I wasn't lying about shitting my pants. Two appearances in local civil court was not the same thing as potentially ending up before the state supreme court to argue precedence for trademark law. I wasn't sweating from nervousness. *No.* The office was just hot that day.

I had gotten about fifteen minutes into pulling up relevant case law when my desk phone rang. It rarely did that. It was an internal call. "Lucas Warren," I answered.

"Mr. Drake would like a word," the secretary said.

I choked on my own tongue. "Sorry, I… Mr. Drake? This is Lucas *Warren*. Floor five? I'm a… well, I'm nobody. You might want Lucas De—"

"Mr. Drake is aware of who you are," she assured me. "I have the right Lucas. Please head up right away."

She hung up, so I hung up, but I couldn't quite get out of the seat right away. The phone would ring any second with a curt apology for the misunderstanding. When it didn't, I practically leapt out of my chair to get to the elevator.

I'd already kept the owner of Camelot Legal Services waiting half a minute.

Chapter 2 - Lucas

I only stopped long enough to snag a paper towel in the bathroom and use it to wipe my forehead and neck. I wasn't normally this sweaty; it had been a fucking day already, and it wasn't even noon.

Mr. Drake's secretary was a slim-looking woman with black hair that hung in a bob around a triangular face and was shinier than any hair I had ever seen in my life. I had never laid eyes on her before—I had never been above the eighth floor and this was the fifteenth floor. The top floor. The place where the boss of bosses had an office that sprawled out to take up the entire level, with the small exceptions of a lavish washroom and a small waiting area with his secretary's desk.

"I'm, uh…"

She eyed me. "Lucas Warren." She said it like she was providing me with obvious information. Which she was—I'd basically forgotten my own name. She waved a pen at the door. "Mr. Drake will see you."

Yes. Yes, he would. My mind swirled with all the horrible possibilities. It was Gregg—it had to be. He'd called up and said that I'd stuck my newbie fingers where they had no business being, and that I was going to fuck up a huge potential account for the firm and Templar Industries was a fifty-billion dollar a year company and Mr. Drake was going to personally fire me and probably make sure I never worked in law anywhere, ever again.

My hands were shaking as I turned the elaborate iron handle of his office door and poked my head through first. "Mr. Drake?" I asked. "You… wanted to see me?"

"Come in, Lucas," he called.

I had seen pictures of Mr. Drake. Once, I saw a video. It was for the holiday party. For the most part, he stayed out of things. He was an attorney, of course, but the last time he'd taken a case himself was way before my time. He was old, I knew that. Well… in his seventies, at least, and he was a something-something-the fourth, who inherited the firm from his father and his father and so on going all the way back.

For a man in his seventies… he was in remarkably good form.

He was standing by his desk, pouring a drink. I closed the door quietly behind me and tried to avoid stepping on the immaculate ebony floor as I crossed a room big enough to fit a football field in. At least, it seemed that way. The ceilings were vaulted, at least twenty feet, with elaborate gold crown molding that led to stone columns. Cavernous—I never really had a clear idea of what that word meant but this place definitely captured it.

And Mr. Drake?

They say that some people have 'gravitas'. Mr. Drake had that. He had his own little planet worth of it. The closer I got, the more I could actually feel—physically *feel*—a kind of power radiating off him like his own personal sun. He was tall, a little over six feet at least, certainly taller than me, with jet black hair swept back into something bygone and classy in a way I hadn't seen outside of a photo before. Wings of white swept back from his temples, and where I kind of expected more wrinkles and spots at his age, instead he had skin that just looked weathered and rugged. His bright blue eyes sparkled with amusement when he turned to offer me a glass of something amber colored and probably worth more than I got paid.

I averted my eyes from his chest when he faced me. There was muscle under his shirt and jacket. That just showed me his hands, though—one hidden in his pocket, the other grasping his own glass. That visible hand? Sexy as fuck. Manicured nails, thick, strong fingers, and just the right dusting of fine hair over his knuckles and the back. He was hairy, I gathered, and usually that wasn't especially attractive—I didn't mind it, but didn't look for it—but on him it somehow made me want to see him with his clothes off.

"So," he said, his voice booming in the *cavernous* room, "you're Lucas Warren."

"Um," I said. And then got the rest out. "Yes. Yes, sir, I'm Lucas Warren, sir. It's an honor to meet you, I never imagined... I mean..."

"Relax, son," he said. "Have a seat. Please."

I took that as an order, and nearly spilled my drink putting my ass in a chair. Relaxing was harder to do under orders, turns out. "Mr. Drake," I said, "I just want to say that I've spoken with Gregg and I fully understand that he is the more qualified attorney to represent Templar Industries and I already have a plan worked out to convince Mr. Kelley that I'm—"

"I didn't call you up for that," he said as he pulled his own chair out of the way. "We won't be representing Templar Industries, Lucas. I don't like how they do business. Distasteful. They can go somewhere else. I've already made the call myself."

Relief mixed with mortal panic made for a violent cocktail in my brain. Surely, if Mr. Drake had decided, then I was in the clear—except, I didn't think Gregg would see it that way. "Okay," I said. "Then... if I may ask, sir... why...?"

"Did I want to see you?" He offered. He smiled as he sipped his drink. "Gregg... is it *Stancher?*"

"Staucher," I offered, and winced. "I mean... I think probably you could call him anything you wanted?"

That made Mr. Drake laugh. It was the open, genuine laugh of a man with literally nothing to fear. Probably not even death or taxes, by the look of him. "I guess I could at that. I'll remember that one. Anyway, he did call one of the senior partners, who in turn did call me. I was surprised that Mr. Kelley took such a keen interest in one of our fresh attorneys. So I had a look at your file. You've done good work for us."

Now that really was confusing. "Sir? I mean... thank you. I'm just not..." I started to set my drink aside, and thought better of it. Instead, I sipped it. Liquid gold hummed down my throat, spreading gentle warmth. I stared at the glass. "Wow. That's... is that whiskey? It tastes amazing."

"It's 212 years old," Mr. Drake said. Casually. Like he had hundreds of them and they cost him a few pennies to pick up at the liquor store.

If I could have, and if it wouldn't be rude, I would have reverse-swallowed the stuff back into the cup and poured it back where it rightfully belonged. I was a nobody—I didn't drink two-hundred-year-old whiskey. It was wasted on me. "Wow. Wow… um, I don't want to get into any trouble, sir. I can't tell you what it means to meet you, but I think there's been some kind of mistake? Because my file is all just… filing stuff, and legal research that any paralegal could do—not that I'm complaining, I'm really not, it's a blessing to be here and I know the competition was fierce—and there were these two civil cases but honestly it didn't do anything for the firm, it was just a throwaway case and took like a few weeks each. I don't want to misrepresent myself, is the thing. I would hate to waste your time."

"You're a nervous sort, are you?" he asked.

"Only when it really counts," I replied. I kicked myself inwardly. Awesome. Was it too soon to blame the whiskey?

But Mr. Drake was smiling still, maybe even a little more. "Lucas," he said, "you've got a good sense of humor. That's important in this business. Not a lot of people realize it. And you're a looker, too. That doesn't hurt in the courtroom. Let me ask you something—where do you see yourself in, say, five years? Got a plan? Thinking of… settling down, getting married, family, anything like that?"

Now, my employment law was pretty weak where it didn't pertain directly to my job. But I was pretty sure that was the sort of thing an employer wasn't supposed to ask. Or maybe, that was just for interviews? I did have the job already. Still, the answer was easy enough to give honestly. "I hadn't planned on it, sir. Not that I'm opposed, I'm just… I'm only twenty-eight, you know? I feel like it's a little early. I'm focused on my career. I hope that I'll be good enough to maybe…" Dared I try and swing this in my favor? That, I decided to blame on the whiskey. "…I'd like to make junior partner. I realize five years isn't a lot of time, really it's more of a ten-year—"

"I think you could do it," he said.

This was all so confusing. "Why? Sorry—I don't mean to… why do you think that?"

"A feeling," he said. "I tend to trust them. Let me ask you something, Lucas, and forgive me if it sounds inappropriate, I assure you it isn't meant inappropriately—I'd like to take you to dinner sometime. This Friday? After work. There's a restaurant uptown that makes a veal steak you'd never believe if you didn't eat it yourself. I'd love to have a longer talk about your future."

Reading is a room is an essential skill for any attorney to have, and usually I had it in spades. But at that particular moment I could have sworn that Mr. Caleb Drake was asking me out on more than just a work dinner. That had to be wishful thinking, though. Not that I was wishing for it or anything. I mean, he was fifty years older than me, almost, even if he did look unthinkably hot lounging in that chair across from me, his finger stroking the crystal of his tumbler in ways that made me wonder what else he could do with it.

I had to decide, and quickly. So I chose the path that potentially led to career advancement. After all, if it really was just a work dinner then it could be a huge opportunity. Maybe he wanted to mentor me. Why look that gift horse in the mouth? And while the ethics of fucking one's way to the top were certainly questionable—well, all right, there was no question about the ethics, I guess, they were pretty clear-cut on the matter—I did find myself thinking there were worse people to have to fuck to get there if that's what this was. And, I'd been single since before I started law school.

"Friday," I said. "Sure. Yes. That would be."

He arched an eyebrow.

"That would be great," I corrected. "Nice, I mean. Or… not nice, I mean more like professional. Or… I accept your invitation, Mr. Drake. Jesus. Sorry."

"Perfectly all right," he said. "Finish that up and get back to work. I'm gonna have a case on your desk in the next couple of hours. I think Mr. Snatch has got a bit too much work on his plate."

I wasn't about to beg the leader of Camelot Legal not to do *anything*, much less give me work, even if it was one of Gregg's accounts. "Yes, sir. Thank you, sir."

"Lucas, call me Caleb."

"Absolutely, sir." I shot the remaining whiskey. It seemed sacrilegious, but he had said to go back to work. "Caleb, I mean, sir."

Mr. Drake—*Caleb*—chuckled softly and waved me off. "See you Friday. Dress well, it's a nice place."

I stood, almost offered my hand but realized he hadn't offered me his so instead I did a strange sort of half-bow, half-wave. "I will." With that, I scurried to the door. I could feel his eyes on me the whole way. In fact, even as I rushed past his secretary and to the elevator, somehow I could *still* feel them on me.

What the fuck was my life about today?

Chapter 3 - Tarin

"I've got a lead on another omega," I told Reece when we were finally alone. The Spitfire Ranch was sprawling, but somehow it seemed that between myself, Reece, two other dragons, the midwife-to-be Mercy Brave, Reece's mate Matthew, their impossible daughter Danni—the first female dragon in eight hundred years, though we were yet to see if she could actually shift—and Matthew's friend Yuri, the place felt... cramped. There was just the one house with a second being built, as well as a barn loft where I lived, but everyone tended to congregate in what was unofficially considered Reece and Matthew's place.

Reece looked up as I pulled the door to the barn closed behind me. He was in the process of repairing a tractor—as if it were remotely necessary, or he'd ever laid hands on the inside of a human machine before. The ranch was only a ranch in the technical sense—in practical terms, there were no livestock, no crops, no anything related to *being* a ranch. Not yet, anyway. Reece had some wild ideas about that.

"Did you hear me?" I asked. "My people in Atlanta have a bead on another omega."

Reece nodded. "I heard you."

"So?" I pressed, closing the distance between us. I peered into the mess of metal that was the tractor's engine under the raised hood. "We should go get him."

Reece sighed, and picked through his tools. "By get him, do you mean talk to him?"

"I mean bring him here, where he'll be safe," I clarified. Although I did feel like 'get him' pretty much covered it all.

"Is he a ranch hand, or a farmer?" Reece wondered. "Someone with an agrarian skillset that would be of use here? Or, for that matter, entice him to relocate his life to a ranch?"

I waved a hand at the barn walls and the land beyond it. "This isn't really a ranch, Reece. It's a base. A haven. The whole point of it is to build a new community. Dragons and the sacred omegas, midwives—isn't it?"

He picked up a ratchet but apparently thought better of it. "I should review the manual again, I think. This place is not a ranch or farm, no. Not yet. But if it does not become that, we will arouse suspicion from the surrounding villages. Even if they only believe us to be wealthy pretenders, it will spread, and our enemies will seek us out. Obviously, Tarin, I am in favor of collecting more omegas if they are out there to collect—but you cannot simply go to and get them, and expect them to come peacefully. They must be *recruited*, not snatched, or this will never work. Not for long, at any rate. Not as long as we need it to."

"I didn't mean kidnap him," I muttered. "But we should reach out. Maybe send Matthew to—"

"No." Reece folded his arms over his chest. His nostrils flared once. "Matthew does not leave the ranch without me, and I do not leave without Danni, and I am not taking Danni abroad."

I held my hands up, and waited until Reece calmed to say anything else. I understood, of course, but when it came to his mate, he was more dragon than man. "I spoke out of turn," I said. "But we have to send someone."

"If you believe you can convince him," Reece said, "and you agree not to perform any abductions, then you could go."

Well, that was a rub. "Atlanta is Calavastrix's territory."

Reece gave a thoughtful grunt. "True enough. But that merely means you're the only person suited to go. Calavastrix, to my knowledge, spends the majority of his time in his human form. He enjoys the lavishness of human luxury. He runs a law firm, I believe, but I do not recall the name of it. Sasha would, more likely. His brood brother has dealings. I have not crossed paths with Calavastrix in more than a century."

"Camelot Legal Services," I provided.

He arched an eyebrow at me.

"I don't go near him, but I keep my ears open," I said. "That's... sort of part of the issue."

"What exactly is the issue?"

I rubbed the back of my neck. "Now, hear me out first—you and I both know that if the elders get their claws on the omegas, they'll start farming for mates or something. They'll all be better off with us and this new 'society' you're thinking about than they will be with them."

"You are concerned that Calavastrix will lodge a formal claim on the omega?" Reece frowned. "That seems a reasonable assumption, if he were made aware."

"The omega in question works for him," I said. "Or, rather, works in his firm. Or at least the building, there are four other businesses there, on the lower floors. He's got a law degree, though, so it tracks. My people have spotted him coming in and out a few times. Kid named Lucas Warren. Direct descendant of Bennet Warren, who went off the radar around 1505. Guess his family settled in Ireland, then shipped off to Georgia about the eighteenth century."

Reece's attitude changed instantly. "You believe it would be wise to collect an omega out from under the nose of Calavastrix the Storm? Tarin."

Here came the lecture. For all Reece claimed to be an outcast in spirit, he still had so much of the old world in him. There was no point avoiding it so I clasped my hands behind my back to wait it out.

"If we are to expect any hope of success in this venture," Reece began, "we must rely on a degree of discretion. If Calavastrix were to become aware of your presence, or the presence of this omega—if indeed he is not yet aware—do you not think he would hunt a missing omega down to the ends of the Earth, and perhaps lay utter waste to those foolish enough to steal his treasure from within his own abode? Or even alert the rest of the elders, or the Ancients, to our activities and bring down the wrath of them all?"

"However discreet we are," I countered, "this place doesn't work with one mated dragon and a couple of outcasts. It's already risky, Reece. We have to grow. Don't you think that if we had enough omegas here, and enough dragons, that we'd have the leverage to chart our own course? What's more important to the Ancients, you think—tradition and law, or life and a future for our people?"

Reece snorted softly and leaned against the tractor. "Honestly? I'm not sure those two things would be considered mutually exclusive. If they saw us as a legitimate enough threat to the natural order as they see it, they might elect to kill every dragon here and take the omegas for themselves. I am not opposed to recruiting more omegas, if you will, Tarin. I am simply reluctant to approach this particular one."

"Well, you're not gonna single-handedly revive our race with Matthew," I spat. "He can only have so many babies, so fast, and each one is a mouth to feed and a young dragon just waiting to set fire to something and call attention. One you can manage. Two? Three?"

Maybe that was a mistake. Reece radiated heat, his fire glowing in his eyes. "I will manage my family," he said darkly. "You came here asking for permission, it seemed. It is denied."

"You don't run this place," I pointed out.

"My mate owns this place in my name," he said calmly. "If there is a leader here, it is I. Do not bring the wrath of the Elders and Ancients down on our heads, Tarin. Doing so will endanger my family. I trust that the implications are clear?"

I'd been in my human form long enough that my dragon was a distant thing, locked away nearly three hundred years ago so that each passing century made me more and more man, less and less dragon. But dragons were jealous creatures, prone to infighting and politicking. I couldn't help a flare of suspicion that Reece preferred to be the only dragon on the ranch actually making a family.

That wasn't fair, of course. Just an old lizard instinct. I brushed it aside. He was right—I'd come to get permission. And he'd said no because he was thinking of his family. I could understand that well enough.

"How about if—" I started, unwilling to entirely drop the subject yet, but the barn door creaked open. It was Sasha, his green eyes dark with concern.

"We have a visitor," he said. "Reece, you should probably come and meet him."

"Who is he?" Reece asked.

Sasha chuffed. "Wolven. Pack leader. He wishes to discuss peace terms."

"I was not aware we were at war," Reece grumbled. "This is no doubt about Joseph. I am coming. Tarin—this discussion is ended, yes?"

I looked away, and let him leave.

The discussion was ended, yes.

But just because I'd come to ask permission, didn't mean I actually *needed* permission. Reece had valid points, and I took them into consideration as I left the barn and headed down to the end of the long driveway leading to what would one day be a small courtyard around which the houses were arrayed. Where my car was.

It had been centuries since I took to the skies. It would have been faster to fly to Atlanta, of course, but Reece had said it himself. I was the ideal candidate to retrieve Lucas Warren.

That was really all the permission I cared to get.

Chapter 4 - Lucas

"You're really going to do this?" Brenda asked. I'd invited her to go shopping after work the day I was supposed to meet Mr. Drake for dinner, and now she was helping me make decisions. "The blue tie is cuter. But seriously, you do have any idea what happens to *women* when they sleep with their bosses?"

"I'm not going to sleep with him," I insisted for the tenth time, and began tying the blue paisley tie. Brenda was no fashionista but then neither was I—a second opinion from anyone was better than my own, probably. "We're going to have dinner and talk about my future with Camelot and if things go in that direction I'll just politely excuse myself."

Brenda gave a mirthless laugh. "You do that and you're going to learn a hard lesson about powerful men. Look, I hope that it's just a business dinner and that you get showered with promotions and that you remember me when you're a big-shot lawyer because I need a raise to finish law school—but honey, men like Drake don't swoop up plucky new attorneys and turn them into princes. Believe me, I've seen this story a million times."

I adjusted the tie, folded my collar down and briefly reconsidered my entire life. "You don't think this all looks... I don't know, like I'm trying to hard?"

"That depends," she mused. "You going for top or bottom?"

"Har har," I groaned and turned to face her directly instead of watching her in the mirror. "What am I supposed to do? Say no? I have to at least meet with him, he could get me blacklisted basically anywhere in the world. If I don't go, I may as well pick another career, except he could probably make sure I never work anywhere again. I'll be flipping burgers at a fast food joint for the rest of my life. Actually, we represent about a dozen fast food chains so..."

She stood and took my cheeks in her hands to make me look her in the eye. "Lucas, this is exactly what I mean. There's an imbalance of power here; even if he was straight up husband material that would be too much pressure. What happens if you turn out to really like him, but then can basically never leave?"

I took her hands away and held them. "I know that you're concerned, and I know you're just looking out. I'm not going to lie—Mr. Drake is... really hot. I'm not interested in being anyone's house husband or kept boy, and while the prospect of fucking my way to the top in record time is admittedly attractive—"

"So stupid," she muttered.

"—it would be *stupid* and I know better," I agreed. "So text me at about eight, or eight fifteen, and if things are getting creepy I will make an excuse and a quick exit."

"And then go straight to HR and get a lawyer," she suggested.

I grimaced as I let her hands go. "You know, the trick about suing a law firm is that they're a *law firm.* I don't want to get branded as the guy who can't play nice."

"Wow," Brenda said, eyes wide. She snorted. "Welcome to our world, you're officially an honorary woman."

I gave myself one last cursory look in the mirror before I grabbed my keys. Brenda walked out with me, and when we reached the sidewalk outside my condo building, she gave me a long, tight hug. "I'll text at eight o'clock sharp that your dog just went to the vet after breaking a leg trying to save your dying mother who is in the hospital."

I laughed, and let her go. "Yeah, okay. If I don't text back, I'm tied up in his gold-plated basement. Otherwise, I'll let you know how it's going."

Brenda shook her head slowly. "Please don't joke like that."

"See you tomorrow for brunch," I said. "I'll let you know how big his dick is."

"You're not funny," she reminded me. "Record everything just in case. See you then."

I was early to Madison's, the reservations-only, booked-out-six-months-in-advance, high-end steakhouse where you could allegedly order things like giraffe or lion steaks if you had an in with the chef. Ethical considerations aside, the place could paper their walls with awards and stars and supposedly Gordon Ramsay dropped by every time he was in the area.

Expensive didn't touch this place. Without Mr. Drake, I couldn't even get in to wait. Instead I stood on the sidewalk, watching the minutes tick by. I'd been so anxious when I left the condo that it didn't even occur to me that the drive was only going to take fifteen minutes. It was closer to my place than I realized.

About fifteen minutes before we were meant to meet, I sensed a familiar presence like some kind of Jedi—that gentle, radiating sense of warmth that tickled something in my stomach. I turned, confused, but expecting to see Mr. Drake standing there watching me like the heroine in some romantic comedy or maybe a Lifetime original thriller about a stalker boss. Instead, though, it was someone else.

He was dressed in a cheap suit, wearing tennis shoes, and cloaked in a tan wool trench coat. A dark brown trilby hat was tilted forward on his head. I had a sudden flashback to my childhood, watching the Dick Tracy movie with my mom before I was old enough to have good judgment. He was older, handsome, his jaw covered with salt-and-pepper stubble. It was uncanny the way he exuded the same kind of presence that Mr. Drake did, and I was struck speechless trying to figure it out.

When I didn't speak, he did. "Pardon me," he said. "You must be Lucas, right? Lucas Warren?"

I glanced at the door to Madison's warily, checking that the host at the door was in sight. "Yes, I am. Sorry, have we met? I'm really bad with faces."

He smiled, and I had to make myself stay on guard. "I don't believe so. My name is Tarin."

I returned the smile but slipped my hands into my pockets. "Nice to meet you, Tarin. I'd chat but I'm headed in. Meeting someone."

He glanced at the door, then at me. Something crossed his face too quickly to read it properly, but it looked almost like panic. "Yes," he said. "With Caleb Drake?"

"I..." How would he know? Was there already a rumor mill running? I didn't recognize Tarin—who hadn't given a last name, which I found strange—from the building. "Who are you again? I mean, what do you do?"

"I'm Mr. Drake's driver," he said. "Sorry, I should have opened with that. He didn't give a very good description, just said you'd be out front waiting and that you were—pardon me— that you were a handsome young man. Mr. Drake got held up, and wanted me to come and get you. He's having dinner prepared at his home."

Well, there it was then. Mr. Drake *had* given signals, and now he was moving things to his place. I could hear Brenda as if she were standing next to me, telling me to call her, make an excuse, go home.

But if I did that, there was no telling what the next foray would look like. I didn't dare risk my job, not over an invitation. And so far that's all it was, right? God, that even sounded naïve in my own head.

"I don't mean to rush you," Tarin said apologetically, "but I wouldn't like to keep the boss waiting. You know how he gets."

I didn't, actually. I wasn't sure anyone did, but maybe his driver had seen more of the elusive millionaire. Or billionaire. I actually wasn't sure what Mr. Drake was worth but it was a bigger number than I could count to in a day, I was pretty sure. "I... just give me one second."

Tarin nodded, glanced at the street—in both directions—and took a step back to check his own phone. "Just gonna let him know I'm looking for you," he said. "Buy a little time."

"Thanks," I muttered, and texted Brenda. *"Got invited to Drake's place for dinner."*

She must have been watching her phone. The response was almost instant. *"Definitely a hard no."*

"Can't just bail," I shot back.

"Sure can."

I huffed quietly to myself, and checked to see Tarin anxiously tapping on his own phone. I started to text Brenda back, to tell her the emergency exit text plan was still in effect, but halfway through it there was a crash down past the end of the street, two cars colliding hard. "Oh, shit," I said, startled out of my skin almost. "Jesus, that sounded awful."

"Crap," Tarin moaned. "That's the street I was gonna take, too. Look, we're already gonna run late, I need this job..."

"It's fine," I breathed impatiently. "Sorry, I just needed to... uh, check my schedule. Where's the car?"

"Just down on the curb," he said, gesturing to the opposite intersection from the crash.

I sighed, and waved for him to lead me to it. Dinner at Mr. Drake's house. *Fuck*. I wished I didn't have such mixed feelings. And the weird aura around this other guy, Tarin, was a curiosity that complicated the matter in a way I couldn't quite put my finger on. Maybe it was just a sexy older man vibe that I hadn't been sensitive to before. All me, some kind of projection phenomenon borne of an almost six-year dry spell. I did *have* Grindr on my phone, I just never had time to try it out. I had the wild thought of hooking up with the driver on the way to Mr. Drake's mansion—which is what I imagined he lived in—and indulged a private smile.

But I wasn't that kind of boy and probably it would just be awkward and leave me ruffled and rumpled and embarrassed to meet my boss. I wished I had Brenda's legendary confidence and game.

The car was a classic Lincoln, rather than a Jaguar or a Rolls or whatever rich people got ferried around in. And it was a little dusty. "You drive for Mr. Drake?"

Tarin opened the back door for me and glanced at the state of the car. "Had a lot of errands to run today, it was clean this morning. I do it first thing. Mr. Drake is more practical than people usually give him credit for."

Maybe I had misjudged the man. I paused with one hand on the door to get in. "Are you two… related or something? You kind of give off the same sort of, I don't know—vibe?"

Tarin snorted. "Usually no one notices. We're cousins. Second cousins, actually. Great guy, don't get me wrong, but he definitely got the looks and the money, you know? Still, it's a good gig. You mind?"

That probably explained it. I smiled sympathetically as I got in. "Must be some family."

"You have no idea," Tarin muttered, and closed the door. He got into the front, pulled away from the curb, and took the next intersection going south to get around the crash.

Must have been some other rich person headed to Madison's. I winced at the sight but also felt a slight tickle of *schadenfreude* no doubt born of petty envy.

The shiny white car that had been hit was definitely a Rolls Royce.

Chapter 5 - Tarin

Don't panic, I told myself as I pulled onto Highway 75 and scrambled for my next step.

It had taken a few calls and some coordination to get eyes on Lucas Warren while I made the drive east to Georgia. That part had been easy enough. My dragonmarked were numerous, and there were still several spread over the East Coast that had once been where I made my home. They had remained loyal over the generations, in exchange for my periodic help for their families. I didn't have the Hoard anymore, but three hundred years was more than enough time to amass my own modest fortune.

When they'd let me know that Lucas had left his house well-dressed and stopped at the most expensive restaurant in the city, I had hoped that he'd simply gone there to meet some rich suitor. Guessing it was Calavastrix himself had been an instinct. One that I dreaded learning was accurate.

And not only had I stolen an omega that Calavastrix had no doubt identified and begun to court—I'd arranged for one of my dragonmarked to wreck his car.

Reece was going to kill me. If Calavastrix the Storm didn't get to me first.

And fuck me, but I hadn't expected that an omega in close proximity would have such an effect. It was no wonder Reece and Matthew mated. How could they have helped it? I could feel my dragon form closer to my skin than I had in the last two hundred years, surging back with a sudden insistence as if it could break through the bindings of the Ancients by sheer force of will and arousal.

"Where exactly does Mr. Drake live?" Lucas asked from the back seat. He'd been on his phone. Hopefully not texting with the dragon of Atlanta.

"Confidential I'm afraid," I said into the rearview mirror.

Lucas' face pinched with incredulity. "We're going there now, it's not like I can't just look at the street number on the gate. Or portcullis or whatever."

Of course, he'd be a smart one. My luck. "I just follow orders," I said. "Sorry. It's a bit of a drive. Music?"

Lucas slumped in his seat, sullen, and went back to his phone.

I had to say something to keep him distracted. "So, you and the boss, huh? I, ah... he's pretty picky, hasn't had a boyfriend in ages."

"Oh, we're not," Lucas said quickly, straightening. "He's my boss, it's a business thing."

I grunted, smiling. Sure, it was. At least Lucas seemed slightly offended at the idea. I could use that. "That so? Funny, he made it sound like he had plans."

"Plans?" Lucas asked.

With a shrug, I caught his eye in the rearview. "Yeah, you know. Plans. Wine and dine, all that good stuff. He's got an appetite. Last kid I took out there had a great night. They all do, far as I can tell."

I saw the twist in his lips as it hit him. He looked out the window.

"But hey," I said, drawing his attention back, "he talks very highly of you. I think this could be different."

"He does?" Lucas wondered. "We've only met once. I'm pretty sure he didn't even know my name before this week."

That was only a small relief. They hadn't mated then, and if Lucas had been claimed I would feel it. Or rather, not feel it—Matthew didn't put off this kind of magnetic pull anymore, but when I'd first spotted him, I'd felt a bit of it even at a distance. "I just mean he's pretty taken with you," I said, and gambled on his flat expression. "Says you could really go places, if he likes you."

"Likes me," Lucas muttered. "What does that mean?"

"You know," I said, oozing suggestion. "Let's just say, if he has a good time... good things happen."

The disgusted look that took over Lucas' face was precisely what I hoped for. He put a hand to his stomach. "Shit," he breathed, softly enough that I only heard it because I was listening closely.

Now the question was—what kind of man was Lucas Warren? I had an inkling, but I'd given all the push I felt I safely could. It was in his court now.

He was quiet for a long time. I took an exit headed west. If Lucas knew the area, he would start getting more suspicious soon.

Fortunately, he never made it that far. "Hey, um... I just got a text from my sister. I hate to cancel on Mr. Drake, really, but it looks like my dog just went to the emergency vet. I should get back. It's terrible for me to ask this but do you think you could take me back to the city and drop me off at my car? It's really urgent."

Now that, I wasn't expecting. Anyone who said no to that was the worst kind of asshole. If I'd really been Calavastrix's driver, I would have been dragonmarked more than likely and been that kind of asshole. But Lucas expected it to work.

I slowed a bit, and peered at him in the rearview mirror. "Really?"

"Mm hmm," Lucas said, and held his phone up where, sure enough there was a text from someone—Brenda—letting him know his dog was at the vet. Convenient. I upgraded him in my estimation from 'smart one' to 'rather clever'.

"Yeah, sure," I said. "Let me get turned around."

While I made a show of looking for spot to do so, I played out a few different strategies in my head. His dog wasn't sick—I was pretty sure he didn't *have* a dog, though it was possible my people had missed that detail. So this was an escape option. Which meant he'd soured on the idea of meeting with Calavastrix. Did I play it hard or soft?

I made the turn after deciding, and gave an exaggerated sigh as I pulled to the side of the road and put the car in park.

"What are you doing?" Lucas asked.

"Listen," I said, my voice thick with sympathy, "I'm guessing you weren't expecting tonight to be a… well, you know. Quite like that. I don't really blame you for bailing out. You okay?"

His face was stiff and wary as he tried to judge whether I was going to talk him back into it or not. Finally, though, he cracked. "I… I'm sorry, I don't want to cause you problems, Tarin. Really. You can tell him I jumped out of the car if you need to. I'm fine, I just… I had this stupid idea in my head that this really was about work. For a man like Mr. Drake to even notice me, professionally I mean, felt… I don't know. Your cousin is kind of a legend, you know?"

I snorted. "Yeah. Yeah, he is that. Sorry about it. He can be a dick. Thinks all that money and power and status mean he can just do whatever he wants to whoever he wants. The whole family is like that, honestly."

"Everyone but you?" Lucas wondered. "The driver?"

I didn't have to fake the laugh. "Yeah, my side of the family we're, ah… working class, you'd say. Hey… I'll come up with a good story for Cala—for Caleb, and make sure he's not on your case. This is a little forward and I know you just went through something that sucked but, um… you wanna maybe grab a bite to eat? I know a place not far from here. Not as fancy as Caleb can afford, but good food. I know the folks there. No pressure, just—seems like you had kind of a shitty night."

"Oh," Lucas said, "Tarin, that's not…"

"Promise," I said, "no funny business."

"I wouldn't want you to get in trouble," he explained. "You seem like a nice guy. Really."

"Cuz can't fire me," I said. "Rest of the family would eat him alive. But it's your choice. Dinner, then home to your sick dog; that's it, I promise."

He locked his jaw, lips working as he clearly weighed the possibility. He was feeling the natural attraction between us, that much I knew for certain. If he'd understood it more he might have resisted, but as far as he could tell—and from what I gathered from Matthew—it was deep, animal, and mysterious.

I was a bastard for leveraging it, but the thought of anyone locked up in a dungeon somewhere, forced to breed not only new dragons but also new omegas was enough to let me set the ethics of the alternative aside. Abduction or not, in the end Lucas would be far happier out of Calavastrix's claws than in them.

He finally smiled, biting his lip in a way that made *me* want to bite them, too. "This is definitely the strangest entry into dinner with a gentleman that I can remember. Guess it makes a good story. Sure. Mind if I stay in the back seat? It's gonna sound silly but… kind of lets me imagine I actually have my own driver."

"Sure thing," I said, chuckling as I put the car into drive. "We're not far. Best barbecue in Georgia, hands down."

"As long as there's booze, too," Lucas said, "it could be mac and cheese."

I turned us around and headed back west again. There really was a restaurant about ten miles ahead, where I'd switched out my car for the Lincoln. And I did know the owners.

They were dragonmarked, my people. And the next part of this was going to be pleasant enough but I did not look forward to what came after.

Just don't panic, I reminded myself. *It's for his own good.*

Chapter 6 - Lucas

It was spontaneous, and possibly career suicide, and more than a few times during the drive to the side-of-the-road joint that Tarin drove us to I considered changing my mind. I had turned down an obvious invitation to sleep with one of the richest—if not *the* richest—most powerful men in Atlanta, probably in Georgia, and possibly even the whole country. I tried to calculate a price tag on my dignity and couldn't do it, though, so I let Tarin keep driving until he parked in front of a ramshackle-looking place with an unlit sign.

There were street lights in the dirt parking lot, and other cars as well. Through the windows, I could see a handful of people at tables with beers and food. It was, in fact, a restaurant and not his secret murder shack. I relaxed a bit.

"Sit tight," Tarin said. "I'll get the door."

"Oh, you don't have to—" I started, but when I tried to open the door it wouldn't go. A chill shivered along my spine.

He opened the door for me. "Sorry, it's got the child lock on. Just procedure, I should have said something, but usually everyone expects me to open and close the door, you know?"

"It's fine," I said. I cleared my throat as I got out, and tried not to look like I'd just had a moment of panic.

No one would describe me as spontaneous. Even accepting a dinner invitation from my boss had been purely about calculation and foresight. Probably, this was one of the many reasons I'd never had a stable relationship—I was *too* stable to make something that chaotic actually work.

As soon as I was standing next to Tarin, I did feel more at ease, though. We were on equal footing now, and while the sudden twist in events did make a part of my brain begin to scream at me to get back on my usual routine... there was another part urging me to be curious. He was handsome, after all, and nice enough. He'd given me the honest truth about Mr. Drake, even perhaps at the cost of his job. I didn't owe him a date—if that's what this was—but I did kind of feel like he'd earned it. And boy, had it been a long time.

"So," I said as we walked toward the door of the place, "this one of those old family diners where they've been making the same apple pie for six generations?"

Tarin chuckled and pulled the door open for me. "Something like that, actually. I believe it's been here since... about 1915."

I whistled. The place certainly looked like it could be that old. "Predates both of us, huh?"

"Mm hmm," Tarin hummed. "By the bar, in the corner."

It was an intimate space, a bit out of sight from the rest of the tables and patrons. Definitely a date table. The floor was clean, the bar shiny and polished, and the seats around the table were comfortable and not sticky. Not that I expected the place to be dirty inside. Well... maybe a little bit.

A rail-thin black woman emerged from the kitchen, wiping her hands on a blue apron. She beamed when she saw Tarin and surprised me by smiling almost as wide at me. "My, my, look what the cat dragged in," she said. "Lord—ah, lordy me, if it isn't *Tarin*. Pleased to have you again."

"Always happy to see your face, Annette," Tarin said. "This is Lucas."

"Lucas," the woman breathed, and put a hand to her chest briefly before she seemingly composed herself. "Well, I… I'm just so happy to have you here, too."

Something odd passed between Tarin and Annette. I shelved it to shake her hand, and then listened as she described the night's fare with more enthusiasm than I thought I had ever seen in a backwoods little diner. Not that I had much experience—maybe she was always just happy to have anyone find the place. I gathered it was actually her family's place, and that she was head chef.

"Annette," Tarin said, "all of that sounds unbelievable. I think I'll have the mock-turtle soup. Your grandpa's recipe?"

"The only one worth making," she agreed. "And you, Lucas?"

I ordered the pork chops, which underwent some secret spicing process, and kept my face polite and friendly as Annette withdrew to go make our food straight away.

Tarin seemed slightly sheepish when she was gone.

"I seem to recall your side of the family is what I would call 'working class'?" I inquired. I jerked a thumb at the closing kitchen door. "What was that? Are you a local celebrity?"

He made a dismissive noise and shook his head slowly. "No, no. I, ah… helped renovate the place when they were in hard times about… uh, twenty or so years ago."

It wasn't falling apart, but if it had been twenty years then the place had seen a lot of hard times since then. "That was kind of you. You usually have sort of a white savior thing going on?"

"Now," he said, pointing at me, "that's hardly fair. Annette's family and mine have a long history is all. My side of the family, I mean. We've been coming here a long time, and when it took a hit we didn't want to see it fail. Believe me, with the right resources Annette and her father are more than capable of managing their own affairs."

I raised my hands in defeat. "All right, I was just making a joke. It really is sweet. I grew up in a pretty small town, Cumming, and… it's bigger now but even when I was a kid there wasn't a place that had some long family history with mine. So. Are you Mr. Drake's driver full-time?"

"You can call him Caleb when he's not around, you know," Tarin said. He rolled his eyes. "The man thinks a lot of himself as it is, I'd hate to report back to him and see the smugness."

"Are you?" I asked.

He raised a questioning eyebrow.

"Going to report back to him." I rested my elbows on the table. "It's just, I'm a little worried that if Mr.—I mean, if *Caleb*—finds out that I ditched him like this… it could be my job."

"I don't think that's going to be an issue," Tarin said softly. "Speaking of, though—what do you do for him?"

"I'm sort of an attorney," I said. "At least in theory. I mean I got my degrees, and passed the bar, and got a job at a law firm."

Tarin cocked his head a little to one side. "But?"

I spread my hands. "But I don't do very much attorney-ing there. It's complicated, there's a whole hierarchy—a pecking order—and I'm basically at the bottom of it, just above a paralegal. Paying dues and all that. Don't get me wrong, Camelot Legal is… well, from there you can go anywhere. So in ten years, maybe fifteen, I could be running for AG, or state legislature, or in private practice."

"Ten to *fifteen* years?" Tarin's eyes widened. "But that's a big chunk of life, isn't it?"

"Spoken like someone who was born with rather more privilege than they realize," I shot back. "Yeah, it's a chunk of life. I'll be in my forties before my career is really all that impressive. That's how it goes. Doctors, lawyers—it's a mid-life investment."

He looked bewildered by the idea. "But your life is… I mean *life*—it's short. Is this really what you want to do with it?"

I laughed. "I'm about eighty grand in the hole at this point so I really hope so."

"Seriously," he pressed. "Is this what you want, Lucas? Toiling away until your life is half gone? This is your passion?"

"Passion," I echoed, smiling. "Come on. I don't have the luxury of passion, Tarin, who does? You might not have gotten the notice, but I'm a millennial, you know? Student debt, half-million dollar one-room condos, hell, a wrecked climate. I mean, I want to do good things, help people but… Who has space for passion? I'll earn that, and retire at sixty something, and be passionate about things when I'm old. Assuming there's anything left to be passionate about. Oh, please—I don't need your sympathy."

The look on his face had gone from bewildered to almost abjectly sad. "It's not sympathy," he said. "We all choose our paths. For the most part. I'm just curious, though. Is that why you went into law or…?"

"I didn't want to be an attorney when I was five, if that's what you mean," I offered.

He looked me over. "Then what did you want to be?"

Gosh, it felt like two lifetimes ago. I had to think about it. "I think when I was five I wanted to be an astronaut. But not like an actual astronaut—I wanted to be lost in space. Meeting aliens and zooming through asteroid fields and shouting at a robot not to tell me the odds."

"Droid," Tarin said.

"What?"

He grinned. "C-3PO was a droid, not a robot. Not strictly speaking."

I giggled at that and nudged his leg under the table with the tip of my shoe. "Nerd."

"Guilty," he said. "I find stories fascinating. I've got a lot of free time, so I read, see movies, go to shows."

"Caleb only need a driver once a day?" I asked.

Tarin's face was caught in amber for a moment. It passed quickly, though, and he shrugged, sobering. "I'm not his only driver. He's got three, actually. Mostly I work nights, so."

"A little handout from cousin?" I joked.

He seemed to take it the right way, smirking. "You might say that, yes. He's got everything in the world, after all. Might as well take what I can, when I can."

"Fair enough," I agreed.

We chatted back and forth like that for a little while before Annette came out of the kitchen with a young man, both of them laden with plates. They set our food out, gave us napkins and silverware, and set down two beers we hadn't ordered but which I wasn't about to turn down.

I held the bottle up to toast, and Tarin joined me. "To… very unusual drivers," I said.

Tarin bobbed his head. "And to surprising young would-be astronauts."

I sipped it, and exhaled relief when it was exactly what I needed. I took my first bite of the pork chop and almost came in my pants, it was so good. Smoked to perfection, and spiced with something I couldn't quite identify—a little bitter, but between some kind of citrus-based reduction and the smoky flavor it just blended right in. "This," I muttered around a bite, "is the single best piece of food I have ever eaten. I can't believe this place is out here in the middle of nowhere, Annette should be raking in cash in Atlanta."

"She likes to make the food herself," Tarin explained. "I've suggested before that she move shop but this was her grandfather's dream project, and her father's *passion*, if you will, so she prefers to stay put. Besides, there are some benefits to being outside the city proper."

"If one of those is making food like this," I said, and sipped my beer again, "then I guess she's in the right place."

"There's a smoking shed out back in fact." He waved his fork in the direction of the kitchen. "Hard to get a permit for that in the city."

"I could see that." I devoured the plate like I'd never had food before, and made my way through the first beer and then a second as I did. By the time I finished, I was not only sated but utterly exhausted.

"Must be the food," Tarin said. "It can have that effect. Should we get going? I can take you home."

I nodded, the grogginess threatening to overtake me. "Yeah," I muttered. "Yeah, I think I could use my bed. And to contemplate my future because… I'm guessing I, uh…"

"Lucas?" Tarin asked. "God, you must be tired. Come on then."

Tarin left cash on the table, and waved to Annette as we left. I had only had the two beers, but apparently they went right to my head. That would teach me to skip lunch. And maybe it was the tipsiness, or the insane series of events, or the way Tarin looked at me—I didn't really know—but when the door to Annette's restaurant closed behind us and I had my arm looped through Tarin's elbow, I looked up at him and smiled. And then I kissed him.

His lips weren't just warm, they were hot. He froze at first, shocked by my forwardness. Hell, so was I. It wasn't like me, really. And yet there was just something about him, about his kindness, about that easy but nervous smile that made me tingle inside. He relaxed after a few moments, and kissed me back. My head spun, and I ran a hand over his shirt, under his jacket. His hands grazed my arms and when I pressed against him, I could feel how hard he was just from a kiss.

"If I wasn't so tired," I muttered as I finally let his lips go, "this might be a much longer night."

"I should…" Tarin cleared his throat. "Um, I should get you into the car then."

He urged me off the deck and I stumbled along beside him. By the time we got to the car, I realized it had to be more than just exhaustion and alcohol. My limbs were starting to go almost numb, and I couldn't keep my eyes open any longer. It came on in a sudden rush, far too quickly to be natural. I slumped, and Tarin caught me.

For the few moments that I was still conscious, I felt like such an idiot for kissing him.

Drugged. *Oh, fuck. No, no, no.* I attempted to push him off me and call for help but my voice barely worked and all that came out was a groan. The world spun around me, and the car he opened the door to wasn't the one he'd picked me up in.

"I'm so sorry," he muttered as I faded. "I promise, I'll explain everything when you wake up. It's for your own good, Lucas. I would never harm…"

I didn't catch the rest.

Chapter 7 - Tarin

Annette had her instructions, and would dispose of the car. I'd transferred plenty of money to her account before I left Comfort to help her pay to do it right. As far as anyone was concerned, Lucas was picked up in front of the restaurant and then disappeared from the radar. It made me sick to think how he would react, or what the consequences would be. I angled the rearview mirror to keep an eye on him, and couldn't help staring at this peaceful face. He was beautiful, objectively—but I knew some of that was the attraction between our two natures. That brief kiss had bowled me right over, struck me like a hammer until my whole body rang with the impact.

Whether that was nature or just old-fashioned attraction, or a bit of both, didn't really matter at this point. After this, he would never trust me. That was fine—he'd be free, and aware of who and what he truly was, and not locked up somewhere pumping out babies. I didn't kid myself about having the moral high ground or anything—but if it was shades of gray I at least wasn't as far into the black as Calavastrix.

The elder dragon was going to be hunting for us. He would have centuries to carry that grudge around, as well—millennia, even. It was only a matter of time. But a lot could change between now and when he finally found us.

Reece was going to be furious.

I drove fast, on a full tank, without stopping until the tank was nearly empty, and then chose a gas station in the middle of nowhere, with no cameras at the pumps, and paid cash. There were only a few more hours before Lucas woke up; the cocktail that Annette had given him was safe, but consequently not terribly strong. Eight hours of driving had us about an hour west of New Orleans before Lucas finally groaned softly and began to stir.

This was going to be painful. I spotted a rest area on the highway and was relieved to find it empty when we pulled in. Not much traffic at four in the morning, it seemed.

I took the keys out of the ignition and opened the back door of the car, placed a bottle of water and some Tylenol for the headache he would have on the seat, and waited for Lucas to come around.

It would have been easier to keep him drugged the whole trip, which was only fifteen or so hours in total—but I hoped that this way he might get a chance to listen and be more cooperative when we reached the ranch. I stood some distance away, and watched as he came to in stages. First tossing and turning as if having bad dreams, then waking for moments at a time, and finally pushing himself up in a haze of grogginess and confusion.

"Don't be alarmed," I urged gently. "There's water and something for your head there beside you."

He gave me a long, bleary-eyed look of noncomprehension. "Where…"

"You'll get to it," I assured him. "And then you can yell and say whatever you like, and then I'll explain everything."

He blinked rapidly, rubbed his eyes and snatched up the water bottle to drink. After several swallows, he winced and picked up the pills as well but paused. "Fuck," he whispered. "Fucking… you drugged me. You fucking drugged me and—Jesus, where are we? Tarin, you son of a bitch, I *trusted* you and you—oh, God. I've been kidnapped. I—"

"You aren't bound," I pointed out, "or locked in a car or a box. I'm not going to hurt you, Lucas, I swear. Your head hurts, I know, and the pills are just Tylenol. The seal is unbroken, you can check for yourself."

"Gosh," Lucas spat, "thanks so much for thinking of me in the middle of an *abduction*, it's so *courteous* of you. I'm not taking your fucking pills, asshole, I'm calling the police, I… of course, you took my phone, too."

I held it up. "I have it, and I'll give it back to you if you'll hear me out."

"I'm not helpless, you know," he snapped, still in the car and huddled against the far door. It was child-locked, just in case. I couldn't exactly let him run off. "I wrestled in high school and I did jiu-jitsu in college, you want to take me, you're going to have to work for it. People are going to be looking for me, you get that? My boss is—"

"Your boss was going to lock you in a cell somewhere and rape you repeatedly," I said. "And then, very likely, force you to breed and produce offspring, which he would sell to very rich, very powerful men."

Lucas' jaw dropped. He stared at me, clearly unbelieving, and then laughed. "I don't… What the fuck are you even… Jesus, *what*?"

His laughter verged on hysterical. I decided to let him get it out. It was, in all fairness, a very stressful situation and a revelation that almost no one would take seriously until they were hip-deep in the reality of it. When the last titters of it finally faded, he choked off a single sob and drowned it with more water.

"Can I explain myself?" I asked.

In response, Lucas attempted to open the passenger side door next to him, found it locked, and hung his head briefly before he looked up at me with a face full of acid and fury. "What is there to explain, exactly? You drugged me and threw me in the back of—wait, this isn't even the same car, so…" Some new comprehension dawned as he stared around at the interior. "All this was planned. Shit. You're some kind of serial killer, aren't you? That's just my luck, I swear, every time something good happens to me something ten times worse has to follow it to even out the scales."

"I'm not a serial killer," I sighed, and waved him out of the car. "Come on. Get some fresh air, it will help you wake up."

"And if I run?" he asked. "Or is this where you like to do it? I get out, you stab me to death and arrange my corpse artfully on some… where the fuck are we?"

"We're at a rest stop off the highway in Louisiana, not far from New Orleans," I said. "Lucas, I'm not going to stab you, or anything like that. I wish I could make everything perfectly clear for you, but I can't. Where we're going is another eight hours away and when we get there I promise that the people waiting for us can make everything make sense. I can't ask you to trust me after what I did and I do understand that—but if you go back home, if you step foot in Atlanta, your boss is going to find you and I promise, he really will do what I said."

Lucas didn't get out of the car. He stayed crammed against the door, his body taut like he really would fight me off if I came in after him. It made me nervous to get behind the wheel again. I wasn't that worried he would hurt me—I was trapped in my human form but still had a degree of supernatural strength and hardiness. Rather, I imagined him attacking while I was driving. I would likely survive a crash. Lucas potentially would not. If he really did think he was headed toward his death, it might not matter to him.

I didn't *think* he really believed that, though.

"Bullshit," he was muttering, "this is complete bullshit. How the hell does this kind of thing always happen to me?"

"Have you been abducted *before*?" I asked.

Lucas barked a laugh. "Uh, no. But I have a track record with fucking nutjob guys that I hoped was finally over. I should have known the minute you asked to take me to dinner, I'm some kind of magnet for bat-shit crazy."

I tucked that away for later—Matthew, during some of our many 'family' dinners, had told stories about his past and the trail of unstable men behind him. Two wasn't a pattern but one never did know.

"Listen," I said gently, approaching the door but with my hands out in the open, "can you feel that kind of heat between us? The way you get warmer when I'm close? You should be panicked, trying to flee, you should be losing your mind with fear if you really think I mean to harm you—but you're not. Right?"

He snorted. "Clearly, that's not an indicator—I got the same vibe from Caleb and you're saying he planned to turn me into a sex slave so…"

I had to give him that. Still, I pressed on. "That's because in a certain respect he and I are the same."

"Cousins?" Lucas asked blithely, bitterness dripping like something I could have collected in a jar.

"That part isn't actually that far off," I said. "Distant cousins, from several generations back. But more than that. We're the same…" I couldn't say that we were both dragons. He'd want proof, and I couldn't give it to him. "…call it a genotype. And you, well… you're not entirely mundane, Lucas. Other people don't feel what you feel around us. It's a kind of natural attraction, a biological calling. I know that sounds crazy, and you can't take my word for it. Where I'm taking you, there is someone who is the same as you are. He's had time to understand it, get used to it—he can explain it better than I can. If you'll go with me, and meet these people, you'll discover a whole new world you never imagined existed. And after, if you really and truly do not believe us, or you don't like what you find, I will personally put you on a plane and send you back to Atlanta to do whatever you like."

"Easy to say that," Lucas said. "To make me compliant. So that I won't put up a fight. If you really don't mean me any harm, then what you need to do is let me go. I don't want or need *anything* from you, Tarin. I will flag down a car on the highway, go to the nearest airport, and pay for my own goddamn ticket back to Atlanta. Wherever this magical Neverland place of yours is, I don't give a fuck about it. I have a *life*. A career. You just threw a huge fucking wrench into all of it."

It had been easier for Reece. Matthew had been attacked by the Templars. Maybe if I'd waited... but that would have simply complicated things further and put him in greater danger. I didn't regret trying, but I wasn't about to knock Lucas out and drag him all the way to Comfort. It left me with no real choices. "I can drive you back to New Orleans and you can—"

"No," Lucas snapped. "No. You back away from the door, and I will get out and go to the highway. You give me my phone, and I will make my way back to Atlanta and you can fuck yourself and die in a ditch on fire, please."

I had no real right to be stung by that, so I brushed it off. I tossed him his phone, and backed off from the car. "This was clearly a mistake," I said. "I'm sorry. But when you get home, you cannot go back to work. You can't get anywhere near Caleb—Lucas, if you believe nothing else, believe me when I say that he will keep you like a bird in a cage and your life will be unpleasant and very long."

He scooted toward the open door cautiously, and then crept out of it. He was unsteady for a moment and had to brace himself on the door. When I moved to offer him a hand, he glared at me and held up a finger. "Don't."

I ducked my head and backed off. It felt like I had one last chance to plead my case. Or maybe I was out of chances already—either way, I had to try. "Caleb isn't the only potential threat you need to be aware of," I said. "There are others, who will hunt and kill you for what you are. Templars. They have a mark, usually on the chest over the heart—sometimes a tattoo and other times a brand—in the shape of a cross."

"Templars," Lucas muttered. He grew very still. "What do you know about—no. Never mind, I don't want to know and I don't care because everything you've said to me so far has been a complete lie, and I'm not listening to more of it. I'm going to leave now, Tarin. I'm dialing 911"—he tapped the numbers into his phone—"and if I see you, or hear you, or think that you're following me, I will call them and tell them you are armed and the police will show up and shoot you and this will all become a very terminal kind of bad date."

He edged around the door and walked backwards away from me, toward the highway that was barely lit by occasional street lamps, holding up his phone so that I could see his thumb beside the call button.

I stood, trying to decide how this was going to play out. I had hundreds of years of training how to use this human body—I could wait for him to get out of sight, sneak up on him, apprehend him more aggressively and spirit him away to the ranch. He'd be pissed, but Reece or Sasha could shift for him. Matthew could explain things, Mercy could corroborate.

Seeing a dragon didn't convince a person of anything other than that dragons were real, though. Or that they were on a bad trip, and if Lucas didn't accept any of it then we'd be faced with the choice of letting him leave and expose us—or forcing him to stay and be no better than Calavastrix would be.

The indecision kept my feet rooted in place as he finally turned and ran back along the exit ramp toward the highway, already waving his lit phone at the next pair of headlights.

Great fucking job, I chided myself. *Fuck.*

I wasn't about to leave him to the wild, though. I took out my own phone, loaded up the GPS tracker I'd installed on his while he slept, and watched the little dot blinking at me. It took an hour for Lucas to flag down a ride, that little dot hovering by the other side of the highway until, finally, it began to move. I turned the car on, mounted the phone on the dash, and pulled out of the rest stop to follow. When he did get back, and Calavastrix made his move, I would be there.

Chapter 8 - Lucas

"Thank you so much for picking me up," I told the burly looking woman in the driver's seat as she picked up speed. She was dressed in a kind of business casual, like she'd come from something important but not formal. Her hair made me think of Sharon Stone. My mom used to love her movies.

She glanced at me, smiling just a little. "Not a problem. This hour of the night, you're lucky I missed my exit. Don't worry, I'm fine to drive—just been up a long time."

My head still throbbed a little from the tranquilizer Tarin had *drugged* me with. I shifted in the seat and rubbed one temple. "I think I was owed just a little bit of luck at least," I said. "This day… you wouldn't even believe me if I told you how fucked up it was."

"Trust me," she muttered, "couldn't be worse than mine."

"Shit," I breathed, "I'm Lucas, by the way. Lucas Warren. What's your name?"

"Lena." She kept her eyes on the road. "Care to tell me about it? I could use the interaction to keep me alert. We can trade war stories."

I offered a sympathetic groan. "You go first. I need a little distance from mine before I go over it again. You're coming from some kind of, what, business thing? Or a date?"

She quirked an eyebrow at me. "Good eye. Business."

"What do you do?" I asked.

Lena made that same slight smile that didn't quite reach her eyes. "So far, I'm pretty much just a glorified go-fer. I run deliveries, carry messages—pick up the boss' lattes. It's shit work but they're trying to move me up the ladder."

"Sounds like a good thing," I said. "But you don't seem excited. Conditions apply?"

"Yeah," she grunted. "Yeah, they do. I've been with the company a long time—loyalty is a big deal there—and now if I want this promotion, well… I have to prove it. Do some stuff I never expected to have to do…"

"You work for the mob or something?" I wondered, half-joking and half… not.

Lena laughed at that. "No, nothing like that. I have to get rid of someone."

That was a relief. "Oh, I see. I don't envy you at all. I've never been in a position where I had to fire anyone but I was an RA in college and had to have a student removed from the dorms once. It did not feel good, even though he deserved it. He was breaking into the other rooms. Still, made me feel gross."

"I'm sure it did," she said. "So what about you? What kind of sad story put you on a highway in Louisiana at four in the morning?"

"My job," I said, "and then a very bad date. Well, two maybe. I'm not really sure yet."

She shot me a brief, critical eye. "You're not sure if you had two dates? Must not have been very remarkable. And this is an odd place for it. Did you walk from somewhere?"

I wasn't sure how much to tell her. Really, what I wanted was to call a friend, maybe Brenda though… probably she was asleep. But Lena seemed friendly enough. "The details are a little bit confidential," I said, "but basically... I was propositioned by my boss, then picked up by a stranger claiming to be his driver, who then convinced me not to hook up with said boss and then subsequently drugged and abducted me."

Lena barked a short, sharp laugh that she cut off immediately. I could see the incredulity on her face even without looking directly at her, could feel it in the air. "You... you're not serious."

"As a heart attack," I breathed. "Or, you know, an attempted abduction."

"Jesus fuck," she muttered, and quickly crossed herself like a Catholic. "Sorry, Lord. Um... are you okay? Do you need the police or—"

"No," I assured her, rubbing my head again, "no, I don't want to... get anyone involved. It's just too weird and really I'm not sure I can handle a whole thing right now. I really just want to get home."

"I guess so," Lena said. "Well, I'm headed all the way back to Atlanta, you're welcome to come along."

I blinked, watching my own face in the darkened window. "Atlanta," I said. "What makes you think I'm... that's a crazy coincidence. You going all that way. Going on business for this job, or...? I mean, you can just drop me off in New Orleans. I can catch a plane from there."

"It's no trouble," she insisted. "And I could use the company. I'm sorry, aren't you going to Atlanta? I could swear you told me that when you got in."

My head was still foggy. I didn't think I had said that, though. "Um... maybe," I said. "Still, long car rides they, ah... make me nauseous. I throw up, have panic attacks; it's really awful. I'd love to keep you company but flying will be easier for me."

"By the time you get a plane and land we would have gotten there hours before," she pointed out. "It'll be faster in the end. I'll even stop and get us some snacks at the next gas station. You seem like a nice enough guy."

Lena seemed like a nice enough woman. But there was something uneasy in the air. I'm not remotely a religious person, I don't even believe in shit like karma or synchronicity or whatever new age nonsense people are into lately. The idea that someone just happened to be one of the only cars on the highway, headed to Atlanta, at the precise moment that I needed a ride away from this nightmare was a bit... difficult to accept.

"What company do you work for again?" I asked. "I don't think you said or maybe I missed it."

She glanced at me. "I didn't say. Probably shouldn't."

"Signed an NDA?" I pressed. "Must be something serious then. Private security? You've got some military background, I'd guess."

Lena whistled. "All right, you've gotta tell me what gave it away."

"My cousin Mireille is in the navy," I said. "The hair, the build, the way you talk. Kind of reminds me of her."

"You'd be surprised how often I get that kind of thing," Lena said. "Must have one of those faces. You know—I kind of look like everyone."

I nodded. That she was coincidentally on her way to Atlanta strained belief—but what strained it even more was the thought that maybe it wasn't an accident at all. Because what were the chances that I would not only be propositioned by my boss, then abducted by some stranger who thought my boss was trying to human traffic me, and then *on top of that* get picked up by someone else who had some kind of plan for me. Serial killer? Sent by Caleb? A friend of Tarin's meant to lure me into a false sense of security before delivering me back to him?

All of it sounded progressively more insane and paranoid. But if it was going to happen to anyone, I couldn't quite bring myself to believe that it wouldn't be me. After all, it was a numbers game, right? Something like this practically had to happen to someone.

"You know," I said, "the more I think about New Orleans the more I think... maybe all this is for a reason. That maybe I'm just meant to make a big change. I know it sounds crazy but I think I'd rather start over there than go back to Atlanta."

Lena eyed me sideways. "Oh, yeah? Sounds like sort of a rash decision. After what you've been through, I mean."

"All the same," I replied, trying to keep it light. How hard would she push for me to end up back in Atlanta? "I've got a string of shitty relationships behind me, only one real friend, a boss who's probably going to fire me, and a family that... well, they don't entirely connect, you could say. Why not just move on, wipe the slate? We're going to pass it pretty soon, you can just drop me off."

"Isn't all your stuff in Atlanta?" she asked.

I unclenched my jaw. Important to stay loose, not freak out. "Funny thing; I don't actually think I told you I'm from Atlanta, Lena."

Lena sighed. "I guess you didn't, Lucas. Doesn't really change the facts, though."

"You work for Mr. Drake," I said. It was the only thing that made sense. The only reason someone would insist on taking me back there. Shit, had Tarin somehow been telling the truth?

"Now why would Mr. Drake go to all the trouble of sending someone to follow you around and bring you back there?" she asked. "You're just some junior lawyer, aren't you?"

A chill ran through me, right to the tips of my fingers. Adrenaline washed into my brain and set off a series of blaring, panicked neurological klaxons. I thought about the rest of what Tarin had said—the stuff that I brushed off as a fabrication to keep me with him. If not a friend of Tarin's and not working for Caleb then...

"Are you... do you work for Templar Industries?" I asked.

She laughed quietly, mirthlessly and glanced at me with a look of appreciation as she took one hand off the wheel. "Wow. You are well-informed and quite sharp. I admit, I'm impressed. Are we going to do this the hard way? Because you seem nice enough and I'm guessing you aren't a highly trained soldier like me."

She wasn't wrong about that. I'd sort of played up my experience with Tarin in an attempt to bluff my way out of a confrontation. I was starting to think maybe he was more honest than I gave him credit for. Even if I hadn't been bluffing, though, Tarin didn't have a gun.

Lena did. She produced it from between her seat and the console and rested it on her thigh, one finger brushing the trigger. "If you're wondering," she said, "I'm a very good shot, in fact."

"I wasn't," I muttered. "Are you… going to kill me?"

"No," she said, but drawn out like she hadn't made her mind up yet. "But I'm not obligated to deliver you alive to Atlanta, so that's something to think about."

It was too much for one day, or two days, or a week—or a lifetime, honestly. Two abductions in one day. What the fuck was so special about me? Whatever it was, I wanted to return it for a refund. But since I was guessing Lena knew, I decided to make the most of the moment. "What is it about me?" I asked. "First my boss, then Tarin, then you?"

She *hmphed* and shrugged one shoulder. "If you don't know, you probably don't need to be burdened with it. It's not really your fault or anything, if it makes you feel better. Just an accident of birth."

"It really doesn't make me feel better," I shot back. "What accident?"

"Not an accident," she corrected me, "and accident *of birth*. That it's you is the accident. That it's anyone at all is very much on purpose. One that's at odds with little things like the survival of our species and God's plan for this Earth."

All the breath left me and I had a hard time inhaling again. When I did manage to gulp down some air, it was with the sure knowledge that there were only a few such breaths left for me. "Is it… is this because I'm… gay?"

Lena's face screwed up with incredulity. "What? Of course not. I don't have a problem with gay people. Or trans people or anyone else. I'm gay, too, Lucas, thank you."

"Well, then what the fuck, Lena?" I demanded. "If you're going to maybe kill me or maybe not, then you may as well come out and say it."

"Lucas," she sighed, "no one needs to kill you."

I hoped my grunt of disgust was acidic enough. "Gee, that's good news."

"You just have to be sterilized," she went on. "You're an omega, and unfortunately if you had kids, they might grow up to overthrow human kind as the dominant species."

Oh, was that all?

"Well, before that happens," I said, "I have to piss. You want me to do that in your car seat, or can we stop?"

"We can stop," Lena said. "Pretty sure I can easily run you down and break your kneecaps if I need to. I'm faster than I look. Plus, we need gas."

I didn't respond to that, instead staring out the window again, my thoughts spinning, trying to spit out something like a plan to get away. The only real plan that kept coming back again and again wasn't a plan at all. It was a fantasy.

Part of me desperately hoped that Tarin had defied my wishes and followed me after all. Somehow, I didn't think that was the kind of luck I had at the moment.

Chapter 9 - Tarin

I kept one eye on the phone screen and the other on the pair of tiny red lights far ahead of me on the highway. They disappeared around a corner or over a hill a few times, but Lucas' dot on the screen didn't go away, or stop because he threw the phone out the window or anything. He didn't realize I was following him using it or he'd have turned it off.

When I caught up to him, I wasn't sure what I was going to say. *"Super sorry about how I kidnapped you, can we try this again?"* It didn't seem like that would work out very well.

As a very last resort, there was always the worst possible alternative. I did have chloroform in the trunk. It was awful, and I would never forgive myself for it—one of countless times I wished I hadn't gone quite so native these past three hundred years—but it would get the job done. I could zip-tie his hands and feet and just hand him off to Matthew and Reece when I got back to the ranch.

I really did hope the first option would work out.

After about an hour and a half, just past New Orleans, they took an exit. By the time I reached it, the phone had stopped. I pulled off to follow, and pulled into the parking lot of a gas station. There were only two cars in the lot, and one of them was at the pumps. A tall, broad-shouldered woman with short blonde hair pumped gas in a cheap suit. The car was nice. There was no one else in it.

I guessed that Lucas might be inside. His phone still showed as being in the car, if the GPS was accurate.

Something about the woman set off instincts. She looked dangerous—the way she held herself, the stillness she maintained as she waited for the pump and the flat, unaffected expression all said 'this is a very patient, watchful person.' When I first took human form after my sentencing, and was forced to live among them full-time, human expressions were at times confusing. Give it a few centuries, though, and you become something of an expert at just about anything.

I only glanced at her before I pulled into a parking spot by the store, got out and stretched as if I'd been on a very long drive—which, in fact, I had so it wasn't a difficult role to play—and blearily rubbed my eyes before I strode into the convenience store. I stopped at the counter first, scanning the tops of shelves for signs of Lucas' head. Nothing. Bathroom?

"I'm gonna grab a cup of coffee," I told the man at the counter, and laid a five-dollar bill on the counter. "Keep the change, please."

The old-timer shrugged as if nothing in the world could possibly interest or surprise him anymore, and took the fiver. I went to the coffee station, poured a cup, and checked the corner of my eye to confirm that the woman was still there—and that she was observing the store through the big, dirty windows.

Definitely something about her, then.

I walked along the rows of shelves until I found a place where the two of us couldn't see one another, and spotted the bathrooms. If I ducked down a bit I could make it to the door there without her seeing me.

"Is there a back door here?" I called.

The old man didn't answer. Maybe he was deaf and mute as well as apathetic.

I ducked down, slipped behind the nearest shelf, and made my way across the store to the bathrooms. The door to the men's room was locked.

I knocked. What was the worst that could happen?

There was no answer, but I heard the faintest sound of shoes shuffling. Someone was in there. Hiding. It made my pulse suddenly jump, and I almost leaned out to check on the woman at the pump.

I knocked again. "Lucas? It's... Tarin. I know you don't want anything to do with me now but—"

The knob clicked, the handle turned, and the door was flung wide as Lucas grabbed me and dragged me inside.

Shock and worry each had a quick say, before reasoning jumped in and stated the obvious as I stared down at Lucas' frightened face. "The woman outside, is she—"

"Templar Industries," he said. "She says I'm not human; or some kind of... omega something—what is that? Is that why *you* grabbed me? What does she want?"

I stared at him. "She's a Templar?"

"I guess?" Lucas said. He waved frantically at the closed door. "She's got a gun. Said she might kill me, and that Templar Industries wants to sterilize me for the good of all mankind or some shit. What the hell is going on? And... wait, how did you find me?"

I grimaced and showed him my phone. "While you were sleeping—er, unconscious, sorry—I used your thumb to get into your phone and turn your GPS on. Just in case. And as for the rest... she's not lying about your being an omega. I don't think we have time to talk about it here, but I—"

The bell above the door in the main store rang. There were no windows in here. The only way out was through the store. Lucas put his hands over his mouth and closed his eyes tight for a moment as if holding in a scream. His eyes were puffy, I realized—he'd been in here crying. It twisted my heart to see it, and I had to force down an instinct to pull him to me. Biology, I reminded myself. Nothing more than that.

A plan. I needed a thorough plan. I was old, and canny, and strong—but I was far from immortal and in this form I was vulnerable. The woman would know how to use her gun, and more than that. I had to get the drop on her. And there was really only one way to accomplish that.

"You have to go," I told Lucas. I put my hands on his shoulder when he began to protest. "Listen to me—you have to go out, go with her to the car. I need her distracted. Demand she buy you food. A lot of it. Make her carry the bag."

"She's armed, Tarin, you—"

I shushed him, as there was a knock on the door. "Lucas? Come on out, please. Pretty sure it doesn't take more than a few minutes. I know you're in there."

He shivered under my grasp. I leaned to whisper in his ear, "Go with her, and complain about the man in the bathroom as if he's a stranger that hit on you. She doesn't recognize me, she saw me when I came in. Go. I know what I'm doing."

I straightened. "It's just a blowjob, boy," I said louder, with a thick southern drawl. "Don't get your panties in a bunch."

Lucas shot me a look of utter disdain, but answered in kind. "Fuck off, old man," he spat. "I'm not your fucking hooker."

I gave him a quick nod and urged him to the door.

As he unlocked it I slipped into the stall. "Whatever, cocktease."

"Problems?" the woman asked. "Why was the door locked?"

"Let's go," Lucas said. "Just some asshole hick."

There was a pause. "Want me to shoot him?"

Lucas choked. "What? No, of course not—Jesus, Lena, what the fuck?"

The door closed. I barely heard Lena's voice outside the door, "I was kidding, obviously."

I waited a moment longer, then left the bathroom and peeked around the edge of the nearest shelf. I wouldn't have a large window. They made their way to the counter, where Lena paid for gas, it sounded like, and a stack of snacks. Lucas kept plucking things from the racks just in front of the counter, seemingly at random, and piling them on.

"I think that's probably enough," Lena said.

"I think maybe you've got a company card," Lucas replied, "and that under the circumstances you can buy me whatever the fuck I want, don't you?"

She snorted, and pulled a card from her wallet. "All of this. Thanks."

While the man at the counter checked her out, I crept around to the back of the store and stayed out of sight. There were cameras, but the rack of monitors at the counter didn't face the customer side. If the old man noticed, he didn't care. He didn't even respond to Lena, just rang up the pile of candy and bagged chips and whatever else Lucas had gotten his hands on.

By the time he gruffly let her know the total, about two hundred dollars, and asked if she wanted cash back, I was as close to the door as I could get without being seen. I waited. She paid, the old man bagged the groceries and handed them to her.

"Take those," she told Lucas.

"Carry your own damn groceries," Lucas shot back. Good boy. "Women, am I right?"

The old man gave a short, raspy sort of chuckle. The next sound was a plastic bag being snatched off a counter. "Long trip to Atlanta," Lena said, and made it sound like a threat.

A second later, the bell to the door rang, and two sets of footsteps marched out.

I slipped around the shelf and rushed the door, shushing the old man as I intercepted it before it rang the bell. He didn't seem remotely concerned. I wondered what kind of shit he'd seen before this.

I made it to Lena about half a second before she caught on and turned. The bag was in her right hand, and she had to drop it to reach for her gun. That heartbeat long delay was precisely what I needed to tackle her against the side of the car.

The moment her back struck, she brought a knee up to my groin that I barely managed to turn aside with my thigh. I did not manage to spot the elbow she threw next, though, and it smashed into my temple. My world spun, half my face seemed to go both numb and turn into a bruise at the same time. Eyesight on the left side of my face went dark.

I didn't need to see, though, to grab her by the lapels of her jacket and twist sideways to hurl her away from the car and onto the ground. Her feet left the cement and she went careening away to land with a grunt and a curse. As she scrambled to get up, I staggered toward her half blind and kicked hard at her midsection as her hand again disappeared into her coat for the gun. The toe of my boot connected and she gave a retching, coughing sound before she curled briefly around her midsection. Her hand came up, though, and it had the gun in it.

"Get behind the car!" I barked, and hoped that Lucas listened before I stomped down on the Templar's wrist. She howled, and the crunching of bones contracted muscles. The gun thundered.

I dropped to a knee and smashed my fist into the side of her face. When that didn't do it, I tried again, and again, until finally her eyes were rolling and blood coursed from a split on her temple.

I took the gun from weak fingers and considered killing her. There was a camera above the door, and it was pointed right at us. Instead, I turned, and fired into the two tires on my side of her car. They hissed, and flattened, and I ejected the clip, cleared the chamber, and released the slide. I tossed the pieces in different directions, and then turned to give Lena a final kick to the side of the head.

If she was dead, she deserved it. If not, I hoped to be too far gone for it to matter when she recovered herself. There were a lot of back roads between us and the ranch.

I found Lucas cowering on the other side of the car, his hands over his head as if waiting for debris to crash down on him. "Come on," I said. "We have to go. She can't follow yet but she will, or someone else will. We need to get out of here."

Lucas nodded, got unsteadily to his feet. He looked over the car, and saw Lena. He took a sharp step back, horrified, and looked away with one hand over his mouth. "Holy shit... what did you—"

"She'd have killed you," I said. "She'd have killed me. I'll explain while we drive, but trust me that the Templars are fanatical murderers. She's alive and that's more than she deserves. We need to go, Lucas. Now."

He shook his head like he needed to dislodge the image from his eyes, and pulled at the handle to the driver's side door. "I need my phone, but the car's locked."

"No time," I told him. "We can't afford to waste a second. You can use mine. Let's go."

He hesitated a second longer, then forced out a frustrated breath and stormed past me toward my car. "Fine," he growled. "And then you need to tell me everything and it had better make sense."

I followed and we both threw ourselves into the car. As I sped away from the place and started to lay it all out, however, I didn't think there was any version of it that was going to make sense anytime soon.

Chapter 10 - Lucas

"So let me just... make sure I'm hearing all of this correctly," I said to Tarin once he laid out his version of the... *circumstances*. "I'm a 'sacred' omega, which is a kind of breeding mare for *dragons*, who are all male because the *Templars* killed off all dragon females centuries before and now you're collecting *omegas* like Pokémon to help save your species from extinction, while the Templars are hunting us down to kill us off to keep your species from taking over—whether you would do that or not—and some of your people, like Mr. Drake, masquerade as humans and want to round us up if they can find us and make a lot more of us by forcing us to breed, and you found me using spies that are out there *looking* for us. But you and your people are somehow *different* than Drake and his people."

Tarin nodded, eyes intent on the road as he drove well over the speed limit for a dark, though gradually lightening, rural road that kept us off the highway. "I think you took some liberties there," he said, "but those are the bones of it, yes."

"And you can prove any of this?" I asked. "Because I think you know that sounds like fantasy."

"I suppose I could get you pregnant," Tarin mused.

When that was all he said, I snorted. "You know, I'm not sure if that was the punchline or the setup, but either way you are very bad at jokes."

"I'm only half joking," he said. "Besides, you'd have to wait a few months before you knew for sure if I was serious. Still, there's part of the process that you'd be hard-pressed to explain."

"Process?" I pinched my eyebrows together. "What process?"

"Getting pregnant," he clarified, blithe as he cast me a dubious look. "You're aware how it works?"

A little heat went to my cheeks. "I certainly *thought* I did. There are supposed to be at least a few perks to being gay, you know, and not accidentally having children is one of them. So are you saying that if I had ever had unprotected sex, I was at risk of getting pregnant?"

Tarin chuckled, shaking his head. He glanced at the rearview mirror as he did. He did that every few minutes. "A human wouldn't be able to impregnate you. Only a dragon. The process is biological but also mystical in nature."

"Because if there are dragons," I muttered, "of course there must be magic, too."

"Obviously," he said. "You're taking this much better than I expected. Well done."

I rolled my eyes. "I don't think I am. I think I'm just in shock from all the abductions and violence. This is not a normal day."

He took a turn onto a gravel road. "If you'd listened to me to begin with..."

"Do you hear yourself when you talk?" I asked. "Tell me one person you can think of that would have responded positively to being drugged and kidnapped."

"Fair," he countered, "but you have to admit that if I'd told you all this over dinner you wouldn't have come with me."

That was definitely true. I sulked against the door, arms folded, still not sure what I thought about any of it. Obviously it was all bullshit. The question was—why? I entertained some obviously delusional theories to try and explain it. One of them bordered on plausible if I considered that fabulously wealthy people were frequently unhinged. That was: Mr. Drake had somehow set all of this up as an elaborate, well-funded, reality TV-style prank. There were cameras everywhere, and at some point we would finally stop—probably the moment I announced that I believed what Tarin was telling me—and everyone at Camelot Legal would come out from behind some scenery laughing and clapping and it would turn out to be some kind of hazing scenario.

I did say 'delusional' theories.

Sherlock Holmes supposedly said in one of those books that when all other possibilities have been exhausted then whatever remains, however impossible, must nonetheless be true. Or something like it, at any rate. I was not so out of possibilities that I had to go looking at the impossible explanations just yet.

"Do all dragons look like people?" I asked, needing to break that pointless loop in my brain long enough to let all the facts to date churn in my unconscious. I'd come to some critical insights on cases that way. "Or is 'dragon' some kind of metaphor?"

"Not a metaphor," he said. "And no, they don't. Well... not always. We're shape shifters—we can look like people, or like dragons, and our dragon forms are mutable. Large, small, something in between."

"Can you fly?" I asked.

Tarin nodded.

"Are you aerodynamic?" I pressed. "Hollow-boned? Do you flap your wings like a bat? You know this designer figured out how humans with wings could fly, and he had to keep changing things until the human looked like a bird for it to work."

He eyed me critically. "If I didn't know you better, I'd wonder if you rambled when you were anxious."

"I do, as a matter of fact." I slumped down into the seat. "But that doesn't really change the question. How do dragons fly?"

"A combination of aerodynamic evolution and magnetic interaction," he said. "We can sense and interact with the earth's magnetic field, use it to reduce the need for lift, and therefore thrust."

I grunted. "Fine, okay. So why don't we pull over and you show me. Or do you only change on a full moon or something?"

Tarin's jaw muscle twitched, and he winced as if I'd pinched him. "You'll have to wait until we reach Comfort for that. I'm... ill-equipped."

"You have to admit that does seem rather convenient," I pointed out. The world outside was beginning to get greener, the trees thicker. I was entirely lost but it looked like we were on the verge of driving into dense forest. "So what, you can't get your dragon up?"

When he replied, it was with none of the smart-ass tone he'd had a moment before. "You might say it was... taken from me. I haven't been in my scales for a very long time."

"Cursed by a witch?" I guessed.

"No," he said softly, and took another turn, this time onto a paved but very narrow road through the forest, "by my own people."

I had to remind myself that there were people in the world who could become so immersed in their own fantasies that they believed them wholeheartedly. Just because Tarin seemed suddenly to be struggling under an immense weight didn't mean that what he was saying was true—just that he believed it was. Even so... I couldn't help wondering. "Why would they do that?"

"I saved a town," he said. "And the three hundred or so people that lived there. Most of them, anyway. I lost twelve."

I studied what I could see of his face, looking for some sign of insanity as if it were the sort of thing you could see right up front—even though I knew from experience that wasn't the case. "That doesn't exactly make a good case for dragons as the good guys."

"I suppose it doesn't."

"So what was the problem?" I pressed. "Why punish you for helping people?"

He sighed, and shrugged one shoulder. "We have laws," he explained. "One of them is to keep ourselves hidden. When we first arrived here, we were more open. The response was not welcoming, so we went into hiding. My people are very strict, we have a rigidly hierarchical society—the Ancients lay down the law, and we follow it or pay the penalty. I lived in a small town in Virginia at the time, and when the British attacked we were unprepared. Out of the way. My only chance to ensure that these people I lived among didn't perish was to defend them myself. In human form, we're every bit as vulnerable as you are. Well... nearly, in any case. So I changed, and ran them off. Word spread quickly, my people came for me and because of the nature of my abuse, I was bound into this form, so that I wouldn't further risk exposing us."

I blinked slowly. "The British? When was this?"

"In 1779," he said. "Pushing close to three centuries now."

"The American Revolution?" My jaw dropped. "You're not... so what, you're immortal?"

"Not remotely," Tarin assured me. "Just very long-lived. I'll die like any other living thing, eventually—especially if something kills me."

That was about the limit of what I was willing to indulge. The way he talked about it all, like it was an old, old pain made me wonder just how invested in this he really was.

Not that I could deny everything he said. Lena *had* confirmed that she was with Templar Industries—which could be the same thing as being 'a Templar'. And she had not equivocated on what was in store for me. If this wasn't an elaborate prank, then whether I really was what Tarin said or not, and whether any of the rest of it was true or not—I was certainly in danger from those people.

If letting Tarin play pretend and live in fantasies was a requirement for getting far away and regrouping somewhere that I could call the police or the FBI and file charges against Templar Industries for sending Lena after me, whatever the reason ultimately was, then it was a small price to pay. And if I had to play along? Well, that wouldn't kill me either. Not like a gun would.

"I'm sorry that happened to you," I said. "It sounds terrible."

Tarin snorted. "There's nothing here for you to indulge, Lucas. I know you don't believe me. Don't worry. We'll be in Comfort soon enough, and then I can prove all of it."

"And if you do," I wondered, "what then? Say I'm what you think—a sacred omega. Then what? You knock me up? Just like that?"

"What?" He looked shocked. "Of course not. Not without your—that is to say, you're not under obligation to have anyone's child, Lucas. The whole point is to keep you from going *in* to that kind of situation. I promise you, I'm not taking you to be a concubine. In all of this, it's your choice."

"And if I don't want to have a dragon baby?" I asked. "What if it's just not in the cards for me; what if I just walk away?"

"Then that will be your choice," he said. "Obviously, I want you to be safe. But if you determine that you want no part of what we're doing there… well, then you will be welcome to go your own way. No one at the ranch will stop you."

I supposed I would find out. As we drove through the dawn, I tried to be intentionally anxious, tried to remind myself that there was someone after me, someone who wanted to kill me or sterilize me, and that I was driving around with someone who was certainly crazy—even if he was telling partial truths.

And yet, even when I tried to feel it, that strange feeling that I had around Tarin, and around Caleb Drake, seemed to work against it. Like some persistent, repeating message:
You're safe here, Lucas.

Tarin would never hurt you.

I did my best not to believe it.

Chapter 11 - Tarin

"I have to pee," Lucas announced, around four hours into our drive. Taking the long way, we were maybe another six hours out from Comfort. We were nowhere remotely close to a place to stop—I had intentionally taken the most rural path I could to avoid both a local Elder, just in case, and to avoid any place with a camera. Bad enough I'd taken Lucas first out from under Calavastrix's nose; now I'd stolen him from the Templars as well.

One whiff of him, possibly by either depending on what kind of intelligence they had on one another, and I'd bring both of those forces to Spitfire Ranch.

"I'll stop at the next shoulder," I told him. "You can go in the woods."

Lucas heaved a heavy sigh but didn't otherwise complain.

Soon enough, there was a narrow side road that had a wide entrance, enough that something large could make the turn easily, and I parked just inside and leaned to look through his window. "Seems okay. Be quick."

"Do we have time for me to stretch my legs a little?" he asked. "Between the two abductions it feels like I've been in a car for… close to forever."

"Can I trust you not to run?"

He rolled his eyes. "No," he drawled, "you can't, because I was a Cub Scout in fifth grade and can easily survive in the wilderness while I make my way back to civilization following the sun and stars and moss on trees."

"That must be why you're so upfront and honest," I muttered. "Scout's honor and all that. The closest town is north, about ten miles. Don't eat any berries that don't look familiar."

We stared at one another a long moment before he grunted and pushed the door open to go.

I did trust him not to run—he had nowhere to go, and no phone to use even if there was service out here. Still, I hadn't stretched my legs in a little while either. I got out and rounded the car to his side while he walked a few yards away from the road, looking for a place to go.

"It's kind of nice out here," he called back. "I haven't taken a vacation in years. Not that this counts. But my family used to go camping a few times a year. Feels like I've been in the city since… well, when I started college at Georgia Tech actually."

"Go Dawgs," I said.

Lucas unzipped as he looked over his shoulder at me. "Uh, that's UGA, asshole. Go Yellowjackets, thank you very much."

"You're a football fan?" I asked.

He laughed. "Not really, no. But the school pride thing is mandatory at both colleges. Day one, they basically strap you to a chair and indoctrinate you for your first week."

"That sounds uncivilized." So was watching a man piss, even from behind, but it was hard for me to look away and leave him to his business, as if it would only take a moment for

Calavastrix himself to swoop down from the sky and snatch him up. Not that he could pull off a maneuver like that in this kind of cover.

"University culture only has to put on a thin veneer of civilization," Lucas said as he shook himself and zipped again. "It's mostly parties, and sex, and drugs if you want them, and generally wasting your youth being irresponsible while you pray that you get a job good enough to pay off your inevitably crippling student loans. Not that I had a ton."

He crept carefully out of the woods, picking through a copse of thorny bushes and poison ivy.

"What made you want to be a lawyer?" I asked as he neared the road.

He reached toward the sky, clasped his hands and stretched his back as he took on a thoughtful expression. "Money was a big part of it," he said. "My family was always poor. Dirt poor, I mean—trailer park, welfare, local meth problem, the works. My dad was injured when I was a kid, working as a contractor. Construction—he lays foundations. Or he did anyway. The surgeries and medications saddled us with about a hundred grand in debt, so we sold everything we had to sell, he and my mom filed for bankruptcy, and it just sort of stuck. By the time I was in high school, I knew I wanted to do something that paid well. Law seemed natural—I wanted to help people in a way that mattered. And I like to argue, in case you couldn't tell."

"I hadn't noticed," I said. "Feeling better?"

He planted his fists on his hips and stomped each foot a couple of times. "A little," he said. "A walk wouldn't be out of place, especially while it's still a little cool. But I also don't want to come back to a posse of Lena's coworkers waiting for us, so…"

The way he gazed out at the greenery and the faint curtain of morning mist that hung in the upper parts of the canopy here—drifting in from the swamplands that weren't far from where we were—made me think maybe it really had been a long time since Lucas saw anything wild and natural. There was a wistful sort of longing there. And we certainly had time for sightseeing later, when we arrived in Comfort, but that place wasn't lush like here. I had whelped deep in the hills of northern England, north of what was now Leeds all these centuries later. A part of me felt a calm peace out here that I thought I could see in Lucas' eyes.

"We're far enough out of the way that we probably have time for a short stroll," I told him. "And I don't think anyone will catch up with us very soon, if they do at all. My legs could use some circulation."

Lucas pursed his lips as he slipped his hands into his pockets and glanced around at the trees. "I mean… if you're sure. How far away are we from where we're going?"

"We'll be there by noon," I said. "Come on. There are trails off of all these dirt roads."

The corner of his mouth tried to twitch up into a smile but he bowed his head a moment, clearly trying to hide it, and then shrugged. "Sure."

I locked up the car and we took the road north until, indeed, we spotted a trail just wide enough for two people to walk. There were tire tracks as well, it was some sort of service road perhaps, but clumps of the more persistent weeds had pushed up through the hard-packed soil. Until we'd walked perhaps a quarter mile down the trail, only the sounds of the forest around kept it from being a walk in silence.

"Are you close with your family?" I finally asked after we paused so that Lucas could breathe in the scent of fresh honeysuckle that clung to a tree where the sun likely managed to shine for a few hours each day. There was something so innocent and childlike about his simple enjoyment that I found myself wondering if he'd escaped a family or if he expected to be some kind of savior for them.

"Kind of," he said. "My dad's older, a baby boomer. Kind of… not all that interested in me. My mom is about twenty years younger than him. I was a bit of an accident, really. Still, she says I was a happy accident, just like her marriage. They never intended to get very serious. Just sort of got that way after a while."

"Do you see them regularly?"

"Are you asking if they'll miss me when I'm gone?" he asked, and straightened from breathing in the flowers to give me a hard stare.

"Of course not," I told him. "I'm just curious."

If I was entirely honest, I was a bit guilty as well—if everything progressed ideally, we would introduce Lucas to a dragon that he connected with, perhaps even fell in love with, and he'd eventually have a child. It would be tricky explaining that to his parents, especially if he saw them more than once a year.

Lucas picked up on that, perhaps. He studied my face until I looked away. "I haven't seen them in a couple of years," he said finally. "We talk every once in a while but… I've just been busy, and it's a long drive down to Tifton, where they live—south Georgia, almost to Florida. Things have been tense with them ever since I came out, so… I keep meaning to make plans to go down more often, though. Just never really seems to be the right time. You know how it goes. Or… I don't know, do you? Are you close with your parents?"

The question caught me a little off guard. I gave a quiet snort. "Of course not."

His eyebrows pinched. "Is that… usual, then?"

"It is," I said. "Sorry—I'm not sure I've ever been asked. Dragon parents are typically absentee. I was one of the last generations born from two dragons, mother and father. We're hatched, you see, over the course of ten to twelve years."

"Uh, you didn't mention—"

"Not in the case of omega birth," I said, smiling. "That would be live birth, and the children are born in their human form. The first change often comes during puberty, rarely earlier. But in the old days and perhaps the future, we were buried in a kind of stone nest, near a natural source of heat. Volcanoes, hot springs, thermal vents. We hatch largely capable of fending for ourselves, so we do. Our parents drive prey to us, and we hunt, and grow, and only occasionally encounter them. There is a formal naming ceremony, but… before and after that, it's entirely possible to never meet them."

Lucas squinted at me. "Like lizard parents."

"Lizard is… something of an epithet for us," I said. "Nonetheless… yes."

"I wouldn't want to have a kid if the father was going to be like my dad," he said. "Not that I'm… I'm just saying, even if I could have a baby myself, and wanted to, I wouldn't do it if the father—the other father—was going to, I don't know, drive rabbits into our yard once a year and otherwise keep a distance."

I cocked my head at him. "So you're open to the idea?"

He plucked a sprig of honeysuckle and waved it under his nose. "I didn't say that," he murmured. "Just, you know—hypothetically."

He inhaled the scent of the flower and cleared his throat. "Honeysuckle always takes me right back to childhood. Reminds me of our yard from when I was little. We had three bushes, they covered most of the fence in the back of the house. I couldn't have been more than three or four, I guess? But it still makes me think of… I don't know. Small places? There was this tree, I don't know what kind it was, but it had a canopy that spread out, with branches that brushed the ground. Inside, it was like a little cave. I would take toys in there and play, and pretend it was a fort. The honeysuckle must have grown right next to it, because I could always smell them in the spring and throughout the summer. I barely remember anything else, of course. But I remember that. Weird how that one thing makes such a big impression. Like, somehow it kind of redeems my whole shitty childhood. Emotionally, anyway. Which I guess is all that counts in the end, right? It's not like I got rickets or tetanus and was crippled for life or something. Even though I certainly could have some of those years."

Something inside me swelled slightly as he spoke. Silly, of course—it was just some childhood memory of his, but there was something achingly poignant about it and the way his eyes lidded slightly as he recalled it. He breathed in the scent of the flowers as if more of it could somehow illuminate the memory further—as if it was something he wanted deeply, but couldn't quite get. His brow knit tightly, and his eyes closed entirely as he inhaled again.

When he opened his eyes, I was staring. He cleared his throat and lowered the honeysuckle from his face. "What?"

I shook my head and remembered to neutralize my facial expression. "We should…"

He tucked the honeysuckle into the pocket of his button-up. "Yeah, I know. I'm ready if you are."

The way he said it, I stood frozen for a heartbeat thinking, for some reason, that he meant… something else. But he strode past me, trailing reason and sense behind him. He meant, of course, that he was ready to *leave* if I was.

How I could have imagined he meant anything else… was a question to worry about once I deposited him at the ranch, and accepted Reece's inevitable banishment.

Chapter 12 - Lucas

The walk in the woods helped clear my head a little bit. Just the last wisps of brain fog and shock that had clung to me since I woke up in Tarin's back seat, but they'd been buzzing around like bees uncertain of where to settle since then. Now, they seemed to have found a place to rest.

The rest of the drive was as pleasant as a possible human trafficking event was going to be. We chatted more about my work, what it was like going to Georgia Tech, and why I hadn't quit my job even though at times it clearly was trying to make me quit. I told him my personal mantra for professional life. "There is no short game," I intoned, "only the long game."

"Interesting," Tarin mused. "I take that to mean you make very few short-term goals?"

"Only when they further a long-term goal," I explained. "And I tend to ignore short-term nuisances. Or, you know, mitigate the irritation with alcohol or something. Not that I drink in response to stress. Well, I do—everyone does. I'm not an alcoholic or anything, though."

"Or neurotic about it in the least," he said, amused at my rambling. "I'm not concerned with your drinking, Lucas."

Neither was I, but the instinct to explain myself to him, to make sure he didn't think poorly of me, was growing stronger every hour we were together. I *wanted* him to like me. I thought maybe he did, too. At the same time, the reasoning part of my brain seemed to understand clearly just how fucked up that was. Sure, Stockholm Syndrome was a legitimate psychological ailment, but I always assumed it took more than a day to kick in. That and a lot more trauma to try and escape from. Was I really that fragile? I reasoned that working for Camelot Legal probably helped whittle me down for it. Maybe this was just the straw that broke the junior lawyer's spirit.

About Tarin, I learned mostly generalities and more of his dragon delusions. He 'had his wings bound' after a short internment that lasted from 1779 to 1795, during which time some very old dragons called 'The Ancients' were apparently woken up from very long naps to deliberate on his fate. It took them a further five years to discuss that, and when it was done he was put in his human form and kept from changing back. His sentence would be up around the time the planet grew too hot for human life and then it wouldn't particularly matter. "Dragons will still be around," he assured me, "we can handle very extreme conditions. But I imagine we'll likely starve or die out from lack of mates. Or perhaps we can manage to clean the world up once there isn't a tide of seven billion people pushing back."

"That is... very bleak," I observed. "And also somehow oddly optimistic."

He shrugged. "Like you said—there is only a long game. Dragons are predisposed to think long-term. Easy to do that, when you expect to be around a very long time."

Tarin told me also about his many travels. It was tricky, getting around the world on foot, then by horse and carriage, but his adventurous spirit really took off around the time that planes became a thing. "That is," he said dourly, "until they became a more secure kind of travel. Now that you need ID and passports and such to get around, well... it's less accessible."

"A thousand something years on the planet and you don't have an ID?" I asked.

"I do," he said, "of course. But not one that will stand up to scrutiny very well. I formed a small company in the late 1800s to manage investments and banking for me, and I utilize a lawyer to move funds around when I need them. A descendant of the people I intervened for when I was sentenced."

I thought about that for a moment, chasing down a stray realization until I finally managed to grab it. "Wait... Annette—is she also a descendant of one of those people?"

Tarin's conspiratorial smile confirmed it but he nodded once. "She is, in fact," he said. "Her ancestors were freed after the villagers pledged their loyalty to me once the British left. I swore them to secrecy, and gave them my word that they and their children would be protected no matter the outcome of the war, even if I had to take them west and build a new country for them myself."

The math was not hard to do. "So... they were slaves."

"Of course not," he said quickly, "I was never cruel to them, those stereotypes are—"

"Annette's ancestors," I clarified. "They would have been slaves in that village. Virginia, pre-revolutionary?"

He frowned. "Those were different times," he said quietly. "However, when I no longer had to blend in among them, freeing Annette's ancestors was my first and only demand. I have seen a number of empires fall from relying too heavily on slavery, and enough human suffering to last me the rest of my days. In part, that is why her family has remained so loyal to me. They are my dragonmarked."

Annette *had* spoken to Tarin with an almost reverent degree of deference, as if he were incredibly important to her. Being the person who paid off some debt or helped save the business didn't seem like enough to engender that sort of enthusiasm.

Being a mythical creature who secretly supported your family for about two and a half centuries, though... that might do it.

I studied Tarin's face from the side. Other than handsome, it looked entirely earnest. Matter-of-fact. Yes, it was possible he was delusional, and that Annette had gotten roped into it somehow. Cult leaders did that sort of thing all the time.

On the other hand, it did fit. It made sense. And it nearly made me tip over the edge into believing everything he'd said so far.

Tarin was either incredibly charming, or being as truthful as he know how to be. Those two options had blended together as we talked, until I realized that I had more or less forgotten just how I ended up in the car with him.

"You're staring," he said softly.

"You're handsome," I said automatically. And while it was true, it had come out by accident. My cheeks warmed, and when I tried to follow up with some other comment to turn it into a joke, or something, nothing came out.

Tarin stared ahead at the road. "I... appreciate the compliment. I made this body myself. I suppose I had several good examples."

There simply was no good response to *that*, so I didn't give one.

And when he didn't return the compliment in kind, I reminded myself that it didn't matter. That didn't make it feel any less disappointing, of course.

We made last half hour or so in silence as the hot Texas sun burned away all the moisture in the air that we'd enjoyed before. The forest and grasslands had given way to baked earth pocked by heavily irrigated plots of farmland, or pastures dotted with cattle. We made one turn after another down bumpy back roads until we reached an old highway that hadn't seen a dollar's worth of infrastructure spending probably since it was first laid.

And at the end of it, we made a right turn onto a gravel road that led about a mile off the highway to a tall, broad ranch gate. Just as Tarin had promised, the title "Spitfire Ranch" stood in big, beaten-iron letters along the top. Some distance beyond even that, a large, two-level farmhouse painted white with bright red shutters, surrounded by copses of colorful flowers, came into view beyond a small natural fence of tall pines.

"It's real," I said quietly. "This place, I mean. I don't know about the rest of it but I admit that up until this moment I honestly kind of thought you might be lying about where we were going."

"I haven't lied to you once," Tarin said. He hummed skeptically. "Well, except at the very beginning, I guess. But now, I can prove the rest to you. Are you ready?"

I rubbed my eyes and tried to laugh but what came out was a kind of nervous choking sound. "Um... for you to prove that there are dragons and also somehow that I can get pregnant? Would anyone reasonably be 'ready' for that?"

He gave a nod of concession. "Fair enough. Then at least, are you ready to meet the others? Probably they will be... unhappy to see me. But I promise, no matter what happens, they will be thrilled to meet you. So if one of them seems a little furious try not to hold it against him. I specifically defied his wishes going to retrieve you. Mm... perhaps keep the bit about your employer and the Templars to yourself."

"Wait, so you weren't even supposed to—"

Before I could finish the thought, a voice boomed from the porch as the door was flung wide. "Come back when you acquire any sense of respect or shame!"

An old man with sunbaked skin, wearing a black Stetson with a natural-looking leather vest, marched out of the house, followed by a younger man in a similar get-up. Both were stacked, like their whole lives consisted of lifting heavy things. A tall, handsome middle-aged fellow seemed to be practically chasing them out.

"I will not entertain a single wolven delegation until you demonstrate your ability to govern your own people," he roared. "Do not violate this territory again or you will learn the nature of consequences in dealings with my dragons. Return when your people are under control!"

The two men fleeing the house hopped into a rugged, ancient white pick-up truck and pulled away from the house. As they passed us, the driver—the older of the two—met my eyes briefly, and then very clearly clocked Tarin's presence in the car. His lips moved as he said something to his partner.

It was brief, and I couldn't tell any more than that, but I had seen more than enough passing meetings with clients, enough people taking last-minute counsel from their lawyers as they entered a room, to know that it was an observation and a comment of some kind. I turned slightly to watch the truck go, and saw the man in the passenger side doing the same.

"What… is that about?" I asked.

Tarin shook his head, grim. "I'm not sure. But… you're about to meet Reece."

"Tarin," Reece boomed as he stormed toward the car. "What. Have. You. Done?"

With a long, shaky exhale, Tarin opened his door. "Stay inside until I call for you."

He left and approached the bigger man. They exchanged quieter but obviously tense words before finally Reece looked over Tarin's shoulder at me, gave Tarin a disgusted look and finally waved a hand harshly in what was obviously a "get out of my sight" gesture.

Tarin stiffened, looked over his shoulder and waved me out of the car. I almost didn't respond. Reece looked *angry*, and even dangerous—like a man who might fly off the handle any moment now. But Tarin waved again, and I got out, closed the door behind me, and stood by it nervously, my stomach fluttering with the need to decide whether I was about to run or fight.

Reece, however, appeared to soften a little as he muttered something I couldn't hear to Tarin. Tarin gave a nod, shot me a hopeful, encouraging look, and then… left.

I watched him go as Reece approached me, and felt a visceral kind of pull toward him. He couldn't just leave me here—was he being thrown out or something? He was the only person in this place that I knew, assuming there even *was* anyone besides the man I'd just seen throw three people off his property. Was there some protocol I didn't know about that would earn me the same fate?

"You must be Lucas," Reece said, his voice significantly toned down and civil. Despite Tarin's describing him as a dragon as well, he didn't have the same aura that Tarin did—that peculiar warmth and strange halo of safety that he shared with Caleb Drake. "I am Reece Stiles. I must apologize, with deepest sincerity, for the means by which you come here. I assure you, my… *friend* was expressly forbidden from stealing away with you, or even making contact."

I opened my mouth to say that he *had* supposedly saved me from a life of alleged sexual slavery as well as a very much not-merely-alleged assassin-slash-hitperson, but somehow I suspected that would only make things worse for Tarin; hence his admonition before. "It, ah... he didn't treat me poorly," I said. "Or... anyway, it got significantly better after the first little bit. Is he going to be okay? I mean, it looked like he, um... will I see him again?"

Reece peered at me, then looked in Tarin's direction before he made a soft, curious little grunt, as if coming to a surprising but not world-shattering revelation. He nodded slowly. "Yes, I think you will. Tarin informed me that you have been made aware of the nature of this place, though he has not presented clear proof of his assertions."

The man almost spoke like a very old lawyer. It took my brain a few seconds to make the necessary adjustments to the odd cadence and choice of words he used. "He... yes, he told me some things."

"Then understand," Reece said, "the security of this place is my highest priority and concern. My mate and my child live here. Their safety is first in every decision I make. I am not angry with you at all. It was clearly not your choice. But I must decide what consequences Tarin will bear for potentially bringing danger to my family."

"I hope you go easy on him," I said.

Again, that same assessing, revelatory look. But this time Reece only bobbed his head and then turned toward the house. "Come then," he said. "Let me introduce you. Welcome to Spitfire Ranch. I fear you have come at a complicated time, but you are welcome."

"Complicated?" I asked as I caught up. "Those men that were leaving just now?"

"Indeed," Reece sighed.

"What's the problem?" I followed him up the steps to the door. "I'm a lawyer. Not technically licensed in Texas but... maybe I can help."

"Doubtful," he said as he pulled the door open for me. "It is not a legal dispute."

"What kind of problem is it, then?"

Reece gestured me into the house, his expression dark. "It seems we may be about to go to war."

Chapter 13 - Lucas

Bewildered by what exactly Reece meant about that, I followed him into the house when he invited me. At the threshold, I looked in the direction Tarin had gone. "Where did Tarin go?"

"To contemplate the ramifications of his choices," Reece said. He led me inside the house. "We both needed time to cool down. Are you hungry? There is food. I believe my mate is in the kitchen, helping to prepare for lunch."

In answer, my stomach growled. Reece glanced back at me. I smiled weakly. "I guess that's a yes."

"Then you have arrived at an opportune moment," he said. We reached a wider doorway at the end of the hall, and he stepped aside to let me pass through first. "Just through here. Matthew—we have a new guest."

I went into the kitchen ahead of Reece to find a tall, dark-haired man who looked about my age at a large, wood-topped kitchen island. There were plates stacked on one corner, and he was finishing making a sandwich while another man, blond and wiry, cut another one and stacked it on a platter. It was the dark-haired man that smiled at Reece like they were obviously in love, then turned a slightly less amorous smile on me. Still warm, though. "I see. So that's where Tarin went, I take it."

A woman with a mound of coppery dreadlocks on her head emerged from a door that led outside. She had a plump baby on her hip and was in the midst of some soothing diatribe in baby speak when her eyes lit up to see me. "Oh! Is this the new one?"

"That's Mercy," Matthew said. His smile became strained. "Mercy, meet…?"

"Lucas," I offered as I approached the island. "Lucas Warren. Nice to meet you. I think. I'm not totally clear… am I like a guest or…?"

The three of them all grew quizzical.

Reece emerged from behind me to stand near Matthew, arms folded, his expression troubled. "Tarin extended a rather more compulsory invitation than we had discussed."

Matthew peered up at his 'mate', frowning, before he finally seemed to catch on to what Reece meant. He gave me a horrified look and put down the butter knife he'd been using to spread something on the sandwich. "Fuck. Lucas, I'm so, so sorry—I promise, that's not how we do things here. Christ, what was Tarin thinking? Where is he?"

"At the barn," Reece said. "I am going to join him presently. Lucas has had a long trip, and appears to be hungry. If you would feed him, my love, I will deal with Tarin and then we all can address the *other* situation. As if our circumstances were not complex enough. Lucas, our home is your home, for so long as you choose to remain here. You *are* a guest, and if it is your wish you may leave when you choose. Mercy will happily escort you to the airport if you decide that. In the meantime, please eat."

With that, he pulled Matthew into a brief but passionate kiss—chaste enough that I didn't feel like an intruder but so momentarily absorbed that I had the impression the rest of us and the room simply didn't exist for them in that moment. When they parted, Matthew had the kind of grin on his lips that he couldn't have hidden if he'd tried.

"Always with this," the blond said. He wiped his hands on his jeans before he approached me, hand extended. "I am Yuri Kompanichenko. You can call me Yuri, of course."

"And this," Mercy said, waving the baby's hand for her, "is Danni. Matt and Reece's beautiful, adorable, perfect little baby girl, *yesh, she ith, ithn't she? Yes, yes, she is.*"

Mercy devolved quickly into gibberish baby speak as the child broke into the kind of grin that belonged on a baby-food jar and waved her hands excitedly at the attention.

"You... adopted?" I asked Matthew. Somewhat hopefully.

The three of them shared a look that I couldn't decipher before Matthew focused on another sandwich. "Did Tarin... explain to you why he brought you here?"

"He did." I pulled a stool from the side of the island and sat on it. Now that I realized how hungry I was, I couldn't stop staring at the pile of sandwiches. "Um... at least I think he did. Mind telling me your version so I can corroborate? No offense."

"None taken at all," Matthew said. "Yuri, would you tell Sasha we're done here?"

"Yes, boss," Yuri muttered.

From the look Matthew gave him as he left, I gathered he was joking. "There's the short version and the long version," he said when Yuri left through the back door to get 'Sasha'. "You have a preference?"

I shrugged. "Short and factual is ideal."

He nodded once, approving. "All right. Danni is my biological daughter—and Reece's. I gave birth to her. Reece is a dragon. So are Tarin and Sasha. I'm an omega—they call us 'sacred' omegas but I think that's a kind of honorific; dragons are big on tradition—and you wouldn't be here unless you were one or the other. You're not a dragon, so that only leaves the other. Your ancestors from way back were wolven, mostly likely—those are people who can turn into wolves—and when the Templars—who are fanatics who want to kill us and the dragons and probably the wolven too, eventually—killed off all their females, the story goes that the wolven donated some of their omegas to help them survive. The other version of the story says that the dragons took a few for themselves. Either way, in the end, they were altered with magic so that they could bear the children of dragons, and here you and I are. There's an attempted genocide in there for us as well, but it didn't take apparently. Let me... get you a glass of water."

Probably he offered because I had slowly opened my mouth and now stared at him. Not that I had any reason to believe that he wasn't in on the... conspiracy? Joke? But in any case the way he delivered it with such a casual matter of fact attitude made it hard to simply deny that any of it was remotely true. Still. I took the water from him and looked at it for a long moment. "How is any of that possible?"

Matthew chuckled as he shook his head slowly. "Believe me, I know exactly what you're thinking and feeling right now. A little over a year ago I was in exactly the same spot."

"With Reece," I guessed.

"With Reece," he breathed.

The baby cooed, and Matthew looked up from two slices of bread to smile at her. "There's formula in the fridge, Mercy," he said. "I fixed it up earlier."

Mercy gasped with mock surprise at Danni. "Formula? It must be your birthday or something! Come on, let's chow down."

Matthew watched his daughter a moment longer before returning to his work and me. "I didn't believe any of it myself. And then I was pregnant, and then I saw Reece's true form—his dragon—and... I've seen other things since then. It's a lot, and I don't blame you one bit for being skeptical. Just be glad you got here before the Templars found you. Reece had to, ah... help me out of a tight spot with them. Twice, actually."

I shifted uncomfortably on the stool. "Yeah. Tarin, um... had to do something similar. This woman picked me up. She had a gun, works for Templar Industries—who I was about to start representing in a trademark case. Or, I don't know—maybe that was all a ruse? It sort of seemed like it was too good to be true when it happened. We stopped, and Tarin caught up and..."

Matthew grimaced. "I know. They are particular when it comes to us. But trust me, the Templars are fanatics. If he hadn't killed her, she would have—"

"Oh, Jesus, no," I said quickly, "he didn't kill her. I think he would have but... it was at a convenience store, and there were cameras and it's bad enough that he's on video having beaten her like he did. And he snuck up on her so in any court in the country they'd convict him for aggravated assault. Maybe attempted murder, too. It was bad."

He had frozen. Mercy had, too, at the fridge, with a bottle of pale liquid in one hand.

"He didn't kill her?" Matthew asked.

I shook my head.

"Are you sure she didn't follow you?" he pressed. "You didn't see any cars behind you on the way here? What kind of cover did you drive through—was there open sky?"

It was difficult to see what the problem was, and only moments before Matthew had seemed like a nice enough person—but it was obvious he was upset not that Tarin had nearly beaten a woman to death but that he *hadn't* beaten her death. "I don't... I'm not really sure. I don't think so? We did most of the drive through a national forest, there were trees, but—"

"It's all right." He held a hand up. "It's fine. It's not your fault... here. Have something to eat. The others will be in soon, we can talk about it then."

"Is there a problem?" I asked. "I mean... I know these people are bad news but that was a long way away. She was unconscious when we left, it isn't like she could have gotten up and come after us."

Mercy placed the bottle in a pot on the stove and lit the burner. "Don't be so sure. They don't give up. They've been looking for this place for the last year. They've got satellites, spies, government officials in their pockets. If she knew you were coming this direction... it's more information to go on."

My stomach sank. Whether I believed all of it or not, Lena had definitely intended to hurt me, or take me somewhere to be hurt—that much, I was certain was real. I hadn't even considered the idea of being spied on by satellites or that an entire organization was dedicated to hunting me down. How had this place even stayed secret if that were true?

"For now," Matthew said, "try not to worry. Take a plate. Eat something."

The pile of sandwiches was nothing short of prodigious. "How many people are here?"

"Seven," he said, "including you. Three dragons, though, and they eat. A lot. Please—there's plenty."

At his insistence, I took a plate and put a sandwich on it. When I took a bite, that's all I needed to give in to my hunger and wolf the rest down. By the time I finished, Yuri returned with another man, broad and tall with sandy hair and blue eyes that were almost inhumanly clear. He radiated that feeling that both Tarin and Caleb Drake did.

His eyes met mine. "Ah."

"Sasha," Matthew said, "this is Lucas. Lucas—Sasha."

"Dragon," I said. "Right?"

Sasha nodded. "Dragon. You're catching on, I take it."

"There's this feeling..." I muttered. "So is that... what is that exactly?"

Matthew chuckled. "Magic, basically. Chemicals, too; pheromones, that sort of thing. I've been curious about it myself and finally have some lab equipment on the way but... right now it's a bit of a mystery."

"I don't get it from Reece, though," I said.

He pursed his lips thoughtfully at that. "Interesting. Maybe that's because we're mated."

Sasha took three of the sandwiches and piled them on a plate. "I assumed Reece knew," he said. "Now that the two of you belong to one another, he does not appeal to omegas in the same way. Only to you. Likewise, you do not appeal to other dragons. Not chemically, in any case—you are still very attractive."

Matthew rolled his eyes. "All dragons are incorrigible flirts."

"Not all of us," Sasha said as he left the island to find a seat at the large table that filled half the room behind me. "And I'll thank you not to generalize—it treads perilously close to racism, and you should know better."

More eye rolling, but Matthew didn't dignify the complaint with a response.

"So what I feel for Tarin," I said, my voice lowered to nearly a whisper, "it's just... I mean it's not actually real or anything?"

Yuri gave a quiet laugh as he joined Sasha at that table, and Mercy shot me an amused little grin before she took the newly warmed bottle and the baby to the table as well.

Matthew had raised an eyebrow. "I would say it's as real as falling for anyone else," he said. "Just chemicals in your brain. Why? Are you sweet on him?"

In answer, I snatched another sandwich from the plate, and stuffed it into my face. Matthew only laughed, and took the platter to the table. I took the stack of remaining plates, and for the next few minutes at least I didn't really *feel* like a prisoner.

And I found that the more I listened to them chatter about the business of the ranch… the more I started to really worry where Tarin was, and how much trouble he was in.

But, like Matthew said—it was just chemicals. Chemicals and magic.

Chapter 14 -Tarin

"The ignorance, the audacity, and the lack of moral fortitude is simply astounding to me," Reece said, calmer now—not that it was any better like that. We were in the barn, where he had summarily banished me to once I announced to him that I had retrieved Lucas.

"I'll take audacity and some moral flexibility," I shot back, "but not ignorance, Reece. I spotted the opportunity, I knew what Calavastrix would do, I knew the Templars were going to get him on their radar sooner or later, and I acted to save a life. To save an *omega*. Surely you're happy we've found another and that he's here and safe."

Reece's eyes bulged. "Safe? Tarin, he is only marginally safer here now, and at the expense of everyone else. And this Templar that sought him? If you did not kill her, then she will be redoubling her efforts to find him. Likely with help. Once they identify our location, they will come in force."

"Then make peace with the wolven, and bring on more of the outcasts," I urged him. "We need all the allies we can get anyway. Now even more so. This is the beginnings of an entire generation, Reece, can't you see that? It's not about your mate and child anymore—not exclusively. It's time for us to start building this place up, we can add more security, magical and otherwise. I'll liquidate all of my accrued wealth, you draw what you reasonably can from the Hoard, Sasha has his own resources. Between you and him, you can lay magical protections and—"

"And this place can become a prison for all of us," Reece cut in. He forestalled my next argument with a furious look. "The purpose of this place... we were meant to be quiet, unobtrusive, out of the way. That is the only tactic that can successfully keep us hidden. You've brought all manner of threats to our doorstep with this. I hope very much that it was worth it. I assume the two of you have not yet consummated as mates?"

I balked. "Are you kidding me? No, of course we haven't. I abducted him, he doesn't... it's not going to be like that. I thought maybe he and Sasha would hit it off. Besides, I can feel the pull but I don't even know if I can breed. I've had sex with other men in the past few hundred years, but never knotted any of them. Maybe it's an omega thing, or maybe my body just won't make the necessary shift for it. Even if there was any possibility of us becoming involved, I doubt we could get pregnant."

Reece sighed as he turned away from me and raked fingers through his head. "So, not only did you snatch a person of the street—literally—you also hoped to then force not only him, but Sasha to breed?"

"Not force, obviously," I countered. "Just... you know, gently encourage or something. I guess."

The idea of Sasha charming Lucas to the point that they might go that far made me decidedly uncomfortable. That was fair enough. I had found him, brought him here, saved him. It was natural to feel some degree of possessiveness. I could get over it if there was some spark of attraction between them. There almost certainly would be. But Reece had it all wrong—I had no intention of forcing anyone to do anything.

"He's here now," I said as I waited for Reece to turn back to me. "That's done, and it will play out however it does. Tell me about the wolven. What happened? Why were you running them off when we arrived? Is there anything I can do to help? I've got contacts up north who can—"

"We may be well past any negotiating window," he said as he faced me. Apparently he was fine to drop the subject of Lucas for the moment, at least. "Over the past several days, we've met with the two you saw—alpha of a local pack and his son—to discuss the terms of our presence here. They include Comfort in their unofficial territory. If we were another pack, they would have run us out. Because we're not wolven, and not officially claiming territory like other dragons, it's unclear what the protocol is. We were trying to figure it out when Yuri and Sasha discovered scouts probing the ranch. Again, it's a question of protocol and where the lines are drawn, but Sasha seemed to think they were assessing the terrain, looking for ingress and egress, learning the layout and hazards. Perhaps, preparing for a coordinated assault. I don't know for sure, but when I asked that it cease, it was not well-received."

My heart sped up, and the fire that was just out of reach swelled in my stomach. "So I may have just delivered Lucas to an impending shitstorm is what you're saying."

Reece quirked his head quizzically to one side. "Perhaps more importantly," he said slowly, "what we have built here is at risk."

"Obviously," I agreed. "I'm just concerned that—"

"You're concerned for Lucas," Reece cut me off, "that much is clear."

I shrugged. "I feel responsible for him."

"Is that all?" he wondered.

The quiet that descended was thick, and pointed. I snorted softly and looked away from his critical eyes. "Obviously, there's some... natural attraction but it's just the Call. Now that we're here, we'll spend a few days apart and..." I spread my hands, helpless. "What do you want from me?"

"For you to think a few steps ahead, for a start," he grumbled.

I met his glower and held it with my own. "I'm thinking several dozen steps ahead. We have another omega here, we have a chance to convince him it's worth it to be here, and we're better positioned than we were before I left. The wolven are a nuisance, nothing more. The Templars are a threat, but one we can manage. The elders don't know where we are and won't exactly go flying through the skies to find us. Meanwhile, we continue to grow, which means that Matthew's and Danni's futures are more secure. You're welcome."

Reece sneered at me, but his expression smoothed somewhat a heartbeat later. His shoulders sagged slightly, and he walked to the barn door where he paused with one hand on it. "Matthew was preparing lunch. You may as well join us."

"So I'm not kicked out?" I asked.

"If I could afford to…" but he shook his head and pushed through the door.

I waited a few moments before following. Maybe being around Lucas just now wasn't the best idea. If I gave him some time, he might find himself attracted to Sasha, and then perhaps there would be a future for him here. Sasha was a good man, a good dragon—honorable, thoughtful, wise. And he had his scales, and his fire. If push came to shove, he could protect Lucas. I didn't know if I could.

The thought twisted my insides. I had to rationalize it away before I could follow Reece up to the house.

When I arrived in the kitchen and dining room to find the rest of the residents of Spitfire Ranch arranged around the table, everyone around it quieted. Except for Lucas. He straightened when the conversation they were having suddenly stopped, and then looked around to spot me at the back door. "Tarin! You're joining us after all?"

"He is," Reece said, and pulled out the chair next to Lucas before taking his own seat beside Matthew at the far end.

There were other chairs. But I took the one next to Lucas both to give him a familiar face and to avoid further complicating things with Reece. I was passed the platter of remaining sandwiches and a plate, and tried to focus on eating as the conversation resumed.

Lucas leaned toward me, his voice low. "I guess you got a bit of a talking-to?"

Reece undoubtedly could hear us, but he didn't turn his eyes our direction. "Something like that," I replied. "Lucas, I want to apologize again for the way I—"

He grunted. "You should pick another line of work, you know. You're terrible at the whole human trafficking thing. Maybe just get a job as an *actual* driver."

I chuckled weakly at that. "I'll consider it. Ah, abductions were never really meant to be a full-time gig anyway."

"So what happens next?" he asked. "I still haven't seen a single dragon and I'm not pregnant, and there are no pregnant men here, so."

Matthew cleared his throat, drawing the attention of all around the table. He shared a meaningful look with Reece, who suppressed a smile and gave a nod. "Actually," Matthew said, "Lucas, you're not entirely correct about that. Everyone… now seems like an opportune time to announce the good news. Reece and I… have a second little hatchling on the way."

Mercy let out a long, satisfied groan. "Finally! Goddess alive, keeping that secret has been twisting all my chi up into knots. We've known for a week!"

I flinched slightly as I glanced at Reece. "A week? That's… before I left, isn't it?"

"I didn't know either," Sasha pointed out. He raised his water glass. "A toast to the happy parents. May your brood continue to swell, may all your heirs be blessed with the fire. *Ast Nahar, ro'essa tra'Shaina.*"

"By the old fire," I translated for Lucas, "may the ancestors be merciful."

Lucas seemed slightly confused by that, but he raised his glass as well, and we toasted to Reece and Matthew's good fortune together.

When lunch was finished, and the plates were put away in the dishwasher, the rest of the work of the day had to be done. Reece waved Sasha and me to the door. "Come. We are raising the last wall of the new house."

"I'll help," Lucas offered. "Not much else to do here at the moment."

Reece and Sasha both shook their heads. "I am sorry," Reece said, "but that would not be safe. As an omega you are far too—"

Lucas cleared his throat, put his hands up, and stared them both down. "That's a good place to stop," he told them both. "I've been around construction sites before, I can hammer and screw with the best of them, and I'm not about to be told that because I can supposedly make babies, I now have to be surrounded by soft things and no corners and kept safe in some padded room so that I can squirt out some kids. Whether that's true or not, I can use the distraction since you all are trying very hard to turn my world inside out. So you lead the way."

Sasha bit a lip and turned to leave. Reece looked to me for support. I only shrugged and waved a hand at all of Lucas. "Trust me, he doesn't give up. I'll look after him."

That earned me an eye-roll from Lucas, but Reece relented silently and gave the young man a nod before he sighed and pushed through the back door.

Lucas looked up at me, still mildly irritated. "Is that gonna be a whole thing here?"

"Only if you stay," I said. "And if you do stay... perhaps not for very long, it looks like."

"Oh, so dragons are patriarchal children," he muttered. "Good to know."

I laughed, and held the door open for him as we left. When I glanced back into the kitchen, Matthew was grinning at me and Mercy had her arms folded over her chest.

"I like him," she mused.

So did I, but I didn't say it out loud there. I just followed along behind Lucas as he stalked after Reece and Sasha to the build site and tried to get comfortable with the idea that he would never be mine.

Chapter 15 – Lucas

In the course of raising the wall, both Reece and Sasha ultimately removed their shirts and tucked them into their belts. Tarin did not, and he was sweating more than either of them but seemed intent on enduring it without complaint. Only because he didn't, I kept mine on, and by the time the wall was up, and secured, I was soaked through—everything damp, from top to bottom, including the insides of my shoes.

The house was going to be small when it was finished, but had obvious room to grow. Tarin explained that, long-term, the plan was to build several of them—enough to house a small community of dragons and omegas, where they could raise their children in safety and privacy.

"There will be a wall around the property eventually," Reece explained. "Stone and metal, which will hold the enchantments for longer than a wooden fence."

"So a compound," I said. "You know… Texas has something of a history with that sort of thing. Not sure that's the best direction to take this place."

"We have to protect our people," Tarin said.

I snorted, and accepted the water bottle Tarin passed to me. After I took a few gulps, I shrugged, beginning to mull the possibilities over in my head. "I'm sure the good folks in Waco said the same thing."

"Do you have a better suggestion?" Reece asked.

I could hear the skepticism in his voice. A big secure compound was, for some reason, the first thing people went to when they wanted to form their own insular society. I wasn't even sure that was a good idea at all, to be honest—but it was possible there were alternatives that wouldn't bring down the marshals or the FBI. "Maybe," I said. "Let me think about it for a little bit."

"Lucas is a lawyer," Tarin reminded them. "It may be worth giving him time to consider the problem."

Reece pursed his lips, gave me a nod, and turned to survey the work we'd done. None of the 'dragons' seemed to have suffered much with the work of hoisting the fourth wall into place, but I was sweaty, and sore, and tuckered out from only around four hours of hard labor. The sun was heading toward the trees that lined the edges of the ranch, warning that it was starting to feel the length of the day as well.

"Think I could shower somewhere?" I asked.

"There is a facility nearby in the barn," Reece said without looking back. "Tarin can show you. He lives in the loft above."

I did not miss Tarin's sudden shift in demeanor when he rubbed the back of his neck. "The bathroom in the house is more private," he said, "and sometimes the hot water takes time to reach the barn…"

"Barn sounds perfect," I told him. "Lead the way?"

Reece glanced over his shoulder, and something probably passed between him and Tarin but it was mysterious to me. Tarin didn't answer me right away.

"Matthew and Yuri and Mercy seem lovely," I explained, touching Tarin's elbow to get his attention fully, "but a moment away from it all to decompress would be nice. I promise not to judge your barn-keeping."

He gave a mirthless kind of laugh, short and defensive, but gave up and held a hand out toward the wide stretch of grassy hills to the west. "This way then."

We left Sasha and Reece, who began to talk about the next stages of the build, and strolled out into what was probably meant to be a pasture. "So do you all actually have animals on this ranch? Horses, or cows, or, I don't know… goats or something?"

"Not yet," Tarin admitted. "We're currently focused on development. However, there is a hope that we will acquire some livestock in the next year or so. Goats are actually a high priority. They breed quickly, and the children will need a consistent supply of food when they reach their shifting age."

"Shifting age," I echoed.

Tarin nodded. "Around puberty, they will feel the first stirring of the fire. It will urge their bodies into dragon form—small, at first—and with that will come a great hunger as both bodies grow and they learn to move from one shape to the other. In their scales, they will need food. Like goats."

I processed that, and imagined teenage dragons rampaging through the local countryside, eating people's cattle. That… would draw attention. It made me wonder as well why dragons hadn't drawn attention *yet*.

But the walk to the barn proved to be short. We crested a hill, and it was at the bottom of the slope, beside what was likely once a wheat field. I pointed toward the unworked land. "What about all that? Planning for farm as well?"

"I have some familiarity with farming," Tarin said. "Reece and Sasha never really needed the skill and of course Matthew, Yuri, and Mercy are all… unfamiliar with agrarian life. Though, Mercy has an extensive collection of herbs accruing in a small patch at the house. It isn't a priority."

"It should be." I followed Tarin down the hillside toward the big brown barn that had seen better days but still looked solid. "If you were actually using this place like a ranch or farm, you'd be able to apply for all sorts of grants and assistance."

"We aren't actually a farm," he pointed out.

I sighed. "That's exactly why I mention it. If you had more of a presence in the world, under the right auspices, then you inherit a lot of additional protections automatically. You all seemed to be worried about other dragons, and the Templars, and the wolven—have you even considered protecting yourselves as people? As legal entities? Instead of dragons?"

Tarin didn't answer. Instead, he stared off across the old field until we reached the barn doors. There he crossed his arms over his chest and paused, looking over the edge of the field where it met the grass. The green there had started to spread, but slowly in the dry heat. "What would that look like, do you think? These... legal protections or whatever."

"A lot like they look for everyone," I said. "Of course, you'd need to do things like register birth certificates for the children, and I'm guessing you don't want the speculation associated with not having a mother. But there are always extenuating circumstances to leverage. Then of course being registered as a business of some kind, especially in agriculture, easily covers up the presence of extra housing here. Everyone can be listed as an employee... I don't know. I'd have to spend some time with a small legal library for Texas and see what I could figure out."

"You'd do that?" Tarin asked. "After... everything?"

"I'm a law nerd," I admitted. "It's not really about you, or the people here. Not that I don't... I just think that even if you're all a little crazy or something, everyone here seems happy. Assuming you didn't kidnap a baby, well, I don't see why you shouldn't be allowed to have your tribe, you know? I went into law, ultimately, to help people."

Tarin held my eyes for several breaths before he looked away and opened the door. "It's, ah... right through here."

"Into the murder barn," I muttered. But I went through the door. Inside it was about as 'barn' as a barn ought to be. There was a tractor in the middle of it, smelling faintly of old plant matter and oil, the hood opened up to expose the engine inside. Tools that looked new rested in a red wooden toolbox underneath. The ground was mostly clean, dirt but with no trace of hay or detritus other than the ground itself. Here and there a few patches of grass had managed to spring up. Narrow shafts of sunlight cut across the dusty air, giving the atmosphere inside an almost fairy-tale look to it.

"Home sweet home," Tarin said as he moved past me to a ladder that led into the loft above. "I haven't gotten around to building stairs yet, but the loft apartment is in better shape than the rest of the place. Come on, I'll show you to the shower."

"Gonna need new clothes too," I told him as he climbed up. I followed, admittedly a little charmed by all of it. I was a city boy—there was something inherently romantic about a barn. 'Rolling in the hay' as the saying went. I did wonder why that was such a popular image...

The loft above the main barn was finished off. At one end of the landing that the ladder reached, there was a plain wooden door that led into a room that probably took up half of the upper level. The floors here were polished hardwood with a couple of rugs, a window looked out over the old field on one side and out over the hills and to the main house on the other. There was only a walk-in shower, rather than a bathtub, with a small toilet and sink crammed into the space as well. The rest of it was made up of one long studio space, with only a sink, a narrow counter, and a few drawers to serve as a 'kitchen'. Probably, it was the living quarters for some ranch hand once upon a time.

"Quaint," I admitted.

"Thank you," Tarin said. "It's not exactly a vast cave deep in the mountains, but those days are pretty much behind me at this point."

I laughed, but it seemed he wasn't making a joke. He looked almost sad, in fact. "So… when do I get confirmation of this whole 'dragon' claim, anyway?"

"Tonight, if I can convince Reece or Sasha of it." He sank onto the edge of the large bed and rested his hands on his knees. "I suspect they'll agree."

Dark was only a few hours away. I started to ask why we needed to wait but the answer occurred to me only a second later. "Because they can't risk being seen."

Tarin nodded. "In the meantime, you are welcome to make this place your home. I can sleep on the ground downstairs, or with Sasha in his room at the house."

"Sasha gets the house and you get this?" I looked around. Not that the place was bad, but it seemed a little distant from the rest of the place.

He looked out the window toward the house. "If something were to happen, and Reece needed backup with scales, Sasha would be able to assist quickly. I wouldn't, and there's a question of space. It's safer that way. I don't mind being out here. I have my privacy, for one, and for another…"

Tarin trailed off as I peeled my shirt away from my skin and draped it over the edge of the sink. I looked up expectantly, and found him staring at me, jaw still open in mid-speech. Did I like it? The way exposing just a bit of myself made him speechless?

Fine, yes—I was a bit flattered. It had been a while, and I didn't put a lot of stock in my appearance; it didn't generally seem to do me much good. But the way his eyes lingered, I found myself remembering our kiss. Even if it was right before the tranquilizers kicked in. It had been nice, and it had been before I thought he was trying to take me somewhere private to murder me. That seemed a lot less likely now. Matthew felt genuine enough, and Mercy just didn't seem the type to be capable of harming even a bug. Reece had been profuse in his apologies. Sasha… I didn't really know much about him, but while raising and securing the wall at the new house he had seemed friendly enough. Yuri seemed like my people—sarcastic, a little nihilistic, and just enough optimism to want to do something with it.

"Sorry," Tarin breathed as he turned away. "I didn't mean to stare."

"It's fine," I said weakly. The shower was only covered with a thin, almost see-through plastic curtain. There was barely any point trying to hide from Tarin if he was going to stay in here. But I popped the button on my slacks and unzipped them, watching to gauge his reaction.

His head turned slightly, but stalled and looked back out the window. He stood and went to the door into the little apartment. "I should give you some privacy, I guess. I'll see if Matt has clothes for you, he's about your size, I think. Maybe jeans with a belt would—"

Whatever 'chemicals and magic' were at work here, they were potent stuff. Once I was shirtless, my pants undone, and watching Tarin squirm just a little bit—and now in such close quarters I could smell the work sweat on him, only barely impinged upon by the grime of a full day in the car—an intense desire kindled from the little pebble-sized coal I had been carefully guarding from any potential fanned right up into a full-blown blaze.

"You could shower with me," I told him. Or I almost did. The last half of it caught in my throat and instead I choked on it a little and had to clear my throat before stammering it out again and adding, "if you... want to, I mean. We're both dirty, it'll save water... so."

Tarin refused to look at me. "Lucas, after what I did I can't—"

"Sure you can," I said, more confident. "You're attracted to me. Right?"

He laughed quietly and turned to lean against the door, finally looking at me. "Sure, I am. Anyone would be, especially a dragon. Sasha's probably chewing his tongue off to keep from saying anything. You're like... well, you're an aphrodisiac, basically. Spend some time with him, I think you two would—"

"Are you seriously foisting me off on some other dragon that I don't know right now?" I demanded. "Like we could just get in a room together and let nature take its course? I'm not some bitch in heat, Tarin, I'm a human being. Even if I really am configured a bit different, I still am not going to be bred like some prize show dog."

Finally, I got a reaction from him—his face turned pink, and he sputtered an apology. "I didn't mean it like that, obviously." He took a step toward me. "Lucas, I can't... there's nothing I can give you, you see? I can't get you pregnant, can't claim you, can't even—"

I held up a hand and closed the rest of the distance between us. "I hate to pull this card," I said as I plucked at his sweaty tee-shirt, "but... you did drug me and haul me across four state lines. I kind of feel like maybe you owe me?"

A slow, incredulous sort of smile spread over his lips. "You're really going to emotionally blackmail me into it? A shower, is that the deal?"

I shrugged. "Sure. A shower with me, and... then that's it. I'll set up a coffee date with *Sasha* and see if we get to humping, maybe make a few puppies."

"That's not amusing," he lied, smiling a bit wider. "Lucas, are you sure about this?"

With an impatient groan, I took his hands and placed them on my hips, just above my pants. I gave a bit of pressure, pushing them down, and he took the hint, his fingertips slipping under the band of my briefs and slacks. "I'm not sure about anything," I admitted, my voice as husky as I could make it as I pulled at his shirt to start getting it off him, "but you and I have been through some shit and... right now it feels fine. If all this turns out to be real, well... I'm not even sure I want kids anyway, so you're a safe bet, right?"

He nodded slowly, as if in a trance as he reluctantly began to push my briefs down. I was already hard, and it took effort to get them past my erection—when they did, he looked down in time to see my cock spring free and slap against my stomach once before bobbing in the air in front of me, full and throbbing with my heartbeat. A tingle ran up from where his fingers touched my skin, and I pulled his shirt up until he had to let me go to get it off.

Tarin was muscled like I knew he was, and dusted with a salt-and-pepper coat of hair that filled his chest and narrowed to a thick trail over his stomach. His shoulder had hints of it as well, and I ran my hands over all of it, slowly, to find the button of his jeans. It was obvious he was hard inside them.

I did have one moment where I wondered if this was a good idea. If I could trust myself right at that moment, or if there really were chemicals and magic at work. If so, they worked really well—I rationalized my way right around whatever compulsion drove us both by boiling it down to the simplest component parts I could. He was hot, I hadn't been with anyone for a while, and we had the opportunity. All the rest of the stuff that came attached to that... well, I just gently nudged it aside. Sometimes, you just want to get laid.

Chapter 16 - Lucas

"Just a shower," I murmured as I pulled the button free and tugged the zipper down, excited by the way his breath caught and then sped up, "but just in case... do you happen to have a condom around here?"

"I don't," he breathed, "I can't get anyone pregnant and I'm immune to human—*oh*."

I had slipped my hand down his pants to cup his trapped cock. It swelled under my hand, trying to escape, and I curled my fingers under the bulk to heft his balls with it. They were heavy, and tight against his hips despite the heat, like he might come any second. "Now that's something..."

His mouth came for me, but paused just shy of my lips. Hot breath washed over my mouth, my chin, desperate for me in a way I hadn't seen a man react in... well, come to think of it, never. It was always me, always chasing after some guy that didn't get it, didn't connect, couldn't see how or if I was special. I had never been on the other side of it. Honestly... this was officially my first seduction and I was feeling it. It felt like power. Like he'd do whatever I wanted him to do to sate the growing hunger inside him.

I let my own lips hover just out of reach of his as I pushed my pants the rest of the way down and stepped out of them, then pulled his down as well. He helped, shucking them as we stayed with our lips close enough to feel something electric leaping between them. I wrapped my hand around his cock when it was free and couldn't help smiling with delight at how it filled my hand, and how hard it was, and how he moaned quietly when I gave it the slightest squeeze. He still waited for me, waited for me to call the shots, say what happened and when. Probably, he didn't think he had much of a right to anything else.

I brushed his lips with mine, only enough that he immediately tried to get more before I pulled away. I led him by his manhood toward the shower. "A shower," I reminded him, "remember? That's all you owe me."

He looked down at my hand, and took unsteady steps after me. "Is that all?"

With a grin, I pushed the shower curtain aside. "Gotta wash everything, Tarin. Hygiene's important."

I turned the water on and stroked him with slow, teasing gentleness, enjoying the way his eyelids fluttered and his eyes rolled. When the water was finally warm, I pulled him in and closed the curtain.

There was simple unscented bar soap, cheap shampoo and no conditioner. I let Tarin's cock go to retrieve the former, and let him drink me in with his eyes as I soaped up my hands, and then began to wash him.

He expected, I think, more immediate gratification, but only smiled down at me when I began soaping up his chest, his stomach, his arms—all the while exploring the muscled curves of him. His body wasn't hard, not like some Olympic athlete. His muscle was thick, but soft, his skin hot even in the water. I slipped my fingers into his chest hair a few times, and wondered at the small comfort that gave me. This close, and naked, exploring his body freely, that aura he always had seemed to intensify, until the air around us was nearly vibrating with it.

I left the best part for last. My slick hands trailed over his chest, down his stomach, and I lathered slowly around the root of his cock, along the crease of his hip and thigh where a prominent V led beneath his balls. When he was breathing hard, I looked up at his drunken eyes and slid my fingers under them, massaging gently to clean away the dirt and grime.

Tarin's knees shook slightly. He let out a long exhale that turned into a deep, reverberating groan. One of his hands came up to rest on my shoulder, the other braced against the shower wall.

"Good?" I asked.

"Lucas," he rasped in reply. That was all; just my name. But I'd never heard it on someone's lips quite like that before.

I spread soap further up, my hands gliding lightly over his cock, just teasing at first as it jumped and throbbed in eager response. His hand tightened on my shoulder and I teased the tip of it, careful not to get soap into the slit. He was thick, straight as an arrow, a heavy vein tracking along the top in a lazily winding path almost all the way to the swollen head. I didn't think he was circumcised, but at full mast his foreskin didn't reach all the way up. At the base of his cock, there was another bunch of skin that seemed out of place, but then it wasn't like my sample set was vast.

Each time I tickled the underside of his head, plucking with slippery fingers at the bunched skin there, he gave a quiet, plaintive moan. I wondered how far I would have to push him, how much I'd have to tease him, before he lost control and took over. Maybe he wouldn't. Maybe a guy like Tarin liked it more when I ran things.

I took my hands away, and stepped back to let the water hit him. He seemed to come to his senses gradually, and slowly rinsed himself as he gave me a strange kind of assessing look. "You... have a certain way about you."

"You can say I'm a tease," I muttered, leaning against the wall under the showerhead to watch him move his hands over his body.

"I'm not sure how safe that would be," he complained, but with enough humor that I didn't mind. When he was rinsed, he held his hand out. "I believe it's your turn?"

I handed him the bar of soap, and we did a bit of a circling dance to put him between me and the showerhead. He rubbed the bar between his big hands until there was a thick lather, and then, as if I were made of delicate and expensive crystal, he spread the suds over my shoulder, down my arm, and to my hand. First one arm, then the other, then my neck. Every place he touched me grew warm and stayed that way, and tingles spread over my skin, making hairs stand up and raising bumps that stayed with me.

A sigh escaped me, and with it went more tension than I realized I had been holding onto. Every muscle seemed to melt under his attention, and when his hand glided over my chest and down my stomach, I unconsciously hunched my hips forward. The blade of his hand grazed the root of my cock, and washed the spot with a slow, grinding kind of motion. I bit my lip, let my head roll back, and braced myself against the shower wall.

"Should I...?" Tarin asked.

I opened my eyes to see his sparkling with amusement. "Yeah," I said, grinning. "Hygiene, remember?"

"Is it going to go off on me?" he wondered as he set the bar of soap back into the shower caddy.

I shrugged. "Only if you do it right."

"And is that how you want to... finish?" he asked as his hands scooped under my balls, slow, spreading soap and electricity as they did.

My cock strained, bounced as small muscles reacted automatically, and I answered him with a whine of need that I didn't realize I was going to make. We tabled the question for the moment as he dragged his fingers up and over the tightening mound, and then along the length of me. A drunken haze settled on my brain and I thrust my hips slowly forward until I'd pushed as far as I could, and thought that he might somehow make me float off the floor as he teased with his fingertips all the way up to the ridge of my cockhead, where he tickled with all four fingertips until I was out of my mind, gasping and straining at the sensation.

"Not sure if that's really an answer," he murmured. One hand gripped my cock, and stroked from the tip down to the root, twisting slowly. At the base he squeezed and I let out a choked mix of gasp and moan. "Lucas, what do you want me to do?"

What I wanted was to be dangled over this edge forever, until I forgot who I was, where I came from, what planet I was on... but the heat that had built up between us demanded more. I reached out, grabbed his cock, melted a little more to find it still so hard even though I hadn't touched him in long minutes. "I want this."

"That might not be—"

"You asked," I said, and stroked him once. "I answered. If you don't want to fuck me, I get it, I—"

"That's not it at all," he assured me. He moved closer, until I was pressed against the wall of the shower. His hand still worked between us, and his cock slid against my stomach. He moved slowly, grinding against me as he found my lips.

This time, I let him kiss me, craning my neck just enough to meet his mouth. His tongue pressed against mine, tentative at first, a final request for permission, and I gave it as I parted my lips further and let him in. He caught my lower lip between his, swept his tongue over it and then was inside, tangling with me as he continued to rut against my hip, his hand twisting and stroking in time with a rhythm that seemed to have spread from our hips to our lips. Hot, aching ecstasy rose and fell in time with our bodies. In the space between kisses, just long enough for gasps and breathing, Tarin made low, quiet groans to compete with my increasingly needful whimpers.

When I couldn't take it anymore, I twisted against the wall to face it, and pulled him against me, reaching back so that his cock slipped between my ass cheeks. We were both still slippery with soap and while it wasn't the best lubrication I had a hard time worrying too much about it. I was so hungry for it, I could feel myself relaxing and the second I managed to get his cockhead pressed against me, it almost slipped in.

It would have, if Tarin hadn't pulled back a little. "Here? I don't want to hurt you."

"You won't," I gasped. "Tarin, don't make me rethink this."

"Hungry," he murmured as he pressed against me, his lips at my ear. "I like that. I'll go in slow—"

"Go in however you want, just fucking get inside me," I said, and bucked my hips back against him.

There was resistance, and a short-lived stab of familiar but not remotely frequent enough pain—and when the inner muscle inside me relaxed under the urging of a long, tense breath, Tarin shuddered against me and slipped his free arm around my chest to hold me tight as he pushed in.

The soap was enough. I held my breath, mouth opened wide as he filled me. His cock pressed against my prostate, and my legs wobbled. I had to spread my feet carefully to let more of him in and keep myself steady.

"Are you… is this okay?" he asked, his voice taut.

All I could manage as an answer was to nod my head against the shower wall and his cheek and quietly mewl my pleasure. He was thick, and I was stretched by it, but in such a delectable way that the little bit of sting from it only seemed to add dimension to everything else my nerves were telling me. Signals shot up my spine and flexed muscles automatically so that my hips rocked against his, rubbing that powerful little gland against Tarin's intrusion. The hair over his chest and stomach tickled against my back, and his breath was hot and rough in my ear, and after a moment he began to pump slowly in time with my own rocking. Each time he pulled out it was like being emptied; each time my ass pressed against his hips I had a moment where I never wanted him out of me.

I wasn't going to last long and I didn't really want to. His hand played over my cock carefully, his grip loose, his fingers teasing. Sometimes, when he stroked me all the way down, he'd let his hand slip down to cup my balls, and twice he grabbed them a little tighter and gave them an experimental squeeze. The third time, I reached down to encourage him.

He chuckled in my ear, and his big hand closed over my nuts with warm, firm pressure.

"Just like that," I moaned, and bucked against him. The movement of my hips was countered by a gentle tug of his fist. Then another, more purposeful.

"Harder?" he asked.

I nodded. "Please…"

He pushed deep, filling me until he hit some secret spot inside that I wasn't sure anyone had reached before, and gave my jewels a firm squeeze, pulling up as he did. Fresh new sensations joined the others, and I couldn't help putting my hand over his, squeezing harder to urge him on as he fucked me because I was so close, close enough to look over the edge.

"Fuck," Tarin breathed. "I'm close, I…"

I slammed back against him, taking everything I could. Tarin roared against my neck. His cock swelled. His hand clamped down harder on my balls, pulled as if he were trying to use them to get deeper. I howled against the shower wall in the mix of pain and pleasure that I'd never had the courage to tell anyone I wanted before. And then, as his cock put impossible pressure on my gland, all the little muscles inside me locked up as it was finally too much to hold back. I clawed at his hand and the shower wall as I pushed back against him and shot my load against the tile. It was weak, working against the pressure of being filled. Cum leaked steadily from me, dribbling hot along my shaft to mix with soap around Tarin's grip. Quakes of orgasm rocked through me, filling me up until every muscle was quivering and I knew that I would fall down.

"How are you doing that?" I moaned, trying to make sense of what he was doing to give my prostate that kind of pressure.

"Shit," Tarin growled. "Fuck I… I'm… *Lucas, I'm coming…*"

He did, too. I felt it, felt heat flood me, mingling with my orgasm into something utterly alien, a new, unexplored sort of pleasure that nestled in my stomach and sent out creeping tendrils of ecstasy that seemed to caress my bones. I bucked against Tarin, trying to rub another full orgasm out like some kind of sex-maddened animal with only one purpose, but I couldn't get his cock out. It wasn't thrusting, anymore, it was… it was…

"I…" I laughed, overwhelmed by all of it, "…Tarin, I think I'm… *stuck*. What the fuck?"

Tarin was not laughing. He crushed me to him, breathing hard, and gave a long, strained kind of sound as he clutched at me with desperation that seemed all out of proportion in the moment. Or maybe my ass was that good.

"It's okay," I breathed. "Give it all to me, baby. God, you get thick when you come. It feels good, Tarin. So fucking good…"

"I didn't think…" he started but shuddered again. More heat filled me. Maybe I *was* that good. "…I thought it wasn't possible."

"What?" I asked, and started to pull off because my legs were cramping. It always happened to me when I got off hard and I needed to…

"Tarin?" I asked, starting to panic. "Tarin… I'm… are we really stuck?"

"My knot," Tarin breathed, seemingly so overwhelmed that I thought he would cry. "You brought my knot out. We're tied. I never thought—*oh, stars, I—*"

He came again—or he never stopped. It hit me with a rush of heat all over again, and his hand gripped my balls tight enough that I was this close to a second orgasm. If it hadn't been so fucked up, I might have. "I can't pull away," I reminded him. "Tarin, talk to me, what's going on?"

"I think," he said, his voice breathless, "you... you might have cracked my binding. You've got my knot in you. Until it goes down... we're stuck like this."

I blinked, and strained to try and see him. His eyes were half-lidded, his face flushed. "I'm sorry... *what?*"

Chapter 17 - Tarin

Lucas' panic made him tense momentarily, squeezing my knot. I had forgotten what it felt like. Before my transgression, when the Ancients passed judgment and had me bound into this human form, I had slept with human men and women alike from time to time, and during particularly intense experiences the knot would emerge. After, however… well, the knot was a part of my draconic physiology.

As my body shook, and I crushed Lucas against me to keep him from doing damage to either of us, and a wave of release shot through me and out of me, I couldn't quite make my brain do the necessary reasoning to understand why it was happening now. Distantly, vaguely, some part of my thoughts circled around the answer but it was impossible to think straight with my knot being squeezed.

It was the peak of pleasure, the kind that induced a state of helpless subjugation as nerves sang and muscles tensed and released on automatic, like the stinger of a bee left behind in skin. After nearly three centuries, the prolonged orgasm was crippling. There were tears in my eyes, and deep down I could feel my fire, closer to me than it had been since I was bound.

"Tarin," Lucas hissed, "my legs are cramping. Can we… is there a way we can move?"

I came to enough of my senses that I could nod weakly, and with the utmost care we moved our legs together—Lucas grumbling softly, me struggling to keep my legs under me each time our moving tugged or clenched my knot—until finally we were able to collapse next to one another on the bed.

"I don't believe this," Lucas muttered. "Why wouldn't you tell me about this *before* you fucked me?"

"I didn't think it could happen," I gruffed against his shoulder. "It's not supposed to be able to. Just relax. If you don't stimulate it, it will go down."

Lucas was quiet a moment, then chuckled. "This… is the most ridiculous thing. There's just nothing about being around you that isn't insane, is there? Knotted. Isn't that like… an animal thing or something?"

"Yes," I said. "Dragons, like humans, are a particularly evolved kind of… animal… Lucas, if you want to be free, you can't do that…"

He clenched, squeezing another hot dribble of seed from me. Gooseflesh rose on his skin and I had to force myself to breathe.

"So it's sensitive," he murmured. "How sensitive? I mean, what does it feel like?"

"Like every part of my body is shutting down in favor of trying to get you pregnant," I said. "So unless you want a baby in you, maybe just relax."

He craned his neck to look at me, suspicion and skepticism on display. "Tarin, seriously?"

"It's possible that even though I can knot," I offered, "I can't breed successfully. We… we'll find out, I imagine."

To my surprise, he didn't immediately try to pull off or get angry that I hadn't had a condom on hand. Instead he laid his head back down on my bicep. "Pregnant," he whispered. "You know, I used to want kids. Back before I went to college. Not that I don't now, just... I kind of gave up on the idea. I'd be busy with work until I was forty, probably meet some younger guy then, see him few a few hours once a week until retired and then... I don't know, hire a few houseboys to keep me company."

"Dismal," I replied. I couldn't keep my eyes open. His body was hot around my cock and knot, and the constant trickle of semi-orgasm was fatiguing my body. "You really imagined that for yourself?"

"I don't know," he admitted. He squirmed a bit to press closer to me. "Once I started for Camelot Legal, I saw all the other high-powered, well-paid attorneys that seemed to be always on. None of them were married, none of them had kids. Well, not that lived with them, anyway. The ones that weren't married were divorced. Not that there aren't other ways to do it, but Camelot was the big time for me. Is, I guess. Was? I guess that's up in the air now."

"You could still go back if that was what you wanted." I trailed my fingers down his arm, over his hip, along his thigh.

"Assuming I'm not pregnant," he countered. "Right?"

I didn't know how to answer that. Certainly, if he was, I didn't want my offspring anywhere near Calavastrix or out in the open for the Templars to hunt down. I couldn't very well go with him into the territory of a powerful Elder. Which made me realize the true gravity of my miscalculation. "Can you imagine... being with me?"

"Tarin," Lucas said softly, in a way that I thought might mean the kind of 'no' that anyone would hope to avoid having to say. "I'm not sure this is the time to have that conversation. But... I do *like* you. Chemicals and magic or not. I don't think I can ever let you live down the fact that you drugged me and stuffed me in the back of your car—"

"I did let you go when you demanded it," I reminded him.

He laughed. A long, intoxicating explosion of what I imagined was his tipping point for absurdity. It was infectious, and soon I was laughing with him as his body tensed and squeezed, pulled at the knot until my laughter turned to a groan and I tried to curl us together into a ball as the aching release of another load of seed took me. When I recovered, Lucas' laughing had made a similar transformation. "Maybe it is weird," he said finally, "but it does feel good. Too good—I think my prostate is going to be bruised after this."

Experimentally, I bucked my hips sluggishly, rubbing against the gland inside. I could feel it as a pleasant nub of hardness that tweaked the most exposed nerves just at the meeting of each of the two swells. More seed spilled from me, but weakly, and Lucas groaned, his head rolling to expose his neck. Instinct, maybe, like some part of him knew what was supposed to happen.

The desire to claim him was there, but it was distant—like the echo of someone else's feelings. I bit him, but gently and with only the intention of giving him added pleasure. He delighted me by gasping, and reaching up to tangle his fingers in my hair, urging me on for more. I bit harder, and was rewarded when he clenched, and pulled my hand over his hip to grasp his renewed hardness.

"I can come again," he breathed. "Just... do that... stroke me, make me come, please..."

I did, and in short order he gasped for release as his cock burst in my hand, spilling his cum over my knuckles and onto the blanket. I came with him, but it was almost entirely physical this time; the final dregs from the bottom of my balls that, once emptied into him, seemed to signal to my knot that we were done here.

It deflated slowly, until I could pull out. When I did, Lucas made a sound that was half disappointment and half relief. I thought he would get up and leave when he was finally free. Instead, he snuggled close and pulled my arm up to encircle his chest, heedless of the mess. There was really no point now anyway, I supposed. We could just take another shower.

Soon enough, he dozed, and I dozed with him for lack of motivation to do anything else.

When we woke, only a couple of hours had passed. I did not sleep soundly, or entirely. I drifted instead, constantly aware of the sound of his breathing, and the subtle thud of his heart inside his chest. I could just barely feel it under my arm. When he finally stirred, I was roused from my trance-like state, and famished.

"There will be dinner soon," I said. "Are you hungry yet?"

"A little," he said, groggy and only half-awake. "Need to wash up. Again. And get clothes."

"I'll go," I told him.

He held up my hand to display the dried cum over my fingers. "Better shower too."

"If we keep showering like that, we'll both die of hunger," I mused. "Let me rinse off first, and I'll leave you to shower in peace."

I stood, and felt his eyes on me. The shower curtain I left open as I washed my hands, my cock, and rinsed the dried soap from my stomach. He watched me, and I watched him watching me. We watched one another, and there was something there between us that hadn't been addressed. If his mind was anywhere in the general area that mine was... probably it was the utter wrongness of it all.

You weren't supposed to get a mate by metaphorically—or literally—clubbing them over the head and dragging them off to your lair. I was guilty, and now worried that I'd committed him to something he wasn't ready for. If he didn't look particularly worried, well... maybe that was simply because he didn't yet believe. Tonight, he likely would. Either Reece or Sasha would show him their dragon form, and that would remove whatever doubt was left. Maybe he would wait until then to hate me for forcing something on him.

Not that I forced *him*, I reminded myself silently as I stepped out of the shower and grabbed the only towel in the room to dry off with. He stood, his form graceful and liquid, every muscle seemingly eased to a comfortable rubbery state. He sauntered to the shower, his eyes still on me, still not as judgmental as they should have been, and then turned the water on.

I hung the towel, promised him a fresh one, and made my way quickly out of the barn, up the hill and across the field between me and the house.

"Clothes," Matthew said. He looked me up and down, and sniffed. "Did you just shower?"

"Yes," I admitted. "And I left Lucas to shower, so if you have anything you don't mind him wearing, I believe most anything should almost fit. I can run into town tomorrow, maybe pick him up a few things from there."

Matthew eyed me critically, searching my face for something. My chest, my stomach. I wasn't certain what he was looking for, but I had some ideas. He confirmed them when he narrowed his eyes and folded his arms. "Tarin… you know, when Reece and I finish, he has this sort of… sheen to his eyes. Like he does right after he shifts back to human form."

"That sounds like very personal information that I'm not sure Reece would appreciate you sharing," I replied. I searched the kitchen for something to glue my eyes to, but only ended up smoothing imaginary wrinkles from my shirt. "Lucas is probably out of the shower by now."

He led me to his and Reece's room, retrieved a couple of shirts, a couple of pairs of briefs that I couldn't help but notice were of the… enticing variety. He put a pair of jeans on top, along with two bundled sock rolls. "Sorry," he said glibly, "the only underwear I buy are the sexy kind. Reece likes them. I'm sure they'll look good on Lucas, too. You two screwed, didn't you?"

I gaped at him. "Reece is a bad influence on you. I recall you weren't so forward before."

Matthew ignored the comment. "Is he going to get pregnant?"

It was impossible to tell whether Reece's mate was amused or concerned. He knew about my condition. I wondered why he would ask. My answer was honest, though, because it wasn't the sort of thing lying about could possibly change. "We… tied. So I don't know. Possibly."

He nodded slowly, and glanced down the hallway outside their room. "Reece and Sasha went out to check the perimeter, sniff for wolven. I won't tell him, but you should. This is a big deal. We've had some… unexpected sorts of changes, lately. From the claiming, maybe, or from being parents. I don't really know, neither does he. But if Lucas is pregnant, we should talk about them. Me and him, you and Reece. They're not trivial."

My stomach fluttered with sudden nervousness. "He hasn't said anything, what—"

Matthew held up a hand, then waved it to the end of the hallway. "It hasn't come up and we're still navigating things. Go give Lucas some clothes. Yuri and Mercy are starting dinner, I'm about to feed Danni and join them. So was it… I mean, are you and Lucas…?"

"I don't really know," I said. "I suspect we'll have to find out soon enough, though."

"Sooner is always better than later," he said gently, and finally smiled a little. "I'll withhold my congratulations until we know, hm?"

I nodded, and padded down the hallway to return to the barn with Lucas' clothing.

Sooner is always better than later.

Well, maybe that was true. But I couldn't shake the feeling that the timing was terrible either way.

Chapter 18 - Tarin

I did not bring the matter up with Reece. It seemed premature. That night, over dinner, everyone appeared to be aware that Lucas was wearing some of Matt's clothing but there were no comments made—he'd arrived in clothes he'd been wearing for almost a full day, after all. Still, Lucas took his seat beside me at the table, and he was clearly more at ease than before. Eyebrows were raised, meaningful looks were exchanged, but lips remained sealed as far as open speculation was concerned. Thank the Stars, the Ancestors, and the Great Fire.

"So how long before the house in the back is finished?" Lucas asked, as plates and bowls of food rounded the table. It was good food, courtesy of Yuri and Mercy's experimental cooking. Two roasted chickens basted in herbs from Mercy's garden, stuffed with vegetables, with a variety of breads that Matt had been learning to make. The less we had to travel into town, the better.

Sasha shrugged as he passed a pile of rolls to Yuri. "A few weeks, at the most. I've always been interested in electricity and power, ever since it first came into the public eye. Hardly licensed, but I expect to have the electrics finished in the next few days, after we put up the siding. Then it's just plumbing, insulation, windows, and so on."

"And it's just the three of you?" Lucas wondered, looking around at the three dragons at the table. "That's fast."

"When we aren't watching our borders," Sasha said, "it's more or less all we do. Except for Reece's bouts of baby obsession."

Mercy snorted, her finger held tightly by Danni, who was between her and Matthew. "You'll understand when you're a parent."

I caught Sasha's eyes glancing first at Lucas, then at me before he turned his attention to his plate. "Great Fire willing. So Lucas—how are you finding our little 'compound'?"

Lucas didn't look up to answer. "It's very… peaceful. I mentioned to Tarin that you should consider incorporating, turning the place into a real business. When you're a mysterious, isolated community with little outside contact, it makes it easy to take advantage. What with your various problems."

Reece watched Lucas intently as he spoke. "Were that the case, we would almost certainly invite outsiders. That is something we prefer to avoid."

"On the other hand," Lucas argued, putting his fork down, "as I was telling Tarin—having outside attention on you here means protection. Social protection, as well as potentially legal protection. Whoever it is that you say is after you here, they'll have a much harder time making quiet moves against you if they have to go through the public, law enforcement, newspapers. Take Templar Industries, for example. If they're a cabal of killers, well, they're also a multi-billion dollar corporation. They can't afford public scrutiny, they can't get embroiled in complicated legal battles that would affect their stock prices or… smear their CEO with claims of running an assassination operation. The problem with staying hidden is that when someone wants to hurt you, that's hidden, too."

His eyes hard, Reece turned his attention to me, as if I were meant to somehow put a stop to Lucas' fanciful notions. The problem was, I didn't entirely disagree with him. "He has good points," I said, "and he knows what he's talking about."

"I can see the logic in it," Matthew said. He and Reece locked gazes for a long moment. "By tradition, isn't Sasha technically in charge here? Being the oldest? I wonder what he thinks. Sasha?"

Though that was, very technically, tradition, Sasha had not acted as the leader of the ranch. That responsibility had fallen naturally to Reece—he had financed the purchase in Matthew's name, and as the one among us with a child he had the most at stake in the success of the endeavor. Sasha cleared his throat. "I… believe it could be worth exploring."

That earned Sasha an irritated stare from Reece, but ultimately Reece sighed and considered to possibility. "And you would… represent us in this?"

"Oh," Lucas sputtered, "no, no, I—there's the bar exam to go through again, I'm not licensed in Texas, and most of my work is in civil court…"

"So you don't intend to stay," Reece said.

"Reece, it hasn't even been a day—" I started.

Reece raised his fork to cut me off. "Have you made a decision?"

Lucas seemed to search the table for something to use as a distraction. Finding nothing, and five sets of eyes on him, he squirmed a little in his seat. "I… you all seem fine, but… I have a whole life back in Atlanta. It's not as easy as just deciding to up and move. My family is there, not that I… but there's my job, my apartment, everything I own. My friends, my… everything."

"I completely understand," Matthew said, loudly enough that it was clear he intended to terminate that conversation. "Lucas—you are welcome in our home for as long as you need, but there's no pressure."

Reece bristled. "Obviously, I did not intend to imply—"

"Baby," Matthew said, reaching to put a hand on Reece's arm, "let him eat."

"I'm actually pretty full," Lucas said quietly. He wiped his mouth on his napkin and set it on the table by his half-finished plate before he pushed his chair away from the table to stand. "I'm pretty tired, too, so… if you'll excuse me."

He didn't look at me as he took his plate to the sink and left through the back door. Outside, it was nearing dark, and I worried irrationally about him walking back to the barn—or, god forbid, along the border where some wolven spy might be lurking—but conflict kept my feet from moving. I twitched in my chair, toward the door as it closed.

"What was that about dragons and subtlety you're always talking about?" Matthew wondered at his mate. "Can we not give the poor guy at least a few days before anyone starts haranguing him about joining what probably looks like a cult from the outside?"

"We do not give the appearance of a cult," Reece grumbled. "I only meant to inquire as to whether he had given thought to the matter. If he is going to leave, and is set on it, I am inclined to let him believe whatever he likes so that he will not return to Calavastrix's territory and alert him to our nature and location. Or, for that matter, approaching the press or some other venue of exposure that would put us at risk."

"So you aren't going to reveal yourself until he decides?" I asked. "Reece, we can trust him, Lucas is—"

"And how, I beg," Reece raised his voice, "can you be so certain of this? You have known him all of a day, you have violated his freedom, he has every reason to suspect you, and the rest of us. Whatever else has happened to the boy—"

"He's nearing thirty," I muttered.

"—as I said, *the boy*," Reece went on, "your methods of bringing him here have all but assured that we cannot trust his reactions."

"Reece," Matthew said sharply.

He and I both only just noticed that the rest of the table were deeply engrossed in their plates but not eating. Mercy especially was flushed pink around the cheeks. Even Danni had a wide-eyed sort of wary look on her plump little face. Reece and Matthew almost never argued—at least not in public—and it was unlike Matthew to raise his voice almost at all these days. Not since he'd settled into a comfortable fatherhood.

"Will you take him as a mate or not?" Reece asked, calmer but dispensing now with anything like his so-called subtlety which, as Matthew noted, Reece often claimed was a universal trait among our kind.

I was nearly finished, and sated enough. I got up, and took my plate to the sink before I answered. "I don't know how it went with you and Matthew," I said, "but however it turned out in the end, I'm not making that decision for Lucas."

"Then until he makes it," Reece said, "no one is to reveal their dragon aspect. If he chooses to stay, he may be shown. If he chooses to leave, better that he believe us crazy."

And he would, very likely. It would seem too convenient that the local Lord-and-Master had determined that Lucas had to make his choice blind to the reality of this place, and us. I gave a disgusted grunt, and stormed out as Matthew first called for me and then turned a critical tongue to his mate. I didn't listen to what he said, though, instead stalking out into the evening.

My fire was present, and within reach. Something about Lucas had brought it out and it hadn't quite gone back to wherever it had been bound. As I walked toward the barn to catch up with Lucas, I even tried to shift. Just something small—my inner ears, to maybe get a clear bead on where he was. When that didn't work, I tried my eyes, to cut through the failing light. Nothing. Whatever the interaction between us was, whatever had weakened my binding wasn't enough to get me even partially back into my scales.

Lucas wasn't that far ahead of me, though. I crested the hill, and saw him only just reaching the barn. He didn't go in, instead leaning against the corner to stare out over the old field.

I wanted to go to him. But he had left the table with the clear intent to be alone. Perhaps he needed time to think.

Still, I couldn't make myself turn and go elsewhere either. So instead I settled down on the hill, and watched him along with the last of the evening light, trying fruitlessly to hear his thoughts and offer comfort from the shadows.

Chapter 19 - Lucas

The last bit of dusk died, and a bit at a time the stars came out. It was a cloudless night with half a moon in it, already a quarter of the way risen when darkness fell. Stars pricked through the black until in no more than half an hour they finally shone with full brilliance, filling up the sky. If not for the little bit of light coming from town, the arm of the galaxy would have been visible, I thought.

Call me crazy, but I found myself watching it all happen while I pressed one hand to my stomach. My ass was still a little sore from being with Tarin, and with anyone else it probably would have been one of those uncomfortable but still kind of pleasant reminders. *I got laid, yay!* Instead, it kept reminding me of Matthew, and him saying with total conviction that he'd gotten pregnant and had a baby.

Was I pregnant? I couldn't feel if I was but then, even if there was something happening in there it was, at most, a clump of maybe one or two cells. Or was I even ovulating? My knowledge of how pregnancy worked was thin at best, and maybe the same rules didn't even apply. The whole thing was ludicrous, of course, but I was still nervous. Some little part of me wanted to wait before jumping on the denial or skepticism bandwagon.

And, I supposed, that was because of Tarin. I had such a mixed bag of feelings for the man. He'd saved me, yeah, but also he'd drugged me. I couldn't force myself to separate those two things, they were glued together in my thoughts. He had potentially kept me from making a huge mistake with Caleb Drake, and taken me on a date—well, okay, it turned out to be something of a honeypot—that had been... *nice*. Fun, good conversation, good food. And the sex, well... that 'knot' thing gave him a definite advantage that probably wasn't fair to other guys.

If I took out the drugging and abduction, it was a recipe for something amazing, probably. When I tried to imagine the end of that date going differently—I went home, maybe invited him up, or maybe we went back to his place—it wasn't hard for me to decide that I would have called him again.

Chemicals and magic.

All relationships basically started out with that kind of thing, right?

I felt around my stomach, but still didn't feel any different. At what point did I need to pee on a stick? Did pregnancy tests work on omegas, or whatever?

I sighed, stuck, and took a moment to imagine staying at the ranch. Just as a hypothetical. The stars did help a little bit. But there would be no going to movies, no walking down the block from my apartment to the Starbucks, no going out with Brenda for brunch on the weekends, no impulsive visits to Buckhead to buy a new pair of shoes. Amazon probably delivered here but it just wasn't the same...

A situation like this was supposed to be cut and dry. I just wished that I could somehow confirm for myself that anything Tarin said about Caleb was true. It seemed like the only way to do that, though, would be to go back and find out firsthand. And if he was right...

I shuddered at the thought.

Fuck. Why couldn't my life just go back to being monotonous and boring? Wake up, have coffee, look at the news, go to work, go to lunch, get off work, go home, watch Netflix for like an hour and then go to bed looking at case files and earmarking stuff for tomorrow before I passed out at three in the morning and got up at six to do it all over?

Laying it out like that was a little depressing. I groaned with disgust at the complacency that had entirely taken my life over, and turned away from the field to finally pull the door open and go in. I didn't know if Tarin meant to sleep here tonight or somewhere else. There was the prospect of seeing a real-life dragon at some point but I wasn't about to hold my breath for that.

As I pulled the door open, however, an irregular shape on the hill caught my eye, illuminated by the glow of the moon. I squinted, trying to make it out. When I did, it moved, standing into the clear shape of a man, and descended the hill. Tarin, I guessed. Correctly, when he trotted up to the half-open door. "You all right?"

I looked behind him at the hill where I was pretty sure he'd been sitting. "Were you watching me?"

"Watching *over*," he said. "But... yeah. Just, with the wolven and whatever else—there are coyotes out here, too. But I could see you needed space, so..."

"Uh huh," I grunted. "Well, any schedule for this dragon thing? Because if they want to wait until later, that's fine, I really do need some sleep. You kind of wore me out."

He grinned in a self-conscious sort of way that I instinctively found adorable, but smothered it. "Um... Reece has decided that it isn't prudent to show himself to you unless you decide to, ah, stay here."

I rolled my eyes, but the reasoning did seem sound. "Kind of a catch twenty-two, I guess," I admitted. "If he doesn't and I do leave, what did I see? If he does and I leave, I might tell someone. Right?"

Tarin seemed surprised. "Actually, yes. That's the size of it, more or less."

"I can't really blame him," I said. I pulled the door open the rest of the way, and went in. Tarin followed, but didn't climb up the ladder immediately after me. At the top, I looked down at him. "You coming up?"

"Do you want me to?"

Something in Tarin had definitely changed from when he stuffed me in a car. Maybe that was out of character for him in the first place, or maybe he'd turned a corner? I didn't know, but I also didn't want to sleep in a strange place alone. "Come on," I told him. "We're not doing *that* again, I think I need some time to recover, if you take my meaning. But it's getting cold and this place doesn't look very well insulated."

"It isn't," he agreed, and in a moment was up the ladder, following me to the apartment.

Inside, I kicked off my shoes and slid onto the bed to lie on my side, head propped up on my hand. I drummed my fingers on the comforter, still stained with the mess from before, and looked Tarin over as he leaned against the kitchen counter. "Before," I said, "when we left the gas station, you said I could use your phone. Can I still?"

I was looking for hesitation, and I saw it. He didn't quite trust me not to tell someone where I was, or maybe thought that I would call the police. In the end, he fished it out of his pocket and tossed it onto the bed in front of me. "Do you... I can leave you alone."

He started to leave, and I sat up, scooped the phone off the blanket and shook my head. "You can stay. I just need to call my friend, Brenda. Let her know that I'm... well, I guess just that I won't be back for a while. I can tell her I took some vacation time. Assuming I'm not fired when I don't show up Monday."

He looked like he might leave anyway. I patted the bed near me, though, and he sat down, his back propped against the wall at the head. It took me some thinking, but I recalled Brenda's number and dialed it. Two bars of service, but when it rang it sounded clear enough.

It rang almost through to voicemail before she answered. "I don't want any, please take me off whatever list."

"You're basically the only person on my list," I replied. "If I don't call you, I don't really have anyone else to call. I'll have to have talks with my dad or something and... I would rather gouge my own ears out with rusty skewers to be honest."

"Oh my god," Brenda gasped, entirely out of proportion to the moment, I thought, "Lucas? What the hell happened to you?"

I made a face that she obviously didn't see, and shook my head, "Just... out. I saw you yesterday, it's the weekend, I'm sorry if I—"

"I've been calling you like crazy, what phone are you calling from? The number's blocked."

"Yeah, I lost mine," I said. "I'm using a... someone let me borrow theirs. Sorry, I didn't mean to worry you. But I'm safe and sound, so—"

"I got an email from the *boss*," she said. She lowered her voice like there might be someone else around. "*Everyone* did. He said you two had some meeting, and you didn't show, and he wanted to know who had seen you Friday night. He offered money to anyone who knew where you were, Lucas."

A chill ran down my arms and back, and it must have showed because Tarin sat forward, concerned, and mouthed, "*What?*"

I waved him off. "Uh... yeah, he, um... I think he invited me on a date, or something. I lost my nerve and I guess I kind of ghosted him. He must have really taken it seriously. But I did the right thing, right? I mean, I should have called but... that would have complicated things. Right?"

"I mean..." she sighed. "You could have called me. You ghosted Caleb Drake? Jesus."

"Like I said, I lost my phone."

"Okay," she said. "So, where are you now? Want to meet and decompress?"

Yeah, I should have expected that. She wanted all the gossip. "I'm kind of... not in town. I needed some time off, and after I lost my phone and couldn't call you, I thought maybe I should let you know that I'm, you know, safe and all that. Not dead in a ditch somewhere."

She hmphed quietly. "You want to check your email and maybe let Mr. Drake know that? Or do you just not like your job?"

"I've got vacation time saved up," I said. "I can call HR and... I don't know, get them to give it to me."

Brenda was quiet for a second. "So... you're not coming back in on Monday?"

"I haven't decided yet." I shifted on the bed, trying to shake some of the paranoid feeling that was starting to grow in my stomach. "How much money was he offering?"

"Fifty thousand," she said. When I didn't say anything she hastened to add, "I'm not going to, like, turn you in or something. But it's really weird, right? Like, if I didn't show up to work no one would give a shit. You didn't... I mean, you don't have access to accounts or anything really private, do you? You didn't run off with stuff? Right?"

"Brenda," I chided her, "of course not, I would never. He's just obviously a little obsessed with me, is all."

Tarin made a cutting motion, panicked, across his throat.

I ruffled my brow at him, confused, but the frantic motion stirred up my own unease and whipped it onto a panic as well. "Uh, this guy needs his phone back, Brenda," I said quickly. "Let me call you later, okay?"

Before she even finished saying all right and goodbye, I had hung up. I winced, realizing I hadn't responded in kind. "So?" I demanded from Tarin. "What?"

He took the phone back and left the bed to go to the kitchen, where he took a nail from one of the drawers and used it to pry loose the sim-card slot on the side. "If Calav—if *Caleb Drake* is so anxious to get you back that he's willing to offer money for information on your whereabouts, don't you think he might be willing to spend that same money monitoring people you know?"

He broke the little chip and tossed the pieces into the trashcan under the sink.

"Your number is blocked," I pointed out. "She can't exactly give it to him."

He sighed, shaking his head slowly. "You don't understand how valuable you are to him, or how long he has had to amass resources. Caleb Drake is thousands of years old, Lucas. He will have dragonmarked servants in positions of power all throughout his territory and spies where he can afford to be discreet. If he has anyone in law enforcement…"

"Then… he could manufacture a reason to run a trace on calls to Brenda's phone," I finished. It had been done plenty of times, approved by a judge, in cases of everything from harassment to hunting down deadbeat parents. "What do we do?"

"Hope that he has not evolved sufficiently with the times," Tarin muttered. He rubbed his face. "Shit. I have to tell Reece about this. Not about you, I mean—it wasn't your fault, it was mine. I should have thought about it for just five minutes, but you make me…"

He trailed off, waving a hand as he went to the door.

"Stop," I called, crawling off the bed. "Finish that thought. I make you what, Tarin?"

Tarin looked at the ceiling to keep from meeting my eyes. I took his face in my hands and turned him back to me. "If you can prove it to me," I said, "all of this, that it's real, that there are dragons, and magic, and… vampires and werewolves, and whatever else, then I…"

Rash. It was a rash thing to say. But I finished it anyway. Did I mean it? At the time, I didn't know. "…then I'll stay. I don't know what that means for us. But I'll stay. What were you going to say?"

He took my hands from his face and held them. "That you make me stupid."

I couldn't quite help laughing. Tarin chuckled with me, at least, until I managed to control myself. "To be fair, though… it was a stupid plan. And that was before me. So I'm not sure I can be held entirely responsible."

Tarin grunted concession, and licked his lips as he looked at mine. I wanted him to kiss me. Instead, he began to pull away. "We have to—"

So, I kissed him. Soft, sweet. Calming for both of us, I think. He relaxed, his body sagging somewhat. When I finally let him go, savoring the taste of him on my lower lip, I patted him on the chest. "Kind of a crazy day."

"Only a day?" he wondered.

"Feels like weeks," I said. "I know we have to tell the others. Might as well rip the bandage off. I'll go with you. It's as much my fault as yours."

"It's not," he said. "Anything that happens after this is my fault. And I'm sorry for it. I didn't want it to be like this."

I shrugged, hiding my nervousness about it all with glib nihilism, my preferred defense. "If the rest of my life is any indicator, if it wasn't this, it would have been something else. Let's just go see how much worse it could be, shall we?"

Chapter 20 - Tarin

"So what you mean by this," Reece said, his voice and expression dark, "is that there is some possibility that at any moment Calavastrix may descend on us and take his revenge for your pilfering of his territory."

"I wouldn't say I was pilfered," Lucas muttered. "And what is Calavist—Calaven—Calvin—"

"Calavastrix," I said, enunciating the syllables. "Caleb Drake's draconic name. Or part of it at any rate. He's three millennia old; his full name is more than thirty syllables, one for every century he's roamed the earth."

Lucas' eyes bulged. "Wait, then do you—"

"Perhaps we can educate you at a later date," Reece grumbled. He paced the living room, arms folded, head bowed. "Calavastrix is old and powerful. I have seen what he is capable of once before, in the old country. We can't fight him. Not alone. Are there other outcasts capable of the shift that we could call upon?"

Sasha shrugged. He was on the sofa, brooding as well. No one had taken the news happily, of course. "I contacted several before I came myself. Enthusiasm is... minimal. If, however, they knew that we had discovered another omega? A few might come in the hopes of finding others. They certainly won't get a share of whoever the elders find, assuming there are more."

Lucas bristled at that and held his hands up, stepping between the three of us. "Can we *not* talk about people as if they were... treasures you can hoard and dole out?"

Sasha grimaced. "The reality of the matter is that we can't survive unless we breed. To do that we need dragons, and we need omegas."

"He only means that we have to make the opportunity available," I told Lucas. "Not that we intend to pair them off by force."

"And if none of them that you do find actually want to 'breed'?" he pressed. "Having a baby is a big deal; you realize that, right?"

Reece stiffened. "Of course we are aware of the gravity of childbirth. None are more aware—for us, each new child born is a promise of survival. And what manner of opinion do you have on such things? You may not even be here when these events come to pass."

I stepped in as Reece's voice grew heated. "He's agreed to stick around," I said, "if we can *prove* that what we've told him is true."

Reece raised an eyebrow, and turned it on Lucas. "Is this so?"

Lucas spread his hands. "I can't necessarily promise I'll stay forever but... if you are all what you say you are, and this place is what you say it is, then the least I can do is offer whatever help I can. I could at least stay long enough to help you get incorporated, get you connected to some agricultural grants, help you integrate with the town. And if it turns out I'm—"

"He'll have to pass the bar, of course," I interjected before Lucas could reveal our tryst. "But if it turns out he's able, we can certainly pay him for his services, yes?"

Reece flicked a hand. "That will be no object."

Lucas' jaw was tight, flexed as he clenched his teeth. He looked pointedly anywhere but at me. "Then... who wants to do the honors?"

Sasha stood. "Follow me."

We left the house through the kitchen, into the yard that sprawled out toward the work-in-progress cottage. It was dark enough now that there was little danger of being seen, and late enough that official visitors were unlikely. Reece stopped us just beyond the back porch, while Sasha walked out some distance into the yard, making space for his draconic form.

A pang of jealousy struck me. The memory of being in my scales was old and distant, faded from time spent with a human brain in my skull. From time to time I could recall the rush of fire in my veins, what it felt like to stretch my wings wide, catch the wind, and climb the magnetic lines of the Earth like ropes. But it was always fleeting. Sasha's offense had been minor enough that he kept his scales, his fire, his wings. I didn't know the details—few outcasts were outspoken about how they'd gotten there—but it hadn't been exposure, whatever it was. That sentence was universal. If one couldn't wield their dragon form responsibly, the Ancients reasoned, then one did not deserve its many joys.

Sasha turned to face us, and though it was entirely unnecessary, he stripped his shirt off and cast it aside. Watching Lucas, he then kicked off his boots and shucked the rest of his clothing as well until he stood naked in the grass, a specimen that I knew was beautiful to Lucas. Sasha would have been beautiful to anyone who had an eye for men. Another pluck of jealousy played over my heart, and I quashed it. Lucas was watching but not salivating, as far as I could tell.

Without any further preparation or warning, Sasha took a knee, and exhaled a loud breath. *Showy,* I grumbled to myself. His eyes flashed in the darkness, and then like mist blown away on a breeze, his human form dissolved. A rush of hot wind struck us, and Lucas choked back a gasp as he took a step back. Sasha's form was massive, possibly as large as he could manage, and his great scything claws dug into the earth as he lowered his silvery head. His scales, even in the dark, were a metallic kind of alabaster, catching and glinting with starlight, his eyes aglow with embers of his fire. He let out a long, low rumbling sound as scalding breath passed along his thick, muscular neck. The ridges of horns along his brow and over the crest of his head were short, but thick, and as they led down his neck, they became a cascade of bristles.

With a final snap of wind, he flared his wings out, gave them a stretch and then an experimental flap to shake the stiffness from them. If he'd taken to his scales since we'd arrived here months ago, I hadn't seen it. The rest of his body shivered as no doubt the elation of being back in his true form released tension. It always had for me.

"Fucking hell," Lucas breathed. "So... it's true then. It's real, all of it? Vampires, Werewolves, Dragons? Magic?"

"Wolven," I corrected, mumbling the word as I tried not to let me envy show. "And no one's seen a vampire in centuries, so for all we know they're extinct. But yeah—magic, dragons, and a lot else besides. All eking out their survival in quiet, trying to find peace in a panicked world."

Sasha's snub-nosed face lowered and came close to Lucas, inviting him to touch his snout. I ached for a moment as Lucas' hand rose, but he put it down before he actually touched the smooth scales there. "Okay," he said. "Okay. Uh... so... I can see why you'd want to keep this all quiet. You can... change back or however it works, Sasha. Thanks."

It relieved me, and I feigned a cough to cover the sigh that left me. I relaxed everything with a conscious effort, only just realizing how stiff I'd become.

Sasha crept back, crouched low, and just as when he'd changed into his scales, his form grew misty before it condensed into a human body again. Naked, for the second time, rather than simply manifesting new clothing. He dressed far too slowly.

Lucas, though, didn't watch him. He turned to me instead. "And you... you can't do that?"

"Not for some time now," I said.

He took a shaky, stuttered breath, and then blew it out slowly. "That is a lot to process. A deal is a deal, though. I said I would stay and help, so that's what I'll do. If you don't mind, though, I think... I should probably go to bed. It's late, and I have a feeling I'm not going to sleep well. Tomorrow, we'll talk about what I need to do."

Lucas gave Sasha another quiet 'thanks', and then turned to leave us, headed to the barn.

I looked to Sasha. "You didn't have to take your clothes off."

Sasha only shrugged.

Lucas paused a few yards away, and looked back over his shoulder. "Tarin, you staying up or coming to bed?"

A lot of my previous envy melted away. I found myself shooting Sasha a triumphant kind of smile but smothered it before I embarrassed myself with childish antics. "I'm coming," I assured Lucas.

Reece put a hand on my shoulder. "I expect you to apprise me of your status in the near future, friend."

Not angry at all, not like I half expected him to be. Why, I didn't know—I'd been on Reece's bad side lately, I supposed, and figured it would continue. He smiled now, though, and waved Sasha inside as he left.

I followed Lucas, caught up to him and fell into step beside him.

He surprised me by hooking his arm through mine. "Sasha's a good-looking man, you know. And a fine dragon—I guess. Is he hot for a dragon?"

"Er, his scales are quite well kept," I muttered.

Lucas nudged me in the ribs with his elbow. "You thought I was into him."

"If you were, it would be your choice," I said.

"So you wouldn't mind?" he asked.

I could sense something like a test there. It seemed a little early for that sort of thing. Still, I answered honestly. "I would deal with it."

He hummed thoughtfully. "So... you *would* mind."

"I would," I admitted. "But I don't own you. And if it's children you want—"

"You are all obsessed," he laughed, and let my arm go as we reached the barn. "Please stop bringing up the kids and pregnancy thing. Dragons are enough to deal with for a start. Come on. Let's get some sleep. It's going to be a long couple of weeks. Or months."

"Unless we're all burned to death in our sleep," I quipped.

Lucas frowned at me, as if he were concerned that were a legitimate danger. Which it was, for the rest of us.

"I'm mostly kidding," I said. "Calavastrix would never risk harming you. We're far more likely to be torn apart by angry wolven at the moment, or gunned down by the Templars, or—"

"I get the picture," Lucas breathed. He began the ascent up the ladder. "How about you just keep all that to yourself and let me worry about mundane problems like permits and paperwork and bar exams, hm?"

"So, you're not the least bit interested in Sasha?" I asked as he climbed.

Lucas groaned. "Not yet, I'm not, but then I've never had to deal with a jealous dragon before so who knows? That could change. Come to bed, Tarin."

He reached the top and smiled down at me. "Give me the chance to make you do something stupid, hm?"

Chapter 21 - Lucas

It wasn't safe to contact human resources and ask for my vacation time. When Monday came around, I woke up in a panic. When sleep finally cleared out of my brain, it took most of the day to make peace with the idea that I did not work for the most sought after law firm on the east coast anymore, and the reality of what that meant.

But soon enough there was work to be done, and I managed to throw myself into that as effectively as I did working for Camelot Legal. There were permits to apply for—including a construction permit which no one had bothered to get for the cottage. Then there was registering the ranch with the state and county as an agricultural business under Matt's name. That process took two weeks to get approved, and in the meantime I helped build the cottage against Tarin's every protest, which was daily, and collected a stack of information about how to actually run a farm successfully. Well outside my expertise, but the dragons among us had some general familiarity.

Then there were grants to apply for, even if we didn't get them—start-up grants were notoriously difficult to win, but the point was just to get the name of the ranch out there, make it look legitimate. To actually *make* it legitimate, in fact. Mercy, Yuri and I took trips to local farms to make bids on livestock. Just sheep and goats to start with, as they didn't require the resources that cattle or horses did, and the available areas of the farm seemed best suited for those types of animals, according to an extensive YouTube rabbit hole about animal husbandry.

At the start of every day there was breakfast, which we all took turns making in teams. Midday was almost always lunch unless some of us were off the ranch trying to get it all set up. And at the end of every day, there was Tarin, and me, and the little loft apartment over the barn.

I asked questions, and he answered. He wanted to know about me, my family, my life before this craziness started, so I answered. By and by, we got to know one another. Once it was confirmed that dragons were a real thing, it was easier to let go of my skepticism. Caleb Drake really was Calavastrix, and he very likely would have done to me what Tarin had warned me about—sequestering me in some plush dungeon where I could be bred like a prize pony to make more little dragons and maybe a few more omegas who could grow up to share my fate, safe from the Templars but enslaved for generations to come.

It meant also that Tarin was probably telling the truth about how he was bound in the first place. He'd sacrificed himself—part of himself, at least—to save a town full of people in the Revolutionary War. The descendants of those people had passed along a generational debt of gratitude since then. Some of them, anyway—apparently there were only a few dozen dragonmarked spread around the world, many of whom he'd never even met but who reportedly kept the faith regardless.

All of it was surreal. If not for the work, and Yuri, Matt and Mercy, I might have lost my grip on reality entirely. Somehow, though, I kept my balance. And before I knew it, a month had passed and it was like I'd always been there; or as if I'd always been *meant* to be there. The day we finished the cottage at last—delayed slightly while we got permits and inspections done—it finally dawned on me.

"I don't think I've ever felt like a place was really home before," I said to Matt and Mercy as we took our turn making lunch. It was a Saturday, and the cottage had just been finished. There was some talk of having Tarin and me move in, but I had suggested that maybe it would be best if Mercy and Yuri took it instead. To give Reece and Matt an added bit of privacy. We already had the permits for a second cottage in the works. "That seems sad, right?"

Matt smiled as he sliced bread. "It's not sad. That's kind of how it is with us, I think. Before I met Reece, I had an apartment, and friends, and a career that I thought might go somewhere. But no matter where I was, what I did, who I was with, I just... never felt rooted. Like there was something missing."

Mercy began chopping the cucumbers she'd finished peeling. "There is a lot about the omega thing we don't really know. Lost knowledge, mysteries without recent answers. Matt had a string of bad exes before he met Reece. What about you?"

I shrugged. "I mean... doesn't everyone, until they meet The One?"

She cocked her head to one side. "I've had pretty good relationships. They all ended amiably. The ones with my girlfriends especially."

"You still talk to them all?" I wondered.

Mercy smiled. "No, not really. But none of them were really sad. I believe in living in the moment. When the moment is past, that's where it goes—into the past."

"Mercy is a free spirit," Matt informed me as he passed me a platter of bread to begin stacking with meat and veggies. Sandwiches were easiest for a group our size, and it was rare we broke that tradition. And after a month, that's what it felt like it was. "And one of the gentlest, wisest people I know. You'd never believe she once clubbed a guy over the head with a rock."

I hadn't heard that story yet. I listened as they told it, how Reece and Matt had been captured by Templars, and Mercy had freed Reece before the two of them raced to catch up and save Matt. By the end of it, I had forgotten what I was doing, listening to them tell their respective parts of it. My heart had sped up a bit as well. "That's... insane. How can Templar Industries be allowed to operate like that? It's organized crime. I mean, I knew they had hitmen—and hit*women* for that matter—but an operation like that? How does that slip through so many cracks?"

Matt shrugged. "You're the lawyer."

I drummed my fingers on the countertop. "I am the lawyer," I muttered. "Or I will be in a few weeks, when I take the Texas bar exam. Maybe that's the best way to fight them. Legally. Bring them into the open, put scrutiny on what they do, give the government reasons to freeze their assets and they can't—"

"Doing that," Matt said gently, "would require that we expose everyone else. Even if no one believed that they really were targeting dragons and the men who can get pregnant in defiance of every biological reality we accept, it would still bring questions. It wouldn't be safe."

I had been having the same conversation in various permutations for the past month. The wolven were too numerous to offend, and had to be handled with care because they knew where we lived and could give us up if they wanted. The Templars were rich and powerful and had to be hidden from because if they caught wind, they would breeze in guns blazing. Collecting too many dragon allies in one place might alert the Elders and Ancients to what was going on and they could swoop down and punish us all for our defiance.

It was frustrating. I didn't like violence, but I did love a fight. I loved the courtroom as my battleground, and I loved being able to get behind something right and just. For mighty dragons, all the ones at Spitfire Ranch seemed timid.

I did understand—there was Danni to think of, and the future of a species, and we were small.

And that's when I realized it, really. *We* were small. It made me smile to myself.

"What?" Mercy asked.

"Nothing," I said, piling the final sandwich onto the platter. "Let's get the others in here to eat. I'm starving lately."

Matt eyed me as I took the platter to the table. "Cravings? Or just from working so much?"

I shrugged. "I don't know. Not really cravings... wait, why?"

Mercy took my chin in her fingers and turned me to look at her. She peered into one of my eyes, then the other. "Open up?"

Hesitantly, I did, and she looked for something mysterious in my mouth. "Any soreness?"

I checked my body mentally, my pulse starting to speed up a little. "Um... I don't know, I guess my back has been sore but Tarin rubs it for me and we *did* just finish building the cottage so—"

"We all assume you and Tarin are, you know..." Matt bit his lip, smiling. "Are the two of you using protection?"

Mercy's face split into a grin that was too wide for comfort, her eyes sparkling as she let my chin go. "There's a slight sheen to your irises," she said, "and there are bumps on the back of your tongue."

"Huh?" I stuck a finger in my mouth to feel around, but didn't notice anything different. In fairness, I didn't regularly examine my own tongue. And I hadn't noticed a change in my eyes. "But, Tarin can't... I mean, because of his binding and everything, we didn't think... can he?"

"It's unexplored territory," Mercy breathed, her eyes widening. "Oh, this could mean all sorts of things. We still don't entirely understand all the interactions between dragons and omegas, for all we know his inner dragon is motivated to struggle against the magic keeping him in human form. Oh! Or, it could be *glandular* and have to do with the mingling of pheromones—there is a mystical element to omega physiology, it could be a kind of alchemy we haven't had the chance to—"

"You think I'm pregnant," I said.

Matt shrugged, sympathetic but also slightly amused. He rested one hand on his belly. "It *does* have a tendency to happen. So, you and Tarin *are* intimate, then?"

"Yeah, we are," I muttered, flushing a bit. "But…"

"And has he knotted you yet?" Mercy asked.

My eyes must have nearly come out of my head. "*Mercy*," I whispered, "Jesus. I'm not the kind of guy who kisses and tells."

"It's not a kissing thing," she said. "It's an anal—"

"Yes," I blurted quickly, "yes, he—*that* did… happen. Twice, so far. Once when I first got here, and then about a week ago."

Mercy pursed her lips. "With these kinds of changes, I'm inclined to say it was the first coitus when conception occurred. Congratulations!"

I held both hands up. "Okay, let's all just slow down before everything gets blown out of proportion. I'm not pregnant. I would know, wouldn't I? I mean, I haven't had like… morning sickness, or swelling… things."

Mercy and Matt shared a knowing, private kind of smile.

"That's not really a part of it for us," he said softly as he approached and put a hand on my arm. "Don't get me wrong, it's… a journey, for sure. But an omega pregnancy lasts almost a year. Our trimesters are four months long, most of the really crappy stuff—including, well, *crappy* stuff—doesn't really start until about five months along. Mercy spent a lot of time with me during my first pregnancy, making observations, asking me questions. Lots of questions. Endless… questions." He spared her a glance full of old consternation before going on. "She knows the signs. She spotted them in me, and I know what it feels like. You've been taking hotter showers, for example. Right?"

Had I? I thought back. "Uh… maybe, I guess."

"And you don't sweat as much in the heat," he pressed.

I shrugged at that. "I haven't noticed?"

"Soon you'll lose a taste for vegetables," Matt listed, "start craving more meat and like it less cooked, and then comes the growth phase that happens pretty fast. You'll have a sweet tooth like you can't imagine. I must have eaten pounds of ice cream, cake, candy. Mercy started making batches of caramel."

"I make an incredible caramel," Mercy put in.

I took a step back from him, unsure how to feel about any of it. Yeah, sure, Tarin and I were… having fun, enjoying things, trying not to stress out about the list of terrible things that could happen literally any moment but... a child? Pregnancy? Knowing it was possible was one thing. Knowing it was *happening* was suddenly a very, very different thing entirely. "I... is there a pregnancy test or something? I mean, so that I can be sure?"

Mercy took my hand and pulled me toward the hallway. "As a matter of fact, there is!"

Chapter 22 - Tarin

Lunch was suspiciously quiet. Reece attempted to start a conversation about plans for the second cottage, whether to use the same floor plan as before or come up with something else. Sasha was in favor of using the same plan—mostly because he would be tasked with drawing up new ones, I figured. When Reece asked Yuri and Mercy their opinions, the humans only mumbled something noncommittal. Matthew casually suggested that a second bedroom might be nice, in the event of, "You know… new additions. Smart to plan ahead."

"The floor plan we have is designed to be extensible," Sasha pointed out. "So that they can be built quickly and later expanded as needed."

"Well, we may as well skip a step," Matthew replied.

Lucas seemed to have no opinion. He ate quickly, then seemed uncharacteristically quiet as the taut, forced chatter played out. Reece asked him and Yuri about the livestock, and Yuri answered when Lucas hesitated too long. "We will purchase twelve goats from the Los Santos ranch, and fourteen sheep from Ben's Gulch. Very high quality; is good investment."

Not that Lucas or Yuri either one had extensive experience, but then we dragons only really knew the quality of such animals when we plucked them from the ground on the wing and roasted them in our mouths before eating them. Not that I could even remember the taste of a fresh goat anymore, either.

"I will make the funds available," Reece said.

Lunch was finished. Matthew was the first to stand. Lucas stood with him, and began gathering plates, but Matthew waved him off. "Yuri can help today. Or my *mate* for a pleasant change. You and Tarin should… go enjoy a little quiet time. It's been a long week."

Lucas cleared his throat. "I've… gotta finish writing that soil reclamation grant…"

"It'll be at least another month before we can even think about rehabbing the field," Matthew countered. "An afternoon off sounds good for me, too. This baby is starting to make my back sore."

Since his first child, Matthew had acquired the slightest bit of paunch. If he was showing, I couldn't quite tell, but then, I also was only around for part of his previous pregnancy. Still, it seemed early. "You sound like Lucas," I remarked. "His back has been stiff for…"

I trailed off as Matthew's eyebrows crept up slightly, then fell back into place as if he had reminded them where they belonged. He and Yuri collected the remaining plates and ferried them to the sink.

Mercy's finger tapped on the edge of the table rapidly, and I realized it had been doing that for almost half the meal. She spotted me looking, froze her finger in place, and then pushed away from the table. "I should go clip some herbs. Organize my stones. Um… yes. Bye!"

And off she went as well, leaving Sasha, Reece and I with Lucas at the table.

Lucas pushed away slowly and stood. "A walk... sounds fine," he said. "I'm full, after lunch. It'll be good, let everything settle."

This was not among Lucas' habits. A sliver of panic wormed through my veins and prodded at my heart. He was nervous about something. I tried to compile a list of what he'd accomplished for us in the last month, and it was extensive. Had he decided that it was time for him to go? Had he already told Matthew and the human elements of our ranch family?

Reece seemed to pick up on it as well. The line of his mouth was hard, but he kept it shut as he went to the sink to help with cleanup. Sasha was the only one who seemed nonplussed, but then, he always looked that way, no matter what was happening.

"A walk," I agreed. "I don't think I've taken you up near the bramble yet. Close to the northern fence. I need to look over the fencing there anyway, after we spotted that coyote. I've been putting it off. Want to come with me?"

"Mm hmm," Lucas hummed quietly, and made for the door. Rather quickly.

I rushed after him, shooting Matthew a questioning frown as I went. He shrugged one shoulder and went back to rinsing plates for Reece—whose idea of helping seemed to be passing them to Yuri to actually dry.

Lucas had gained considerable ground by the time I made it to him. I fell into step beside him and found the pace to border on panic.

"So?" I wondered. "That seemed pointed. What's going on?"

"Let's just... let's get further up north," he murmured softly. "Dragon ears?"

Reece and Sasha, along with Mercy, had explained to Lucas some of how dragon physiology worked, how we could selectively enhance our senses by half-shifting our eyes, inner ears, and olfactory organs to take advantage of the heightened senses we possessed when in dragon form without making the full shift. It wasn't a skill that Sasha was totally adept at, but Reece was a veritable master. So whatever Lucas had to say, he was concerned about them hearing. Or just Reece.

I was concerned as well. If he were leaving, Reece would not be happy. He liked Lucas well enough, and had even warmed to the point where, on rare occasions, he attempted a joke. Unfortunately, only Matthew ever laughed at Reece's jokes. They were usually grim, or nonsensical, as if the man hadn't yet spent enough time among humans to grasp their humor.

So we walked in near silence all the way to the north end of the main pasture, where a line of trees that were largely choked by thick, thorny bushes that would begin to bud and bear fruit soon. Blackberries, for the most part, though there were a few raspberry bushes here as well. We had begun to call this place 'the bramble' largely because of these natural barriers that served as a kind of second fence, as well as marking out natural trails through the woods here. The fence was some thirty yards into the tree line.

"We're far enough away," I said when we passed the trees. "And with the trees, Reece won't be able to pick up your voice if you aren't shouting. What is it? No... I probably have some idea. You're leaving, aren't you?"

Lucas didn't answer. He gave me a guilty sort of look that I took as confirmation.

It stabbed me in the heart to think of it. He hadn't promised me anything, of course, only that he would help as much as he could. That didn't quite lessen my pain. If anything it made me realize how much I had grown... attached. "I... thought you were taking the bar exam soon," I said. "I guess when you told me that I assumed you planned—"

"I'm not leaving," he said softly. He rubbed the back of his neck, then dropped the hand to his stomach. "Um... I'm not quite sure how to say this because I never thought I would *need* to say it but..."

My breath caught, and I knew I wouldn't be able to release it until he finished. He seemed to search the ground first, and then my face. "Tarin... Mercy is... fairly certain that I am..."

"Pregnant," I whispered in a harsh exhale. A wash of emotion hit me. Worry, for him and for the future and for us and what we were, if we were really anything, which I wasn't sure of. Elation at the thought of a child. Fear—also at the thought of a child.

Lucas nodded, smiling weakly. "Uh... surprise."

"But I..." I stammered, and put a hand over my mouth, not sure which reaction was going to make it to the front of the line. "I didn't think... I can't even shift my eyes, or any of my senses... I don't even know how this is possible."

"Well apparently," Lucas muttered, "you can shift a few parts. Um... several million very small parts, I would assume."

I stared, struggling to parse the storm of feelings.

Lucas gave me a worried, guilty sort of frown. He seemed to somehow grow smaller. "I'm sorry, Tarin, I just thought—"

"No," I said gently, and pulled him to me. I hugged him as if he might break, unable to bring myself to squeeze him too tightly for fear of hurting him or the baby. If Mercy thought he was pregnant, then he likely was. "Don't do that. This is a happy thing, Lucas. I'm... I'm a lot of things, but happy is among them. Thrilled; I never thought this was possible for me—for *us*... wait, are you...?"

He pulled away, but not entirely, his hands resting on my chest. "I am," he said slowly, his eyes on my neck rather than my face, as if he couldn't quite look at me directly yet, "terrified, for a start. And worried about what will happen if I'm in this state when something happens here, if it's going to. And I'd be lying if I said I was looking forward to the responsibility. I mean, it's a *baby*, Tarin. A little life. So fragile, so... I look at Danni and she seems happy, and I adore her, and I adore Matt, and Matt is an amazing father. So is Reece. Probably you would be too, it's just… My whole life has been work since I was twenty-two years old. I never even took the time to really imagine that I would have a family and now that it looks like I might, I just…"

It shook me to hear it all. But I pushed that reaction aside. "Is any part of you happy for it?"

He nodded slowly. "Yeah," he admitted. "Yeah, of course. But it's kind of just one part, and there are all the others and they are very loud and take up a lot of space. Matt helped, of course, and Mercy. They say they'll be there for the whole thing—"

I lifted his chin and caught his eyes with mine. "Lucas," I said, and kissed him softly on his lips, the tip of his nose and his forehead. "I'll be there, too. You know that. You must know that by now."

He bit his lower lip. "We haven't really had 'the talk'."

"Maybe we haven't needed to," I said. "Or maybe we've been having it for a month. A long, slow, conversation. I've meant every word of it."

"I know you have," he said. His fingers clutched slightly at my chest, reminding me of other moments alone and heating my blood. "I have, too. I just sort of had this whole scene in my mind of… I don't know. Something? Where we say what we feel out loud, and then we decide to get married or whatever the equivalent is for dragons, I guess, and then we'd plan, and discuss the possibilities of having a child together and it would happen like maybe a couple of years from now when we were comfortable and knew one another and were confident we could make it work."

I sighed, and put one hand over one of his to press it tighter against my chest. The other I used to cup his cheek. "You wanted to be certain," I said. "Of me. Before this happened."

He shrugged. "Given how we met… I mean, can you blame me?"

My chest rumbled with a contained chuckle that traveled down his arm and into him, and he suppressed a smile, raising his eyebrows with the now well-worn joke.

"You're never going to let me live that down," I muttered.

"Tarin, it's really not the sort of thing a person lives down," he said. His expression sobered. "Can I count on you?"

In answer, I knelt to one knee and held his hand in mine, staring up at him in the afternoon light. It framed him, the sun just reaching its peak and cutting through the canopy of the pines here in stark blades of gold. "I should have said it before now," I told him. "I do love you, Lucas Warren. Whatever you feel for me, I can promise you that I will be there for you, no matter what happens."

A shy smile spread across his lips. He turned a beautiful shade of blushed pink, and gnawed briefly at his lower lip. "I love you, too, Tarin," he said quietly. "Even if you did drug and kidnap me."

Chapter 23 - Lucas

"If it means staying with me," Tarin said, still on his knees, "and starting a family, you can hold that over me every day for the rest of our lives."

"Rest of my life, anyway," I said. "I mean... you're basically immortal—for all intents and purposes—but I'm not. Right?"

Tarin's chin twitched. "I... don't have an answer for that. What I can tell you is that right now, we can make the most of what we do have."

His lips curled at the corners, and he drew me toward him. He let go of my hands in favor of running his fingers along the edge of my shirt, then under to graze my skin. "I don't think that lunch quite hit the spot. Still a little hungry."

I couldn't help matching his grin as I combed my fingers through his hair. "Mm, is that so? I'm afraid I don't have any snacks on me..."

"Not on you," he murmured, and hooked his fingertips behind my jeans. The button popped. "In you, though?"

I had to bite my lip to keep from giggling. He leaned in, pushed my shirt up with one hand and kissed my stomach, just below my navel. As his other hand pulled the zipper down, he trailed kisses lower. My head spun a little as I let my eyes close and rolled my head back, groaning quietly as he pulled my underwear down to let loose my quickly hardening cock.

His breath spread across my shaft. His tongue trailed over the side of my balls, finding the sensitive nerves at my groin, and I yelped in surprise when he nipped me. It turned into a choked moan as he slid his hands around to my ass and drove his mouth forward to gnaw at the tendon there, his stubble tickling me, his tongue relentless.

I curled my fingers in his hair and gripped a handful as he snuffled and growled, his mouth exploring one side and then the other until my cock was standing hard and straight and leaking slightly. "Tarin..."

He knew. He loved to tease me the way I teased him when we were in bed together; I deserved every bit of anticipation he made me endure. His lips were moist when they traveled gradually up the belly of my shaft, lingering kisses marking out the trail from the seam where the decision was made about what parts I would be born with, all the way up to the tender swell of my sensitive cockhead. There, he flicked his tongue across the little inverted V while I squirmed and tugged at his hair with both hands.

Tarin looked up at me, mischief in his eyes. "Eager?"

I could only look down and nod, my eyebrows knitted with need. The bead of precum over the top of my piss slit was thick, and when his eyes left my face, they went to the clear drop of fluid. He gave a pleased growl, hungry and excited, and wrapped his fingers around my cock. He squeezed, and milked up until a larger gush of precum spilled and began to trickle down my shaft.

His tongue flashed out, caught the drop before it went too far, and I held my breath as he licked up and over to get it all. The silk of his tongue made my knees almost buckle, and if he didn't have one firm hand still on my ass, pinning me between the hand that held my dick, I might have collapsed. But he held me fast, and ended his tasting with a kiss to the very top of my cockhead. Then his lips parted, and he took me in, humming with pleasure as he did.

Tarin had the kind of patience that a person probably only got from being a thousand years old. His tongue swirled over my head, and then the ruffle of skin just below it, scarred from when I was cut before I could make memories. He took me down by millimeters it seemed, savoring every part of me as if he could tell the difference between one bit of flesh and the one just beyond it. I breathed hard, shallow and sharp, and couldn't take my eyes off his lips as I disappeared into his mouth, into the unnatural heat and the gentle suction. I felt my balls tighten, my nerves too overwhelmed already to hold back.

He was a quick study, though, and the moment my breathing changed and my hips thrust slightly forward on their own, he stopped. I rested in his mouth, on his tongue, while my body tried to decide whether it had enough or if it could wait. I breathed deep, filling my lungs and blowing the breath out slowly to stall it from happening. My cock twitched once, twice… but didn't blow just yet.

"Close," I warned him.

He hummed an amused *"mm hmm"* around the mouthful, and resumed his slow conquering. He had to stop two more times before finally I passed the back of his throat and his nose pressed into the carefully groomed patch of hair at the root of me. I could hardly breathe, and every muscle trembled as he held me there, his tongue gyrating as he feigned swallowing. It was a gentle, milking sort of motion that nearly made me come, again, and this time there was a trickle that accompanied a full body wave of pre-orgasmic pleasure.

I clutched at his head. "Tarin, I want to come… please, let me come…"

When he growled around me, the vibration shot through my cock and buzzed in my balls. He sucked harder, withdrawing as he let go of my ass and moved his hand around to grip my nuts instead. His fingers encircled them, getting a firm grasp, and when his lips reached the head of my dick he pulled them, using them as a handhold to pull me back into his mouth. The ache spread through my stomach, recoloring pleasure into something all-consuming. I whined, mewling as I bent at the waist in some attempt to wrap myself around his moving head. He swallowed me down a second time, gave my balls a long tug.

"Please," I begged him, clawing over his shoulder with one hand. "Tarin, *please…*"

He pumped a little faster, adding his hand to my shaft so that each time he came up, his fist twisted around my cockhead. It didn't take long. His pace was slow, deliberate, forceful, and even if I had wanted to resist, there was no way I could have. Tarin had learned me, learned to play my body like a tuned instrument, and delighted in proving it. After what felt like hours balanced on the edge, he finally sucked harder, gave my shaft a slow, corkscrew twist and squeezed hard until it felt like my balls were about to burst.

I sucked in a breath and couldn't let it out again. Muscles in my legs and hips locked rigid. I opened my mouth wide, threw my head back, and dug my fingers into his shoulder and scalp. One more slow twist...

It all came out in a rush. I howled. My knees gave out. I went to the ground and he followed me down, swallowing greedily as I came for him, his fist still holding my balls like he owned them. I writhed on the ground as he worked every drop from me, bucking as my vision whited out and every nerve in my body became overloaded to the point that I lost all sense of everything except the white-hot currents that burned me alive inside. The release threatened to hollow me out, like I could lose myself entirely down Tarin's throat. When the last of the volleys were shot, he slowed his sucking and licking and focused entirely on the top of my cockhead. He knew what it did to me.

I pulled at his hair weakly, a half-hearted effort to pry him off, but he hummed and growled his enjoyment when my body shook uncontrollably and I began to babble nonsense like someone fully possessed by The Spirit. I belonged on the floor of some Pentecostal church, my legs kicking as I spoke in tongues, except somehow I suspected they wouldn't quite appreciate the cause.

When my body finally gave out, and all I could do was mumble and tangle my fingers in Tarin's hair and beg for him to let me rest, he finally let me go. He crawled up my body, kissing my stomach, my chest, my neck, and then settled to one side of me. One hand still stroked me, and I was still hard, but it was gentle now and soothing, rather than the electric torture he'd inflicted a moment ago with his mouth.

"Good?" he asked.

I laughed weakly. "Um, yes. Was that last bit punishment for my abduction joke? Because if all I have to do is say that again, you really *aren't* ever going to hear the end of it."

He breathed against my earlobe, and inhaled the scent of my hair, maybe, before letting out a warning rumble. "That was hardly a taste of what I'll do the next time." His teeth caught my earlobe, nibbling while I sighed with enjoyment, until finally I turned and kissed him.

The taste of me was still on his tongue, heady and musky, and his lips were wet from the work. He was still hungry, apparently. His tongue slipped into my mouth and I welcomed it, suckling lazily until we had to come up for air.

"How about you lie back?" I asked, rolling to my side to face him so that I could reach down and feel how hard he was. Full mast, of course; Tarin got and stayed hard easily. Maybe a dragon thing. Or, I sometimes imagined, maybe it was just me.

But he took my hand and threaded his fingers between mine, brought them to his lips and kissed my knuckles. "Not just now. This was for you. Later tonight—that will be for me."

"Tease," I murmured, but let him kiss me again. And since we weren't going to settle that debt this very moment, I let him help me to my feet. My legs were wobbly, and the blood rushed out of my head, giving me a dizzy spell that Tarin had to steady me from. "So… do we tell everyone? Mercy and Matt know, but the other dragons don't. Yuri probably does. What Mercy knows, he knows usually."

"Yes," Tarin said, brushing a leaf from my hair. I needed to see a barber, badly. "We should tell them. It will affect how Reece makes decisions, and he would be upset if we kept it from him. Plus, once Matthew was three months along, Reece said that his smell changed drastically. I don't think it's the sort of thing we could keep a secret if we had a reason to."

"So…" I sidled close, "…this means we're kind of… making it official then. You and me."

"I guess we are," he agreed.

"So if we're doing that," I said, toying with the button of his pants, "then… I understand there's an extra sort of step that dragons take with their mates?"

Tarin smiled slowly as he rolled his eyes. "Ah. So. Matthew told you about the claiming."

"He did," I agreed. "And about how he and Reece are connected, can sense one another's moods and where they are… and how it's, you know… forever."

His expression grew somewhat more serious, his brows pinching slightly as he examined my eyes. "It is," he confirmed. "Unbreakable, except in death. If you want to wait for that, I would understand."

Forever was a long time. I loved Tarin in this moment, loved the kind of attention he showered on me, loved our sex life, loved that he never seemed to lack for something to say. It was never boring, but then was the first month of any relationship boring? I understood by his tone that he was as much suggesting as he was asking.

And the rational part of me—the part that hadn't just had its balls drained and its head blown off by a crippling orgasm—gave that suggestion a bit of weight. "We can talk about it more later."

"We will," he assured me, trailing knuckles down my cheek, his eyes bright with something that I was pretty sure was love. Not that I quite had anything to compare it to.

Which was why I had to admit that it was a good idea to give this whole 'claiming' thing some thought. It was easy enough to say that I was in love with Tarin. I thought that I was.

But if I was, it was the first time. So how did I even know?

Chapter 24 - Lucas

"So," I said nervously to the gathered residents of Spitfire Ranch, wringing my hands as my anxious smile threatened to make my face hurt, "Tarin and I are… pregnant."

Reece looked to Tarin as if to confirm that what I was saying was true. It was Mercy who answered the unspoken question, though. "We confirmed it earlier today. There's a bun in that oven, for sure."

"So you knew first?" Reece asked her, and then Matt. "You both did, I assume."

Yuri raised his hand. "I did not know. But I am very happy for the both of you. *Vitayu vas.*"

Sasha rubbed his jaw and sniffed at the air before giving Tarin a critical eye. "You going to claim your mate?"

"Sasha," Matt hissed. "That's private?"

The dragon spread his hands. "It's tradition. I'm just asking. You modern omegas are weird about this kind of thing."

"We're not *weird*," Matt shot back, "we just don't jump into eternal marriages quite as quickly in the modern age; you're just *old*."

Tarin cleared his throat loudly to interrupt the argument that was clearly about to start. "We are having that conversation, Mom and Dad," he said. "I think that's sort of between me and Lucas?"

Reece was suspiciously quiet. I watched him, looking for some reaction. Whatever tradition suggested, he was the clear leader at the ranch, and somehow I expected him to be happier. New baby dragons and all that. Instead, he seemed deeply concerned. Begging for some kind of congratulations seemed immature, though, so I tried to ignore it. Now that Sasha was mollified, I accepted hugs from Mercy, Matt, and Yuri, all of whom seemed thrilled.

And after they finished, Sasha sidled up and offered a hug as well. "I am happy for both of you," he assured me. "It's always a happy day when a new hatchling is coming to the world."

"And," Matt added, "your timing is great because the only thing worse than a year of pregnancy is a year of pregnancy on your own. Finally I can bitch to someone who understands."

I chuckled anxiously. "Yeah, I don't know that I'm looking forward to all of that. But we're excited."

"Well," Yuri said, "I will go into town. We must have good lean meat, and beans, and fish liver oil. All very good for growing babies."

"Oh," I said quickly, "I'll go with you."

Reece shook his head. "That is unwise, in your condition—"

"I am at most," I said, loudly enough to cut him off definitively, "a month pregnant, Reece. I can still walk, still shop, and still get my hair cut. Don't worry, I already cut up all my cards; it'll be cash."

Tarin looked like he might pitch his flag up in Reece's camp but when I cut my eyes at him and raised an eyebrow, he only pursed his lips thoughtfully and wisely kept his mouth shut.

"At least take Sasha," Reece said. "In the event that there are any problems. We are not short of people who might wish to do you harm."

"It's been a month," I sighed. "No Calavastrix, no Templars... have we even seen any wolven?"

"When one's enemies appear to have forgotten one," Reece said, "it means only that they are planning, regrouping, and gathering intelligence. Sasha will go."

"We'll take Tarin," I suggested. "Tarin and I can—"

"Tarin cannot protect you from threats if necessary."

Tarin's face turned red. He glanced at me, then dropped his eyes. "He's... not wrong. Take Sasha, just in case. He'll have more warning than I would if anyone happens to be looking for you in town. It's unlikely but... we have to think about the baby. No one would recognize Sasha. He's the better choice."

I worked my jaw for a second, but it was clear that Reece had spoken, Tarin had agreed, and while Sasha looked uncomfortable about it, he also looked determined. There was something inside the tension, something I wasn't sure I could define. Maybe I could ask Matt later, when the dragons were off at the perimeter or something.

"Fine," I said finally. "Let's go, then. I suspect I'm going to need maternity pants or something, and I would kill for a real haircut. Yuri?"

"I will get keys," he muttered, before scurrying out of the living room.

"Be careful," Tarin said softly, and kissed me on the cheek. I followed Yuri out of the house, Sasha trailing behind us, and tried not to be angry. After all, there really were threats out there—and I had to remind myself that Reece and Sasha weren't human. For that matter, no matter how much he looked it, neither was Tarin.

***

"Can I just say," said the sweet, round old lady behind the counter at the only place in Comfort, Texas, where one could buy anything like maternity clothes, "it is so special to see a husband in here buying these for his wife for once. Usually it's just the moms out shopping on their own, you know?"

I forced a smile. "Mm. Thank you. Yeah, we, ah... we like to share the responsibility, you know. She's... making a baby, so. Here I am."

Her eyes crinkled to the point that her eyeballs disappeared, her smile throwing a web of deep lines out across her cheeks and down to her chin. "Well, you're all set. Congratulations and best of luck! Kids are a joy but lord, they are a lot of work!"

I took the bag from the counter and gave her the most polite goodbye I could muster. It wasn't her fault that she was unable to conceive of the reality. I had picked up four pairs of adjustable pants with wide legs that would offer plenty of forgiveness when I swelled up. At

Mercy's suggestion, I'd picked up several small tubs of lotion to minimize stretch marks, and a box of tea that Matt swore by to help with what he promised would be prodigious heartburn the likes of which I had never imagined.

Outside, Sasha stood guard like a… well, like a *guard,* which is very much what he felt like. "All set," I said, holding up the bag. "Barber said the appointment was in an hour. What time is it?"

"Four fifteen," Sasha provided. "You've got twenty minutes."

I looked up at him. "You know, when you look all grim and watchful like that, you do stand out. Even if there were no baddies lurking around, I feel like we could draw attention just from anyone wondering why I have a brooding bodyguard following me around and posting themselves in front of every store I go into."

"I'm not grim," he complained, "but I am watchful. That's the point. There are only three babies in the world at the moment and one of them is yours."

He didn't have to specify which babies he meant. "I get it," I grumbled. "No pressure or anything, right?"

"The future of a species is a great weight to bear on your shoulders," he said. "I suspect there is a great deal of pressure."

I peered up at him, eyes narrowed. "How is it Tarin developed a sense of humor, but you and Reece never did?"

His eyebrow rose. "Tarin has spent almost three centuries as a human. He's adapted."

I sighed and gave up. "Where is Yuri?"

Sasha nodded to a store on the corner. "Groceries. He has an extensive list, plus we need more supplies generally. He knows where we're going. Should we return to the barber?"

"If we can drop this stuff off at the car," I said. "No need to drag it around town."

Sasha gave a very grim-looking nod, took the bag from me even though it wasn't heavy and stalked off down the sidewalk toward where we had parked on the street. I rolled my eyes and followed behind.

When we reached the car, a man in a dark hat was tucking a phone into his pocket near it. He turned, and began to walk away. Some instinct in my brain fired, and at about the same time Sasha thrust the bag at me. "Wait here."

I didn't, of course. As Sasha sped up, the man glanced back and then picked up his pace as well, just shy of a jog.

Whoever he was, he was human enough—Sasha moved a great deal faster, and by the time the man realized he was being pursued, it was too late and he couldn't have outrun a dragon anyway.

I caught up just as Sasha tossed the guy bodily off the sidewalk and into a concrete patch between buildings where something had been torn down many years before. Weeds had sprouted up around the edges, slowly reclaiming the old foundation.

"Sasha, don't kill him," I warned as the dragon loomed over the man with balled fists.

"Who are you?" Sasha demanded.

The man was pale with fear, his hat had fallen off to reveal a mat of black hair that was plastered to his head with sweat. He put his hands up. "Don't," he begged. "I-I'm a private eye. Just doing my job, man."

"Who hired you?" Sasha asked. He took a step forward when the PI tried to scramble back.

"C-Can't tell you that," the PI said. "It's confidential."

"If you're investigating us for some reason," I told him, "you're obligated to tell us why under federal and Texas state law. What's your name?"

"Adrian," he sputtered. "Adrian Long. Here, I've got a card—"

Sasha growled as Adrian reached for his inside jacket pocket. Adrian froze. "What are you?"

"He works out," I said. "Let him get it, Sasha."

Sasha stood down, sort of, and Adrian reached slowly into his pocket and withdrew a little metal holder the size of a business card. He opened it, took out a card and held it up. He flinched when Sasha snatched it from his fingers.

"Keegan and Stone," Sasha read.

"Let me see that," I told him, and took the card when he offered it. I knew this name, and frowned at Adrian. "You were hired by Camelot Legal. Or Caleb Drake. Right?"

"It's confidential, man, I can't—"

Sasha loomed. He was, it turned out, remarkably effective at that. "What is more valuable to you," he asked, his tone dangerous and quiet, "your confidentiality agreement or your limbs? Because I will begin to break them if you do not tell me."

"Jesus," I breathed, and stepped between Sasha and Adrian. "Sasha... we're in public? Adrian—Mr. Long—there's good reason to believe that Caleb Drake hired you to find me so that he can kill me." Minor exaggeration. But not by a lot. "If he hired your firm to look for me, then knowing that you are legally obligated to warn me. Otherwise, you'll be an accessory to murder and you can be sure that as soon as I have a chance I will compose a letter naming you as such in the event of my untimely demise. Just nod your head once if this job is for Camelot Legal or Caleb Drake."

Adrian licked his lips, eyes flashing from me to Sasha and back. He swallowed, then nodded. Once.

Cold flooded me. "Delete the pictures. Please."

A guilty look came to his face. He opened his mouth, closed it, and then exhaled a strained breath. "They... they go to a company server. They've already been delivered, I can't delete them from here. Look I didn't know any of that, I just got the job handed to me by Mr. Stone, I had no idea—"

"Strip," Sasha said.

I frowned up at him. "Huh?"

Adrian had the same question. "Huh?"

Sasha gently nudged me out of the way, and squatted close to Adrian's face. "I said. Strip. It means, take all of your clothing off."

Adrian shuddered, and looked around the empty lot. There was no one nearby that we could see, but that didn't mean there wouldn't be. "I don't… why? What are you going to do?"

"I need to see your body," Sasha explained.

That confused me as much as it did Adrian. And Adrian wasn't that attractive. "What are you talking about?"

Sasha glanced up at me. "If he is Templar or if he works directly for Caleb Drake, he will have a mark. He could be lying."

"I know this firm," I said, waving the card. "Camelot hires them for all their investigative work, it's got his name on it—"

"I could easily acquire cards indicating that I work for the NSA, or that I am the Queen of Great Britain," Sasha said. "There is only one way to be certain. Adrian. Take off your clothes. If I have to do it, the experience will be far less pleasant."

"Fuck," I muttered. "I'll… keep a look out."

I only looked over my shoulder twice. Luckily, we were off Main Street, and Comfort wasn't the sort of town that had a great deal of traffic in general, much less one block from the main thoroughfare. Adrian was hastily stripping down the first time, and the second he stood naked near the brick wall of what looked like an old bank building being manhandled by Sasha as the dragon searched for evidence that Adrian was either Templar or dragonmarked. I didn't envy him the experience—Sasha was not gentle.

When the examination was finally over, Sasha ordered the PI to put his clothes back on. I turned around, and watched the man dress with shaky hands, stumbling twice while he struggled back into his pants. Sasha did not look at all appeased.

"We should take him back with us," he said. "To Reece. Let him deal with this."

By 'deal with this' I suspected that he meant something terminal. "He works for a private investigation firm," I said. "We can't… they will know how to look for him?"

My subtle allusion to murder did not escape Adrian's notice. He looked up from trying to tie his shoe, eyes wide. "I got GPS on me," he said. "On my phone, they know where I am, what I'm doing."

The sound that left Sasha's throat was not human. It reverberated through the empty lot, echoing off the brick walls of the adjoining buildings, so that I could feel it in my bones. A shimmer cascaded down his skin, brief but clearly the ghostly threat of scales. I thought he would change right here, and burn or maybe eat the PI before there was any chance of arguing.

He did not shift. Instead, he hauled Adrian up by his jacket, off the ground, and slammed him against the wall where he pinned him with his fists. "What pictures did you take?"

"T-the car," he said. "A-and you… and him. Going into the store. Getting out of the car. There are others, in other towns. We've got a cell phone record showing he was in the region, but couldn't be sure where."

My mouth was dry. So, somewhere in Atlanta, someone had just gotten a notification. New pictures uploaded. They'd be printing them out, compiling a file to take to Caleb. Comfort wasn't vast, but there was more than one ranch here. I didn't know what address the car was registered to. Maybe it would look like we were passing through? No, that didn't track. I'd made the call a month ago—if we were still here, anyone would assume that it meant we were living in the area.

We were caught. There was just no other way around it. Caleb would be told where we were and then it was only a matter of time before he narrowed it down. Spitfire's permits were recent, there were public records—Caleb would know what to look for and start with the newest purchases in the area.

"Let him go," I said to Sasha, my voice thin and dry. "Just… he can't do any more damage than he already has. We need to get back, tell Reece and the others, make a plan. One way or another… Caleb is coming for me."

Chapter 25 - Tarin

Yuri, Sasha, and Lucas had been gone half an hour when the knock came. Reece looked up, his eyes took on a brief metallic sheen, and he scented at the air. Whatever he smelled, he did not like it. His lip twitched with anger.

"Reece?" Matt asked.

"Stay here," he growled. "Tarin… with me."

We stalked from the den, where we had been discussing potential baby names—well, Matt, Mercy and I had—to the front door of the house. When Reece opened it, three men stood on the other side. Two of them I recognized as the wolven who had been leaving when I arrived with Lucas. The other was unfamiliar, but carried himself in a similar manner. A third, then. Enough to make trouble, if they were determined.

"If you have not come to strike an accord," Reece rumbled, "then we have nothing to discuss. Why are you at my threshold?"

The oldest of the three wolven, a muscular, gray haired old-timer with a square jaw and clear blue eyes that didn't seem to fit with his dark skin, settled his gaze on me. "That makes three," he said. "And the gent that came with you? Another omega?"

"That is none of your concern," Reece said. "You have not answered my question and my patience is very thin of late."

The old-timer, probably the alpha of the bunch given that he stood up front, cocked his head to one side curiously. "A pack of dragons growing every day at the edge of my territory is most certainly my concern. Now I did come around here to come to an agreement. I've pulled my people back from your borders like you so politely asked me to. I called a moot, and the pack council came to terms. May we come in?"

"Only you," Reece said, eyeing the muscle. "They can wait outside."

"I'll leave Shawn," the old-timer said. "Arty goes where I go. He's the future alpha, needs to be part of this discussion. Then it'll be two to two. That's fair."

Reece's jaw twitched, the vein at his temple bulging slightly, but he nodded once and stepped aside.

Arty and the old man came in, and Reece closed the door behind them. The old-timer looked me over once and stuck out a hand. "Don't believe we've been properly introduced," he said. "I'm Hank Blackfur. Alpha of the Black Paw pack, which your lovely colony abuts."

I was aware of the pack itself, but hadn't met the Alpha. Reece had not bothered to apprise me of the progress, if any, that had been made other than that they had come twice before and it had not gone well.

We took them to the kitchen, rather than the den where Reece's mate was. It couldn't have escaped Hank's notice, but he made no comment. Where tradition and hierarchy were paramount to our people, hospitality was a sacred law to the wolven. If Reece worried in the slightest about offending them, I couldn't tell.

"What are these terms?" Reece asked when we were standing, not sitting, around the island in the kitchen.

"Simple enough," Hank said. "Our pack doesn't get on with the Templars, and we aren't fond of your Elders and Ancients either. I'm aware that you're no outcast, yet, but we figure that's a matter of time given… events."

Reece's frown deepened. "And?"

"And," Hank said, "I'm sure you're aware that you folk aren't the only ones having trouble making babies for a while now. Difference is, there's nothing we can do to change that. You can."

"We aren't giving you our omegas," Reece said flatly. "We have claimed our mates, they cannot be separated from us."

Hank leaned on the counter with both hands. "I had something a bit more direct in mind."

"That is?" I asked.

Hank clearly considered Reece to hold equivalent rank to him. He didn't so much as twitch in my direction, holding Reece's gaze instead. "Our histories tell us that it was your people that hooked us up with the Great Mother Wolf in the beginning."

I held in a groan.

Reece did not. "Those stories are old and inaccurate. They are grounded in speculation and myth. Dragons did not create the wolven, or the ursin, or any of the others."

"Well now, see," Hank said, shrugging, "that's the party line your people been toeing for a long while. However, our shamans pass down their dreams from generation to generation. And the Red Creek shaman claims to have a direct line of dreams going right back to the beginning. Says when your people first came along, they needed staff to tend their territories, fight their battles, break kneecaps and such. And to that end, he seems to think you all made our ancestors for that purpose. It tracks. Nobody's got magic like the dragons, and there's not a witch on Earth who stacks up and never was."

"Even so," Reece said, "it is unclear to me what you expect me to do."

Hank straightened, and folded his arms. "Well, I should think that would be fairly obvious. We want you to make us more omegas. You've got the magic for it. You do that for us, and we'll keep an eye out for you. There are what—three of you here? There are at least hundreds of Templars out there, and some of the packs are with them now only because they're looking out for their own people. Cutting deals to get by. Way I see it, you can solve that little problem if your people look like the better option."

"That kind of magic," I cut in, "even if it was real at one time, would only be known by the Ancients. They don't share their secrets and we can't even be sure one among them has lived long enough to remember."

Arty raised his chin. "We thought you might say something like that," he said, and tossed an envelope on the counter. "So did the shaman."

I reached for the envelope but Reece got to it first and held it up. "What's this?"

"A lead," Hank said. "Take a gander."

Reece opened it and drew out papers. I leaned to get a look—sketches, notes. Landscapes, it looked like, and a dragon with long horns and jagged scales. We both shook our heads. "What is this?" Reece asked.

"That," Hank said, "is a recollection from a long, long time gone. The first outcast, says our shaman. As old as any Ancient."

"He could be bones and dust by now," Reece muttered. "What do you expect us to do with drawings and nonsense words?"

"Obviously, it could take some time," Hank said. "But these are images and words from the Dream. Seems some of our folks were there when his sentence was passed. This would have been, oh, eight, nine thousand years past? We'll give you, say, three years to hunt him down and pick his brain. In that time, we'll agree to patrol your borders, assist if you come under attack, and lobby the other packs for support. Black Paw is second largest pack in North America, after the Moon Eaters up in the Canadian Rockies. You want us on your side."

I kept my mouth shut to keep from screwing up the deal. But the chances of finding a dragon who, by the drawing, was already thousands of years old after another eight or nine millennia had passed were more than merely slim. If we assembled every outcast on the globe and had them combing every inch of the earth, it could take decades—and even then we were as likely to find his bones as a living dragon of that age. The oldest of the Ancients was barely ten thousand years old. This one... he would have been one of the originals, perhaps.

Though, in defense of Hank's request, if his people's histories were true, and if such magic was still in the world somewhere, it would be among survivors from the exodus into this world from our long-forgotten homeland.

"You are asking the impossible," Reece said. He put the papers down. "If he still lives, he may be mistaken for a mountain range or slumbering in the depths of the sea."

"Like I said," Hank mused, "it could take some time and we're willing to meet you halfway on that point."

"We cannot know the nature of this magic," Reece went on. "What it entails, if it can be successful even if we were to acquire it somehow. Your people have omegas of your own, you are able to reproduce, and at need you can turn humans—"

"We *could*," Hank corrected. He sighed, and turned around to walk toward the table. Without asking, he pulled a chair out, turned it around and slumped into it. "Nobody's survived the bite in fifty years. Don't know why, no one does. Just stopped working. And it only produced betas in any case. Omega birth rates have dropped. There've been six born in my lifetime. The ones that are of birthing age are reaching their expiration date, the rest will eventually. It's like whatever your people did is wearing off. Ursin keep to themselves, but as far as I know they're in the same boat. No one's even seen a vulpin in recent memory, for all we know they already died out."

Some of the stature and bravado had drained from Hank's posture. He was less an alpha in that moment than an old man worried for the generations he wouldn't be around to witness, seeing them dwindle. I sympathized. Only a little over a year ago, I was looking at the same future for my people.

Reece was as well. He spread the pages out some, fanning them to look them over on the counter. "I was not aware your circumstances had become so dire."

"Between centuries of being hunted," Hank said, "and this... decline of whatever old magic is in our bones, we're running out of road, Reece. Something's gotta change. I don't think we can do it without help from your people, but we've approached the Elders and the Ancients. The council was ready to sell you out, help them hunt for your omegas. The sons of bitches wouldn't give us the time of day to spit, much less hear us out. So—we need you, you need us. If it's a deal, you'll have your territory and we'll enforce it if it comes to blows. We know it's a long shot. But I'd rather throw in with some high-and-mighty lizards than see my people live out the rest of our existence as pets to the fucking Templars."

Reece at last looked to me, seeking some kind of advice or agreement. It was a massive undertaking, and one that was not at all guaranteed of any degree of success. But... for three years, at least, it meant a greater degree of safety, stability. It meant the beginnings of a coalition that might well be the key to our longevity as a colony, if that's what we really were. I gave him a nod. All we could really do was try. And to have an Ancient on our side, even an outcast—it would change things considerably for us, for the better.

He sighed, and nodded slowly as he neatened the stack of sketches. "I believe that you are a man of your word, Hank," he said. "And though you admit to considering our location and circumstances a bartering chip to trade with our enemies, I know well the apathy of the Elders and Ancients. It seems that we do not require trust between us; we have pressing necessity, which is often better."

Hank stood from the chair. "I am a man of my word," he agreed. "And frankly, I'd rather see you lot make it than the others. I'll order patrols, but make sure my people stay on their side of the border. In the next months, I'll see to it the alphas in the region come and make their own agreements as well. Won't be a Templar in Texas who can set foot within fifty miles of your territory without us giving you the heads-up."

We all looked up when the door opened, and Sasha came storming in. He froze when he saw the wolven delegation. There was clear concern on his face, and it made my heart skip a beat. "Sasha? Where's Lucas?"

"I'm here," Lucas said. He pushed past Sasha and paused to take in the scene in the kitchen before he came to my side. "We've... got a problem."

"And what would that be?" Hank asked.

Lucas looked to me in question, as if to ask "Who is this guy?"

I gestured at Hank. "This man is Hank Blackfur. Alpha of a local wolven pack. His son, Arty, will succeed him."

"I remember you," Lucas said, extending a cautious hand to shake with both of them. "You were being run off the ranch last time, if I recall?"

"That's been resolved," I said. "For the moment, at any rate. Hank here has made us a deal, for protection and intelligence."

"That is fortunate," Sasha said. "Because we are going to need it, likely very soon."

Lucas gave Arty and Hank a nervous smile. "How do you two feel about facing down an angry dragon?"

Hank's expression fell until he had a look of sour worry on his face. "Well… shit."

Chapter 26 - Lucas

"Reece—everyone—this is my fault," I said, my eyes burning. "I'm so sorry. If I hadn't called my friend, if I hadn't—"

"The fault lies with Tarin, if anyone," Reece cut in. "And laying blame at all is a fruitless exercise at this point. We must prepare as we are able, and be ready for Calavastrix's arrival. He will come at night, almost certainly, on the wing. That much, at least, grants us some ability to be vigilant."

Tarin raked his fingers through his hair. "Hank," he said, "are you willing to commit your people to this?"

Hank didn't seem to like it, but he nodded. "I'll get a crew of my sharper betas out here. They won't take on a dragon straight on, but they'll distract him and if he takes human form, they'll be worth something."

"See to it," Reece said.

"And our agreement?" Hank asked.

Reece offered his hand. "It is agreed. If we survive, we will seek out this outcast Ancient."

I didn't know what that was about, but was relieved that it wouldn't be just the six of us standing up to Caleb. To *Calavastrix*.

Hank and Arty saw themselves out, and I saw Matt and Mercy by the door into the hallway as they left. Matt looked troubled. "Did I hear that right?"

Reece went to him, and pulled him close. "You did, my love. It would be best if you and Danni were moved somewhere more secure."

Matt looked like he would argue, but he held his tongue and only nodded.

"I'll find us a place outside of town," Mercy said.

"Lucas should go as well," Tarin added. "When Calavastrix comes, it would be better if he weren't here."

"Absolutely not," I said. "No, Tarin—I'm not leaving. And besides, if I wasn't here, he might just avoid setting foot on the ranch, and come looking for me, and if I was with Matt and Mercy and Danni…"

"There is an option," Sasha said. He looked at the two of us. "If Tarin claims his mate, Calavastrix will not be able to sense Lucas' presence. Even if he did arrive here, and even if we did not survive—Lucas would be safe. Only one dragon can claim an omega. Calavastrix the Storm is vicious, and he is without mercy—but he is a traditionalist, bound by the laws of the Ancients. If Lucas is claimed, he will not pursue him. He may not spare us, but Lucas would be safe."

Tarin shifted from one foot to the other, uncomfortable as he glanced sideways at me. "We'll discuss that."

I started to respond but thought better of it. Not here, in front of everyone. Claiming was a big deal. Like getting married, only a lot more permanent. Not that I couldn't see me and Tarin together for a long time, but that kind of commitment... I didn't want this to be the reason we made it.

"Tarin?" I said. "Why don't we... have that talk in private?"

"Go," Reece said. "Sasha—contact any outcasts you can. More of our people here would be better. You may... inform them we have acquired a second omega, if only to convince them that it is a worthwhile fight. Matthew, Mercy—take Yuri and Danni. Use whatever funds you require. Somewhere remote is best. If Calavastrix has employed investigators, it seems prudent to avoid populated areas in the region. Go now. On the wing, Calavastrix could be here by tonight."

Matt took Reece's hand and drew him into the hallway. "We can go soon. Come up and... see me off?"

It didn't take much guessing to decide what he meant by that. I cleared my throat and tugged at Tarin's fingers, tilting my head toward the back door of the kitchen when he looked down at me.

He took the hint, and we excused ourselves from the house.

"What will happen?" I asked, once we were outside and walking toward the barn. "When he comes, I mean."

"It's hard to say," Tarin admitted. "Calavastrix the Storm gets his name for an old tactic he uses in territorial disputes. There hasn't been one for centuries, but he's known to summon lightning storms. If he means to cover his approach, he'll pull something like that, maybe. Or he'll avoid alerting us, and come in hidden behind a glamor. Reece is good at spotting those, so if he chooses that tactic, and Reece is in his scales, we might get some notice."

"I... appreciate the strategic rundown," I said. "I meant more, what happens to us, and this place? Once he knows about it, he could tell others. He's coming for me, right? If it turns out I'm... um, *claimed* and everything... even if we run him off, we're still in danger here."

Tarin squeezed my hand, lifted it to his lips and kissed my fingers. "I don't know. We can't run indefinitely, so we have to stand up to him. If we win this battle, it could be we earn ourselves the right to fight future ones. Dragons are... not like humans. Calavastrix will come with a kind of... formal complaint. If he can't resolve it himself, he'll take it the other Elders. They'll hold a vote of sorts, and make a decision, but that decision must be taken to at least three of the Ancients, and that could take time. If we can defeat him now, we will have that time. He will not attack repeatedly. You could say that it's against the rules of engagement."

"So, it's this fight," I said, "and then we get a reprieve."

He stopped, a few yards from the barn, and turned to face me. "We can leave, if you want. I could take you, we could go far away. I know people who could hide us."

"And you wouldn't feel bad about that?" I asked.

Tarin hung his head. "Of course I would. But Reece would understand. You're my mate, claimed or not. You've got my child in your womb. There's nothing more important than that."

I put my hand over his heart. "Tarin. Of course there is. I... of course I want to protect our baby. But I want to protect our *family*, too. We can't just run out on them. And I don't think you would forgive yourself for doing it if we did."

"I have carried sins with me for centuries," he said. "Guilt from abandoning a fight I can live with. Guilt for seeing you and our child harmed? That I couldn't. It would be the death of me."

"Then," I said, and leaned in to kiss him, "we can just keep that from happening. Now... take me inside, *mate*, and claim me like a proper dragon. I'm sure as hell not going to let Calavastrix breed me like a mare."

Tarin searched my eyes, serious. "It's not something we can ever undo," he said. "If I claim you, it's forever. There's no turning back, no changing your mind."

I bit my lip, nodding. "I know," I said slowly. "And this isn't how I wanted it to go but... it's a matter of faith, I guess. I love you now. You love me. At some point, doesn't everyone in that position have to just believe it can work? May as well believe that now, I guess."

"That doesn't sound enthusiastic," he muttered.

I grinned up at him. "Well, to hear Matt tell it... it has to happen under certain 'circumstances' and I suspect I'll be very, *very* enthusiastic then. If you do it right..."

A low growl escaped his throat, and he nipped at my lower lip. I drank in the radiant warmth between us, and by the time he tugged me toward the barn door, I was already hard, my ass practically tingling with the anticipation of having him inside me again. And by the time we made it to the loft, and he let me undress him, he was just as ready as I was.

Chapter 27 - Tarin

Lucas knelt before me, naked, and looked up at me from his knees, his hands exploring my stomach. He combed his fingers through the hair there, and scratched lightly down until his hands found my cock, swollen to almost painful hardness. I shivered at his touch, his fingertips caressing and teasing as he leaned in and pressed his lips softly to the head of my cock.

His tongue slipped out, tasting me, and his eyes fluttered closed as a smile took him over. "You always taste so good…"

"I can't claim you like this, you know," I told him.

"We've got hours," he murmured. "And if there's a dragon coming to kill us all, I plan to take full advantage."

Both hands settled on my shaft, and he held it like some holy object, his touch feathery light. He parted his lips, and the warm slickness of his mouth invited me in. I groaned, and smoothed his hair as he held my cockhead between his lips and nursed the gush of precum that leaked from me. He made an ecstatic sound as he drank me, and pushed further, until all of me was embraced by his lips and tongue.

He worked me in slow, steady pumps of his mouth and hands, eyebrows knit the same way they were when I held him close and stroked him for hours just to see that expression—as if he could barely understand the pleasure. My mouth hung open, panting as I watched him devour me through eyes that could barely see straight. Each pass of his tongue, every twist of his lips around me made my heart race faster, my cock flexing as nerves were surprised each time at how skillful he was at pleasuring me.

He pulled away only long enough to whisper, "I want to taste you."

Before I could say anything in response, he consumed me again, working faster. The fingers of one hand found my balls and stroked along their underside, lighting up the nerves there so that my breath caught as fresh tingles added to the vortex of sensation. His other hand gripped me tight, stroking in time with his mouth, and each time he came up to swirl his tongue around the head of my dick, he made quiet, desperate sounds of need; as if giving up my seed to his mouth was all he needed to live.

"I'm close," I husked, struggling to stand upright. "Keep going, Lucas…"

Lucas took me out of his mouth only long enough to smile and look up at me. "Feed me, Tarin. Come for me, please…"

It became harder to keep my eyes open, but I forced myself to watch him work, enamored of the pinched look on his brow and the prayer-like way he milked me. The first stirrings of orgasm teased at the root of my cock, swelling me up in his mouth so that he became excited, pumping faster, urging me on. My knot flared, and the hand that teased me below shifted to caress and squeeze there as well, awakening a whole new bundle of nerves that sent a tremble up my spine and down to my feet. I put my hands on his shoulders, gripped them tight to stay standing, and gave a long, deep growl as I tipped slowly over the precipice.

His pace slowed, his lips caught and held the head of my cock and he suckled as he opened his eyes to look up at me, pleading, and then smiling as I bent slightly, let out a cry of pleasure, and then gave him what he demanded from me.

It hit me like a wave, crashing into me at the hips and then surging up through my body and along my limbs. I kept my eyes open only because Lucas held them with his, gleefully accepted my seed as his hand stroked me. He gulped, taking the first few heavy shots, and then plunged down to take in the rest. My nerves became sensitive, raw, and he teased them with tongue and lips, and ran his fingertip along the fat tube of my shaft to collect anything still left there.

When he finally let me go, he licked his lips with satisfaction, wiped his mouth on his arm, and kissed me a final time to gather a last straggling drop.

I hauled him to his feet then, and took charge of his mouth with my own, dipping my tongue past his lips to taste myself mingled with his breath. I walked him back, scooping up his ass with both hands to lift him just enough that I could take him down on the bed easily.

Lucas giggled as we crashed down, and squirmed beneath me so that he could wrap his legs around my waist. "Still got anything left for me?"

"More than enough," I growled. "Your mouth, the way you make me come… it's beautiful."

He craned his neck for more kisses, and I gave them freely, grinding my spit and cum-slicked cock against the cleft of his cheeks until they parted for me and I could prod at his hole instead. When I did, Lucas' head rolled, and he worked his hips to try and get me in. It wasn't nearly slick enough for that yet.

"Knees up," I ordered.

His eyes lit with excitement. For the moment, we were just here, just us, together, enjoying one another's bodies—not waiting for an elder dragon to drop out of the sky on top of us. I lost myself to that as I pulled his knees up, braced his hips on my hands and speared his opening with my tongue.

His reaction was instant and gratifying. Lucas wailed, and pulled his knees closer to his chest, spreading his ass so that I could more easily plunder him. When his wailing quieted only a little, I slipped one hand up to grasp his balls. That changed his tune immediately, and as I lapped and invaded his tight ring, I gave them rhythmic squeezes that had him clawing at the blanket, and my head, and wherever his hands landed as he spoke oaths and prayers with equal force.

"Mine," I growled, my lips brushing his opening. I squeezed his balls tight for emphasis.

He cried out, writhing so that I had to shift to keep his hips up. "Oh, *God*… yes… yours, Tarin… all yours…"

"Mine," I rumbled again, and bit one cheek, then the other.

"Yours," he echoed back. "Fuck, Tarin… take me, claim me… please!"

I wasn't quite done, yet. The power that we passed back and forth was intoxicating, the way Lucas seemed to utterly own me one night and then submit completely the next was like the swinging of a pendulum unfettered by things like gravity or physics, swinging further each time. I lowered his hips, spit on a finger, and worked it into him until I could feel the hard knot of his prostate inside. I gave it a long, firm stroke. His mouth opened in a silent cry, his eyes closed tight as he bucked against me until his voice broke with a keening howl.

"Oh, Tarin—fuck..."

"Mine," I told him, and prodded the sensitive gland again.

He nodded frantically, one hand reached down to grasp at my arm in a mock attempt to stop me. "It's yours, please, just fuck me... *please*, I need you inside, Tarin. fill me up—I'm ready!"

I wanted to tease him more, to suck his cock, swallow his first orgasm and make him beg harder. But my will broke too easily. I craved to be joined with him again, to be buried in him and to hear the sounds he made only when I knotted him. I spit on my hand again for good measure, and stroked myself once to spread it, then pressed the head of my cock against his yielding hole.

It parted before me easily, already loosened and slick from my tongue, and as I teased just the first ring of muscle with the tip of what he wanted, he reached for my hips to pull me in further. I chuckled and caught his hands to hold them, threading my fingers through his. "Look at me, Lucas."

His eyes were wild, rolling like a crazy animal, but he focused them on me, his lips parted with breathy pleas, his brow pinched. His face was beautifully flushed like the rest of him. We held one another's gaze as I thrust slowly forward, recording every twitch of his mouth, every widening of his eyes, every slight wince as he stretched to accept me. My knot was already half swollen with anticipation, and not yet fully relaxed from what he'd done to me before. Lucas swallowed, and moaned, and squeezed my hands with his until finally I was deep enough that the only thing left was my knot.

"Do it," he begged. "All of it, Tarin... I want all of it, please..."

Just to hear him like that made my knot flare wider. I bent, and let go of one of his hands to put the other behind his neck. He bit his lip as I pushed. And then gave a cry of mixed pain and pleasure as I popped through his hole and it closed tight behind the two wide lumps of tender flesh at the base of my cock.

Immediately, his demeanor changed. I only had to rock back and forth a little to massage his gland with the knot, and his eyes moistened as he pulled me to him. I continued the motion, slow and deliberate, until his body began to shake and his heels dug into my ass cheeks.

"It's... so... *fuck,* Tarin..." Lucas wrapped his arms around me, pulled me down until almost all of my weight was on top of him. He kissed and gnawed at my neck and shoulder, with short, sharp mewls of ecstasy. Our bodies grew hot, slick with sweat, and it seemed that we were so tightly crushed to one another that we would turn molten and bleed into one another.

"I'm..." he tried to say.

There was no other warning than that. Suddenly, he dug his fingers into my back, scratching deep as his hole quivered around me, then contracted. Heat spread between our stomachs, and his body practically vibrated. "Claim... me..." he gasped. "Make me... yours..."

In the midst of his orgasm, he threw his head to one side to expose his neck and shoulder. I thrust hard into him, urging his gland to keep pumping, to keep his body locked in this state as I bit down and summoned my fire, willing it to flow into him, to mingle our essences and tie us together forever.

Lucas' body gradually recovered. I felt my own orgasm recede in the face of panic. I bit down again, harder but worried about biting too deep.

Nothing. The fire inside me hit the wall of the binding, and wouldn't flow.

"Tarin?" Lucas' voice was weak, but worried. "Please..."

I drew back, my stomach twisting, my heart shot through with a stabbing pain.

My knot even receded as shame and fury flooded through me. "I... I tried, Lucas..."

"What's wrong?" he asked. "Am I...?"

I shook my head, bereft. "No," I breathed. "My binding... Lucas, I... I'm sorry, my love, I... I can't claim you."

For the first time since I saw the people of that village falling, and knew the sacrifice I would make to save them, a sob wracked my body.

Chapter 28 - Lucas

Matt, Mercy, Yuri, and Danni had all gone when we returned, defeated, to the house. Sasha and Reece stood at the island in the kitchen with a sketch of the property, discussing tactics. "He will not risk starting a fire that could draw so much attention," Reece was saying. "If we draw him into the woods, he will have to take a smaller form, rely on magic, possibly even take human shape. That is our—Tarin, Lucas. What is wrong?"

It had to be obvious that something was. We had held one another after the failed claiming as I consoled Tarin and tried to understand what the problem was. He had enough dragon in him to get me pregnant, it seemed, but claiming was a mystical act. Without access to his fire, to his dragon form…

"You have decided not to claim one another," Sasha said. If I could feel him in the room, then he could feel me. He knew.

Tarin's eyes were still puffy. Somehow, I didn't imagine that dragons cried. I'd been very wrong. The shame in his expression stabbed me, and that knife twisted when he tried to look at me and couldn't. "My binding," he said quietly. "It… won't allow me to claim Lucas."

You would have thought we told them Tarin had cancer. Sasha came to him immediately, and pulled him into a fierce embrace. "My friend…"

Reece only seemed to ever have one of two expressions—dire, which was most of the time, and a particular look he reserved exclusively for Matthew. Now, I knew there was at least one more. He looked like he might weep as well. "Tarin, I am… I do not have words. Lucas—I am deeply grieved for you."

Sasha let Tarin go and looked to Reece. "Perhaps we can loosen the binding? Enough to allow the claiming, at least. Between the two of us—"

"It was a tribunal of Ancients that laid the enchantment," Reece said. "We could make the attempt, but their magic was unimaginable when the sentence was carried out. By now, it is deep in his bones. I do not think we possess either the skill or the strength."

"And," Tarin said, his voice still hoarse, "we don't have the time. Calavastrix will come. Lucas will be unclaimed. He doesn't need to defeat us, only get Lucas in his grip and escape."

I shuddered, and tried to hide it but Tarin saw. He took my hand and held it tight. "Even if we ran now… it would only be a matter of time."

"That can't be all," I said, squeezing his hand back. "I'm not just giving up. If we have the right plan—I could call the police, have them here when he arrives, bring public scrutiny; Calavastrix may be an elusive dragon, but Caleb Drake is a public personality. He can't reveal himself to the world, so he'd have to come as himself, right? And then he couldn't exactly just run off with someone."

Reece didn't like that idea. "That will spread the word far and wide that we are here," he said. "Already we have a tenuous peace with the Black Paw pack, who are between us and the Pajalat. If we become a risk of exposure for them, they may well recall their deal with us. And in the meantime, we will almost certainly draw the direct attention of the Templars."

"We could move," Sasha offered. "Go north into the Rockies. There are a lot of outcasts there, it's not a place any Elder would go lightly."

"And the places where the outcasts live are only livable because it isn't territory any elder wanted," Tarin pointed out. "We can't just pick up and rebuild every couple of years. We have to make this place ours now or it never will be."

"Then," Reece said, "we need to ensure that Calavastrix is forced to take the long path."

"Get permission from your Ancients?" I asked. "If I'm not claimed, though, isn't that—"

"*If*," Reece said.

Tarin's face pinched. He turned to me. "Claiming is an act of intention," he said. "If I can't do it... then there is an alternative. It would keep you safe, it would mean Calavastrix has no power to take you."

I shook my head. "What are you..."

But it dawned on me. In part because Sasha bowed his head and gave a long sigh.

I tried to take a step away from Tarin, but he held my hand fast. "It's not the choice I want to make—"

"It's not your choice at all," I corrected him. "Look, I... this might be dire, and I certainly don't want to be Caleb Drake's plaything but... Tarin, I don't *want* Sasha to claim me. I'm not— *we're* not... no offense, Sasha."

"None is taken," Sasha said softly. "But Lucas... the way that this works, among our people, is that Tarin took you from Calavastrix's territory. He has a right to take you back, and will have the support of the Elders in doing so. If you are unclaimed, you're free game as far as they're concerned."

I shook my head, baffled that we were even having the conversation. "The backwards-ass nature of that aside," I said, "I'm not going to dragon-marry someone to keep myself safe. Tarin—you're the one that I want. You're the one I'm going to raise this baby with. I don't care how it has to happen. That's the end of this discussion. Now. What are the rest of our options? It's going to be us and some wolven against a dragon. How do we make that work?"

Reece's jaw twitched several times, but he didn't press the issue any further at least, and Tarin still held my hand tight but he dropped the subject as well. Sasha's eyes seemed to linger on me for a long moment but he turned to the counter and we joined him.

"Wolven will not prove much of a distraction," Sasha said. "Not unless we can force Calavastrix into a tight place where his size won't be an advantage. We want to draw him into the bramble. I've sent messages to other outcasts but... whether they respond or not, we won't know until or unless they arrive. A few that I have contact with are close enough that they could make it... barring that, it's going to be a direct conflict. Reece and myself against Calavastrix, in whatever form that requires."

I wasn't anything close to a strategist. Not on a battlefield, anyway. Give me a war in a courtroom and there was a good chance I'd be worth something—I was no slouch as a lawyer. I mean... yes, I had only been in a courtroom a couple of times but I took to it like I lived there. This, though, was entirely out of my depth. All I knew for certain was that I wasn't going to run—there would be no point. And more important, I wasn't going to leave Tarin, or abandon this place. Matt, Mercy, even Yuri and hell—even Sasha and Reece in their own way—they all felt important to me. They'd taken on risks having me here, and it didn't seem fair to turn away from them now.

Tarin and I were stuck with this, whatever it was. And even if he never could claim me, then I would just remain unclaimed. If I had enough faith in him to let him try, then I could damn well maintain enough faith to do it the old-fashioned way like any other human couple. Calavastrix would just have to deal with all of us, a united front, and maybe if there was enough opposition...

I bit the inside of my cheek. That... was a terrible idea. I knew better than to say it out loud when it occurred to me. Obviously, we didn't need another set of complications and we'd managed to mostly avoid it so far.

Still—it worked in a courtroom. Give your opponent too much opposition, too many risks to take, make it so complicated that it wasn't worth it, and they would often settle. It wasn't a tactic I particularly cared for but I'd seen Gregg use it and seen him pop the cork of a champagne bottle each time it worked.

I had to at least float the idea.

"The, ah... the wolven," I said hesitantly, interrupting an arcane discussion about magical tactics, "if they were firmly on our side... would they be a formidable enough barrier against the Templars? I mean if it was known that they were a constant presence?"

Reece frowned. Sasha shrugged. "Perhaps," he said, though somewhat skeptical. "They have a history of isolation tactics. They don't like to confront large groups of anything supernatural. It gets messy. Instead they pick us off when we're alone, or when they can draw us out. Not that it will matter if we can't jump this hurdle successfully."

"Uh huh," I grunted. "And... what if we jumped more than one hurdle at the same time, then?"

"Speak plainly," Reece insisted. "We do not have time."

I had to let go of Tarin's hand so that I could clasp mine. The anxiety wasn't quite turned off but it was slightly mitigated. "What if," I started, expecting Reece to shoot the idea down entirely, "we... let the Templars know where we are. I could call my phone. Someone is almost certainly monitoring it. I could get them to get ready, tell them... I don't know, tell them I want like an extraction, that I want to be sterilized. If we time it right, and have the wolven here but hidden, and get them to 'storm' the place when Calavastrix arrives—well, that'll complicate things for him, and the wolven will complicate things for the Templars. They'll know that we've got allies, so will Calavastrix, and we'll get a win that might, I don't know, make the wolven more confident in us?"

"Absolutely—" Reece started.

But Sasha held a hand up. "It's not entirely without merit, Reece."

Reece turned a baleful look on Sasha. "My mate and children, born and unborn, are here. I do not wish to put a pin in the Templars' map."

Sasha spread his hands. "Think about how they operate, though. The reason they steer clear of the wolven is because of their tight pack structure. They go after loners or accost travelers. The ursin even had to change how they live, start forming clans, to protect themselves. The vulpin never did—and now no one's seen one in ages. If we give a show of unity and force, and invite them to witness it, it could put them off."

"They'll likely attempt new tactics," I said. "Templar Industries can attack from a lot of other angles, I imagine. Legally. But at least that's a fight where no one is firing bullets or… throwing magic, or something."

Sasha nodded, more enthusiastic now. "And, if Calavastrix is the only dragon on the field, he makes an attractive target. I doubt the Templars would engage directly, but if we could potentially make this territory too dangerous for him…"

"He might never return," Tarin finished. He looked at me. "That is a bold plan. And a clever one."

"And a very dangerous one," Reece said.

"This is… more your home than it is mine," I admitted. With a sigh, I leaned on the counter. "But running Calavastrix off is a short-term goal. It's one step in a direction that we can't know where it will lead. Long-term thinking is how this place survives for generations, if it's going to last that long. That's what all the permits and grants and planning have been for—to make sure that it's not just tomorrow, but next year, next decade. If we plant this flag now, it will earn interest. The long game is the only game—the short game is just a distraction. I don't know enough about all of these… people to know for sure that this will work. I admit that. But I know how political and legal entanglements play out, and no one wants to be the person walking into a shitstorm on purpose. Even if Calavastrix does get some kind of dispensation from the Elders, or the Ancients—are they really going to want to be on the same field as a bunch of wolven and the Templars? Will the Templars want to stage a massive attack in the middle of Texas?"

Sasha clucked his tongue and smiled. "And will the wolven want to give up this alliance when the Templars are parked near their territory? If we bring more outcasts here, and can tell them it's a safe haven, Hank's pack and others will be looking at a high concentration of firepower and mystical clout. If we can't find the first outcast, we'll need another bargaining chip."

"Long-term thinking," Tarin muttered. His mood had improved. There was still that pain in his eyes, the shame of being unable to make me truly his—the way he understood it—but there was something else there that I hadn't quite expected. Pride?

It made me warm. And all of it made me fired up, as well. Excited for a victory in ways I hadn't been for a while. "So? If we're going to set it up, I'm guessing it has to be soon."

Reece rubbed his forehead, looked to Sasha, then to Tarin. Both of them had said their piece, though, and all that was left was his agreement, if he was going to give it.

"If we alert the Black Paw pack," he said finally, "it may well stretch the limits of their willingness to help. Though they will not appreciate a bit of treachery, I do not think the Templars will pull a trigger if the odds are so significantly against them. Make the call, and if you make contact... indicate to them that there are only the three dragons here, and nothing else. Offer them a time to extract you, if possible—tell them... tell them that you have a list of other omegas and other dragons. Names. That way, they will come prepared to remove you, not simply gun you down."

"I can do that," I agreed.

"This will be incredibly dangerous," Sasha told me. "Calavastrix has laid waste to countries before. If we miscalculate..."

Tarin shrugged. "It's the same as if we simply faced him down ourselves. It's a gamble, but it's what we have. Sasha... walk with me to the bramble. We'll get a better sense of the land."

Sasha frowned. "I know the region like the back of my claws."

"I don't," Tarin countered. "I want to know our full play, and how to navigate it on two legs. Lucas?"

He didn't have a question. Instead, he pulled me to him, kissed me deeply in front of the other two, and gripped my waist tight in both hands. There was tongue, and everything, but I had a hard time being at all modest. When he let me go, he pressed his forehead to mine. "I trust you," he said. "I trust your instincts, and your intellect. And I love you, my mate. No matter what our future together looks like."

"I love you too," I muttered, warm-cheeked with Sasha and Reece looking on. There was pity practically radiating from both of them. I wanted to tell them that we could have something just as deep without the claiming as they had or would have with their mates. The truth was, I didn't know that for sure. It was just a matter of faith, and I supposed it would always have to be.

Tarin kissed me a final time, and led Sasha out the back to go examine the bramble while there was still light.

Reece and I stood in an uncomfortable quiet for a moment.

"It doesn't matter that he can't claim me, you know," I said finally, to break the silence and get us moving toward making this all work. "Humans don't have a need for that and it works out just fine for us."

"Perhaps," Reece said. "I do not pity you, or consider your relationship less than in any way, Lucas. Rather, I only hope that the two of you can find fulfillment. In whatever form that takes. I thank you for remaining with us, and for the work that you have accomplished. And for staying now. It would be safer if you left."

I exhaled slowly, revealing just how nervous I really was, I think. "Well… there's a part of me that feels like I walked out on my own family. Or that we walked out on each other, maybe. I've felt guilty about that for a long time. I'm not inclined to do the same thing again and carry that around with me, too. This is home. It's where my child was conceived, where I fell in love with my mate. Where I hope my child will be born. So. Consider me invested."

He smiled, and gave me a nod of approval. He reached into his back pocket and produced a phone, which he slid across the island counter. "It is not locked. Make what preparations you feel are needed, and make the call. I will attempt to ensure that we have notice when Calavastrix arrives."

I nodded, and he put a hand on my shoulder to squeeze it once before he left through the back of the kitchen.

I took some time to steady myself, think through what I would say and how this all might play out. If the wolven were late, if the Templars were early, if Calavastrix didn't show or go there before anyone else…

All I could do was hope for the best, and control the parts that I could, and trust the others to do the same. I dialed my phone, half expecting it to go straight to voicemail. It rang, at least, so someone had kept it charged.

And, after three rings, someone picked up. "Hello?"

I recognized the voice, and had to force myself to respond. "Lena," I said, and didn't have to pretend to be afraid, "it's… Lucas. Warren. I've made a terrible mistake. I think I need help."

There was a pause, as if she were deciding whether it were a trick. But then, "Tell me where you are."

Chapter 29 - Tarin

"You know the land as well as I do," Sasha said as we reached the edge of the bramble. "What do you want to talk about?"

"I haven't seen it from the sky," I pointed out. "But… yeah. I know it pretty well. It's about Lucas."

Sasha picked a tree and leaned against it, hands in his pockets. "Ah. You want me to, what, convince him that letting me claim him is best?"

"Not exactly," I said. I plucked at one of the bushes. "He's good, you know. I suggested we leave. Even if it would have gutted me. To keep him safe, keep him away from all of this, away from Calavastrix. He was the one that wanted to stay. He deserves our protection, stability."

"I think we've known on another long enough that we don't have to approach an ask sideways, Tarin." Sasha sighed, and looked back toward the house. "What is it you want?"

I braced myself for it, because even thinking it was painful. But it was for the best. Would be, if it came to the worst possible outcome. "When Calavastrix gets here… if it looks like there's a chance he'll take Lucas, if I can't protect him… I want you to claim him."

Sasha raised an eyebrow. "Lucas has said he doesn't want that," he said slowly, "and a battlefield is hardly the place to make that happen?"

I eyed him. "You know there's another way."

He exhaled sharply, and shook his head. "I can't do that to him, Tarin. He'd never forgive me, and he would never forgive *you*."

"He'd come around to you," I said. "He wouldn't be able to help it. It might take a few years, but… at least he'd be free."

"That sounds like a matter of perspective," he shot back. He stood from the tree and came to me, put both hands on my shoulders. "You can't want this."

I shrugged his hands off but stopped short of shoving him away. "Of course I don't. It's not about what I want."

"Is it at all about what he wants?" he asked. "How can you ask me to betray his trust in both of us?"

"Because the alternative is much worse," I snapped. "You know what Calavastrix will do. Having his own private omega, he can breed more by force if he needs to, and sell them off for territory, for resources—and he will. He's only ever cared about power, and he'll have the kind of leverage no other dragon could possibly turn down. How long do you think Lucas can produce children? He's twenty-eight. That's, what, twenty, thirty more years? Their lives are brief. That would be nearly all of it, spent under Calavastrix's claw. He'd go crazy. He'd want to die; he'd try, probably, but that monster would almost certainly see to it that was impossible. And he'd have to be replaced, eventually, by one of his own omega offspring. An endless cycle. I would rather break Lucas' heart once, badly, and lose him to you than see that happen. Sasha, I want you to promise me you'll do this. I'm begging you. I can't. So you have to."

Sasha had taken several steps back. He looked disgusted, ashamed—of me, or of himself for considering it, I didn't know. I didn't care. I didn't need him to be proud of anything, I needed him to ensure Lucas' survival because going to that fate would be worse than death.

"Promise me," I insisted.

His shoulders rose and fell with a heavy sigh. He didn't look at me. "If it is certain," he said. "If I know that it's going to happen, I'll do it. You know that it means you'll have to go. Taking him that way... claiming him with magic—it will change him, and he'll hate you for it."

"I know," I whispered. "But I know also that you would never abuse that power. He'd be safe with you."

Claiming by magic wasn't the same as the bite, made in the midst of passion. It wasn't about openness and it didn't go two ways. It was compulsion, a kind of tether that leveraged the dragon magic already present in an omega's being. It made them subject to the dragon's will. It would be a violation all its own, aside from the betrayal itself. But it was just as permanent as the other way, and would serve the same purpose in the end.

Lucas was already pregnant with my child, but as long as he was unclaimed, he could bear the children of any other dragon. Once Sasha claimed him, if it came to that, he and I would have no more. Only Sasha's seed would take. Calavastrix would know, would be able to feel it, just as if Lucas had consented.

It was horrifying to even consider, much less suggest—or for that matter get Sasha's agreement on. But Lucas couldn't even imagine the stakes and if he did, he was far too stubborn to agree.

"If we get through this and I don't need to claim him," Sasha said, "you need to reconsider what it means to you to protect your mate. There is a point at which taking your mate's fate into your own hands, making decisions for them, even if it is for the best, is no better than being a prisoner."

I only stared at him, unable to muster any expression at all. If I felt it, if I let myself sink into my emotions, I would be more useless for the coming conflict than I already was. "You think I don't know that?"

Sasha shrugged. "Honestly, Tarin? I can't tell."

He left me, and in his absence I wondered if I could either.

***

By the time night approached, two trucks arrived from the Black Paw pack. Hank was among them, of course—no alpha would order his pack to a fight without including himself in the ranks. There were, all told, a dozen of them, men and women, all of them dressed in loose clothing. Two of them were particularly... large.

"These," Hank said when the necessary introductions were finished, "are a couple of friends of the pack. They hole up over in Waring. Tristan and Victor Russel, brothers. Ursin."

Both men were approaching seven feet tall, towering over the small crowd. They sported thick black beards, and were at least as wide as any two wolven put together. They had a wild look about them, like men who lived outside of any proper town.

"It's a pleasure," Tristan said, and his voice more than matched his shape. I could feel it in my bones when he spoke. "Any friend of the Black Paw."

We shook, and Victor echoed his brother's sentiments. "Hank here thinks you folks might be able to work out our problem."

Reece was at least honest about it. "The solution appears remote, but... if there is some hope of it, we will see it accomplished."

"Any idea when this angry dragon might show himself?" Hank asked. "My people are fed and fired up."

"At my best estimate," Reece said, "he has left his territory. Scrying is not my particular specialty, but there are indications in the magnetic currents—"

"He's on his way," Sasha translated.

Reece dipped his head. "So it is. I cannot pinpoint his exact location."

"It's over a thousand miles," I said. "Driving, it's almost fifteen hours. Flying? He could do it in six to eight. Maybe faster."

"He will not approach until it is fully dark," Reece said. "So we have some time to prepare. Sasha and I will show you the grounds, indicate our plan. We do not intend to meet him on friendly ground, and there are ways to mitigate his advantages."

"Show us the way," Hank said. He gave a loud, sharp whistle, and the wolven who were not paying close attention snapped to instantly. I had to admit, having an organized force like they seemed to be was a comfort.

They filed around the house, ursin guests in tow, leaving me alone with Lucas.

Lucas looked up at me, smiling despite all of this, somehow. "It's going to be okay, you know."

"You have remarkable optimism," I replied. "If all that we get out of this is that you survive, that will be enough for—"

He put a finger to my lips. "Tarin," he chided softly, "it's *going to be okay*. I can feel it."

I wanted to say that he didn't know what Calavastrix was capable of, how powerful an elder with full control of his magic would be, or how little a pack of wolven, even twice as many, could possibly matter in the face of that. I did not share his optimism, and the thought of bringing Templars into this mix terrified me even more.

Instead, I tried to soak in some of his hope. "We've come far. I'm very sorry about how you got here, you know. I... made a decision for you, and I shouldn't have."

He sighed, and wrapped his arms around my waist, laid his head on my chest. "It's hard to be all that angry about it now," he admitted. "It'll make a good story for our children."

"More than one?" I wondered.

He shrugged against me and nuzzled harder, as if he could worm his way past my clothing. I wanted him to, very much—to share one more round of lovemaking with him before… well, nothing was certain. "Call it keeping up with the Stileses. And besides, you gotta have a couple so they can keep each other busy, right? I just sort of assume having kids is a lot like having dogs. They need a friend."

I chuckled, and kissed the top of his head. "For you," I muttered, "we will populate the state of Texas with our children if that's what will make you happy."

He groaned. "Uh… let's just start with, like, *two*. And take it from there. If we even can. Do they make dragon birth control?"

"I'm afraid they do not," I said. "Though, Mercy has worked up an herbal cocktail for Matthew. He also doesn't particularly want to choose between sex and pregnancy."

"God bless that woman," Lucas said. He kissed me, erasing some of my worry for a few seconds before he finally pulled away and looked up at the sky. "It'll be dark soon. I told Lena to come and save me around midnight. I guess… we'll find out then, right?"

"I suppose we will," I said.

But I don't think that he and I were talking about the same thing.

Chapter 30 - Lucas

There were a lot of unknowns. Four different 'assets' were meant to be on the field, and they all needed to align more or less in the right order for everything to go off without a hitch. However, over the next few hours, as night crept in and the moon began its climb in earnest, we worked out a simple enough solution for the setup.

Hank and his people would hold back in the bramble, and remain there until Calavastrix arrived, if he did—which Reece seemed certain about. Calavastrix was not a patient sort of dragon, and that seemed right in line with everything I knew about Caleb Drake. I had to agree, this was happening tonight.

But even if it didn't, I had warned Lena that if the Templars were going to come and get me, they'd need to approach from the west, away from the main driveway into the ranch. I would be waiting just past the barn. That would bring them into play somewhat out of sight of the wolven, at least until one of them picked up that there were intruders. By the time the Templars were far enough in to grab me, the wolven would know, and if Calavastrix never showed up then we would have dealt with two out of three issues at least—and that wasn't a failure. It would just make Calavastrix's eventual arrival somewhat less optimistic for an outcome.

If, however, everything went to plan, then we would be mired with the Templars in some kind of standoff just before or just as Calavastrix made his entrance. If he was late to the party, we just had to stall until he arrived and pick the moment to put an end to things if he didn't.

When exactly Lena and her people would get here was another variable. I had warned her of the dragons; she wouldn't come alone. How long it would take to muster Templar forces could easily change when she arrived.

But in all the scenarios that Reece, Hank, Sasha, and the two ursin beasts who happened to have fought in the Second World War discussed—all of those that did not include the Templars, that is—the refrain was the same.

"We have the advantage of both time and place," Tristan said. "Those two are the best to have, even more than numbers and weapons if you play them right."

Having a few more confident voices around eased some of my own anxiety. Not nearly all of it, of course. But it took some of the edge off.

"Ursin are notoriously overconfident," Sasha muttered, as the brothers and the wolven dispersed into the bramble to shift. I caught a few of them stripping down just as they crossed the tree-line, including Tristan, and had to look away when I caught sight of what swung between his legs. That was... not natural.

"I can't imagine why," I breathed. "I should probably take position too, then. Not much of a bait and switch if there's no bait in place."

"Sasha will come with us," Tarin said. "In case Calavastrix spots you from above and tries to go for the grab. Odds are he'll want additional revenge, but there's no way to know until he arrives."

That seemed reasonable, but Sasha didn't seem at all happy about it.

"Better idea?" I asked.

Sasha only shook his head, shot Tristan an absolutely mournful look, and turned to head toward the barn.

"What's that about?" I asked Tarin.

Tarin shrugged on shoulder. "He gets like this before a fight, I think. I wouldn't worry about it."

It raised flags and set off alarms, but then so did every stiff breeze at the moment. I wasn't in the right frame of mind to judge which parts of my anxiety were rational and which were artifacts of my panicked imagination. I tried instead to stay here, in the moment, watchful for whatever happened next.

The three of us arranged ourselves so that I was alone at the top of the hill, with Tarin and Sasha below, out of sight from the field in the west. I found myself wishing we'd managed to plant and grow grain there, just so it wasn't so open and exposed. Not that it mattered. The hills and trees gave enough cover, I supposed, and adding more for the Templars wouldn't have changed anything. I just somehow didn't want to see them coming.

I did, though. From some distance, thanks to the relatively clear night. Just a few hints where the moon and starlight glinted off of metal, but I guessed there were a dozen of them, maybe more. They crept across the field from the southwest, on a slightly different angle than I had suggested—but Hank had made that assumption, and there were even a few scouts posted east and directly south just in case.

"They're here," I whispered, trusting Sasha to hear me.

"Then we're started," he said. "Wait to flag them down until they near the barn."

I assumed they could see me—I wasn't at all hidden, and meant to be bait for Calavastrix. Double duty. So when I saw the first of them pass the field and move into the grass, I stood up and prayed that the intelligence I claimed to have was enough to keep them from shooting.

Just in case, though, Sasha was shifted and the air in front of me grew just slightly opaque. His particular skill was with wind and air and he claimed he could stop a bullet with a thought if he was prepared. I desperately hoped I would not have to test that claim.

One they spotted me, one of the Templars paused, and held up a fist. They made another gesture, and the group fanned out, crouched and so silent that only supernaturally sharp ears could have tracked them.

And they did—I heard the panting of an animal, and glanced back to see one of the wolven, now in the shape of a larger than reasonable wolf, trotting toward us.

"Company," Tarin said. "Bring the rest of them to this end of the woods. Templars. This just got more complicated."

I had to struggle not to look back and see the response.

The Templar who had been giving orders swept a gun with a sight on it across the grass and hills on this side of the barn. They stopped at the barn door, opened it slightly to peer in, then moved along while two other flanked them from behind. I held my ground waiting until they were halfway up the hill to me and then made a show of checking around before I descended.

Three guns were trained on me when I reached them. I stayed clear enough from them that there was space for Sasha's disc of air. Once my eyes adjusted to it, I couldn't even tell it was there, and hoped they didn't either. "I'm Lucas Warren," I said. "You came. Uh… thank you."

They were in combat gear, armored up and wearing helmets with visors. The one in front pushed their visor up. I recognized Lena's face under it. "Guess you got a taste of lizard and didn't like it?"

"I thought it was the lesser of two evils," I said. "You *did* threaten to kill me."

"Still might," she said. She glanced back. "One of you take a team and sweep the barn, the other, go to the house. Kill anything in there."

If I had any remaining doubts about where I stood, they were gone. Not that I had any to speak of. Still. "There are children inside," I said. "Be careful of—"

Lena sneered. "Dragon whelps," she spat. "Not children."

The two other Templars crept off, leaving us alone, as far as Lena was concerned. "You've got names? Locations?"

"Just names," I said. "No precise locations." Where were the wolven? I didn't know how long to keep this conversation going.

"Approximate, then?" She pressed.

I nodded. "States, countries. A few cities. There are"—had I mentioned a number before? Shit, I couldn't remember—"twelve of them, in all."

"Twelve," she echoed. "Twelve omegas? Or twelve dragons?"

"Some of each," I said. "Um… Caleb Drake, for a start."

She snorted. "We already know about that one. Who else do you have?"

I wasn't going to name random names and find out on the news that someone with the same name had died. I shook my head. "Take me out of here, get me somewhere safe, and I'll tell you."

Lena pursed her lips. "The one that took you," she said. "Is he here?"

"Does it matter?"

"It matters," she growled. "I lost two teeth and my head is still pounding. It took me two weeks to say my own name straight. I've got a score to settle. And so do you, it sounds like. Where is he?"

She hadn't mentioned this on the call. It was supposed to be in and out, a quick extraction, they were supposed to turn their backs and get pinned down by the wolven. It was past midnight by now as well—where was Calavastrix?

"I… I don't know," I said. "I had to sneak out, they kept me in a cellar so I wouldn't escape. I took too much of a risk even getting you here. We have to leave before they—"

From off to our right, near the tree line, a shot was fired.

Lena's visor snapped down. She took three quick steps back, her gun trained on me. A second later, there was a vicious snarling sound, joined by another, and then a muffled scream as someone human was, I suspected, taken down and torn apart.

"What the fuck was that?" Lena demanded.

"I don't know," I said, panicked, and put my hands up. "Please don't shoot. We have to go, you have to get me out of here!"

Her rifle twitched. The air in front of me thickened, grew almost hazy. The barrel of Lena's gun dropped an inch, and she looked both ways frantically. "Shit. *Shit*, you little fucker. All units, gun down anything that moves. Magic on the field. Repeat, magic on the field, they were waiting for us."

She pulled the trigger. I didn't even have time to flinch.

Suspended in the air in front of me was a sharp metal tooth. My ears rang from the noise of the gun. A second later, I was off my feet, traveling backward through the air. I saw Tarin pass me, and a second later my world spun as Sasha caught me and twisted to absorb my weight and set me on my feet.

Another shot fired, and another.

Howls erupted from the woods. Voices shouted.

Sasha's skin was shifted to scales along his arms and neck. He held one hand out toward my mate, who was crouched as if waiting for something.

Lena's gun clicked. Sasha lowered his arms, and Tarin lunged out of sight down the hill.

"Help him," I snapped at Sasha, but the dragon had a look of grim determination on his face. He turned to me, and his form dissolved into mist, replaced by a dragon about twice the size of a bull.

"I have one job," he said, his voice booming even as he clearly tried to keep it low. "That is to protect you in Tarin's stead. Stay close to me."

He spread his wings, raised one massive claw and uttered something that must have been draconic, hissing through his teeth and vibrating in my chest. The air around us grew thick, and seconds later the thud of several bullets sounded behind me. I leapt forward, taking cover behind one of Sasha's massive legs, and tried to get my sights on Tarin.

"Where the fuck is—"

I didn't even get the question all the way out before thunder cracked over the ranch.

Sasha froze, and looked up at the darkness. "That's him. Whatever you do—don't leave my side."

Calavastrix had arrived.

Chapter 31 - Tarin

The moment the woman's clip was spent, Sasha dropped the shield. I didn't have to think through what happened next. I threw myself at her, arms wide, and crashed into her with everything I had. The world spun and turned hard as we hit the side of the hill and went rolling down it.

Even in the fall, even without the rifle she had dropped, the Templar didn't let the fall affect her judgment any more than I did. We rolled once, and she landed a knee in my side. As we rolled again, I jammed my fist into her neck. I heard her muffled choking at the same time that her elbow struck my collarbone. Pain exploded. When we finally stopped, I managed to use the last of our momentum to throw her off me at the barn.

She missed the corner by a few feet, saving her spine, and instead glanced off the partially open door. Almost immediately, she was on her feet and reaching for a sidearm. I was just as fast, though, and charged her at full speed. By the time she got the gun up, I was on her again, hurling myself at her with an elbow that I slammed into the front of her visor.

The glass or plastic cracked, her head snapped back, and she fell. The gun dropped, and discharged when it struck the ground. Sharp pain exploded in my leg, nearly buckling me, but the bullet missed the bone and must have gone through because as I rushed to finish her, nothing ground in my calf except the burning pain of muscle fibers that had been split.

Her fall continued as she threw her legs over her and turned it into a backward roll that ended in a half-crouch. She threw the helmet off and met me with a kick as I dove for her. I barely had time to turn it aside, and threw a punch at her face as she spun. She expected it, dropped, and a second later a fresh agony blossomed in my leg as it went out from under me. I hit the ground hard. Air left my lungs.

Her boot came for my face. I rolled, struggling to suck in air. Her weight fell on me, hard, and something in my chest cracked. Before I could even react to it, my vision went briefly white and the side of my head pounded. I swung wild, as hard as I could, and connected with something that made her give a pained, breathless grunt. I hit her in the same spot again, and again, until her weight was off me, and then continued rolling to my stomach to get onto my feet.

She rose at the same time, but weakly. She was trained, and good, but she didn't have my strength and she wasn't protecting a mate and child.

I crouched and prepared to lunge with my good leg when the sound of dragon wings halting a descent cracked through the sky like sharp thunder. A second later, the ground shook as Calavastrix landed.

Both of us reacted the same way. Our eyes went to the hill. He wasn't visible yet, but would be soon. He'd come in a glamour.

"Fuck," she muttered.

One disaster at a time. I charged her, and caught her attention only just before I rammed my elbow into her stomach, taking her up and off her feet. Her elbow struck me hard between the shoulder blades, made my right arm numb, but I drove her back until we found the barn door. I drove her through it.

We tumbled onto the dirt ground inside, where I drove her hard into the floor amid the shattered wood. She wheezed, and tried to kick me off her. I let her, using the lift to get distance. She flopped, trying to get up fast, but failing as the muscles in her stomach refused to unclench from the impact. It was all the time I needed. I leapt forward, and brought my boot down on her knee.

Bone crunched. Other things almost certainly snapped free. She screamed, a sound that she bit off into a growl as she reached to clutch at her ruined joint. Before I could stop her, her hand jerked up, found the toolbox and got her hands on something. I flinched back, but not before something struck me in the forehead. The impact snapped my head back. More pain invaded my skull. I staggered, and my balance was lost. The world tilted and I fell over, onto my side. My broken rib complained again, and this time wouldn't be ignored. When I tried to push myself up, the agony that assaulted me buckled my elbows.

"Fucking... lizard," she huffed.

I groaned with the effort of responding, and had to do it through clenched teeth. "Tell... your people... to focus on the big dragon," I managed. "He'll kill us... all."

"Radio's in my fucking helmet," she shot back. "And fuck you, you all deserve to die. *Son of a bitch*..." she hissed and let out a pained wail that she barely choked off. I craned to see her shaking hands hovering over the crushed knee.

Her helmet. I'd seen it. If I could get to it...

Outside, a dragon roared. Wolven howls filled the air. Gunfire blasted. I hadn't claimed Lucas. I couldn't feel him, couldn't tell if he was safe or alive. Sasha would have him under cover, but if Calavastrix overcame his distractions, he would shred Sasha's magic with barely an effort.

I swallowed hard, and forced myself to push up on my arms through the pain. I managed to get to my knees, and then my feet, and had to clutch at my ribs to keep them from crippling me again.

I left the Templar in the barn and staggered back outside into a warzone. The air buzzed with bullets, zipping like hornets as they split the air, but none of them were pointed at me. I heard a second dragon roar—Reece; I recognized the timbre—and searched frantically for the Templar's helmet. It had to be near the door, where she'd rolled. She'd thrown it back behind her...

My foot connected with it as I searched behind the scuffed grass where we'd tangled, and I picked it up with one hand. Where was the microphone? They wouldn't even listen to me, I imagined, but... I found it and angled the helmet to speak into it. "Templar forces," I groaned, "the large, red dragon is Calavastrix the Storm. He will kill every one of you if you do not concentrate fire. Go for his wings, near the joint."

There was no response, but it was all I had. I tossed the helmet inside to the Templar in the barn and gave her a last furious glare before I made my way up the hill to find Lucas and Sasha. They had to be all right. They had to be, or there was nothing left.

Chapter 32 – Lucas

Sasha had shown me his full size. Bigger than a few elephants, his neck longer than a giraffe. Not like he was at the moment, small enough that he could offer thick cover without losing track of me. But even at full size, he was tiny compared to the monstrosity that shimmered into existence atop four deep gouges in the earth.

Calavastrix was unthinkably large. Larger than the house. Large enough to snap a person up in one bite. Which, a moment later, he did as one of the Templars fired on him. The great dragon's head, bearded with horns and topped by a crest of them longer than I was tall, snapped around almost casually and bit through armor to crush a nuisance. His tail flicked, and another went flying.

Fear like I had never experienced gripped me. The kind that had claws, and teeth, and began to tear at my insides, urging me to run for my life. I was prey—a rabbit, or a deer—in front of that thing. That, I realized, was a true apex predator, and I understood in an instant why the Templars hated them so much.

They were afraid.

With a gust of hot breath that I could feel even from a distance of at least thirty feet or more, those great burning eyes turned toward me and Sasha. The great, red-scaled head tilted, lowered, and turned sideways to peer at me. The voice that came out of it was smoother than I expected, and thrummed in the air. Every hair on my body stood on end. "There you are, little omega. I have come to collect you."

"Stay behind me," Sasha rumbled. He moved to face Calavastrix.

The great dragon's chest vibrated with a chuckle. "Voatristix the Fury," he mused. "How quaint. You will not be missed."

Sasha spoke a word that I could feel in the air, hissing as he swiped a claw. Outside the dome of the shield around us, the wind howled and slammed into the larger dragon. He staggered once before he recovered his balance and snapped off his response in draconic.

The shield around us shattered. Shards of it exploded out from us, creating a momentary disorientation of changed air pressure that popped in my ears. The shards dissipated almost instantly, and Sasha's forelegs collapsed as a second word—magic, I understood—crashed into him and drove him down.

I had scrambled back from fear of being crushed, but even as he fell, Sasha seemed aware of me, throwing his hindlegs sideways to keep from falling onto me.

He wasn't done, though. He roared something else, and the stars were obscured by something long and thick. Calavastrix looked up in time to swivel out of the way as a chunk of ground below where his head had been exploded as if a giant spike had been thrust into it.

Calavastrix moved to respond, but before he could, he jerked in surprise and snapped at his own wing. There had been a constant patter of gunfire already but it seemed suddenly to be focused entirely on the larger dragon. The Templars were taking their shot, going for his wings.

He pulled them in close to his body and turned to bellow at the source. A second later, lightning blinded me, dropping from a clear sky. There was a break in the gunfire, but it renewed a moment later, coming from a different direction.

Wolven howled, cutting through the noise, and as I tried to clear my eyes, I saw the blurred shapes dashing from the woods toward Calavastrix. There was no chance they could hope to take him down, or even make him pause, and he raised a great claw to prove that.

Which, I gathered a second later, was a distraction.

From the sky above Calavastrix, a third dragon plummeted like a meteor. I could see the impact coming, and knew that it would have to be massive, and destructive. I took a step back, my heel caught on a clump of grass and I fell, and then continued to crawl backward as fast as I could.

The ground shook beneath me, and the boom had to have been heard for miles. Reece—it had to be him—plowed into Calavastrix though he was barely half the greater dragon's size. But he had momentum, and that momentum drove Calavastrix into the ground, *hard*.

Instantly, there was fresh noise in the air as the two creatures became tangled. Claws raked over scales, great jaws snapped loud enough to hurt my ears. A gout of flame gushed from one of them but I couldn't tell which. Gunfire continued to rain on them, until the Templars became more concerned with their own survival as the wolven harried them. It was chaos, too much to take in, and my mind was frozen. Sasha continued to growl words in draconic, assaulting Calavastrix every time he spotted an opening—how he did, I had no idea, but gashes appeared on the massive dragon's wings.

"*Lucas,*" Tarin hissed.

Out of the chaos and the terror, a single note of relief cut through to my core. I practically flipped onto my hands and knees at the sound of his voice, and sprinted the few feet to him. "You're alive!"

He barked with pain when I threw my arms around him. "Easy," he grunted. "Ribs. Collarbone. Head, I think. Bad shape."

"Lena?" I asked. "Did you get her? I thought they would withdraw, they were supposed to—"

"She's not going anywhere unless her people take her with them," he said. "We have to draw Calavastrix into the woods, force him to take a smaller shape so that Reece and Sasha can match him, at least physically. We need to get into the woods."

I nodded quickly, and looked over the dark field for a path. "There," I said, pointing, "but there are a lot of guns still firing."

"They'll focus on Calavastrix," he said. "Come on. We have to move."

We started, and he whistled sharply, though it cost him dearly from the look of it. He nearly fell over once the sound was out of his lips. It was enough, though. Several of the wolven peeled off and headed for us, zig-zagging across the grass in a blur as they surrounded us as an escort. If anything, the Templars seemed relieved. Some of them were reloading, others simply turned their weapons back on the tangling behemoths in front of us.

"Tell Sasha that we are moving," Tarin rasped. "I can't… make myself loud enough."

"He's focused on—"

"He knows the plan," Tarin wheezed. "He'll be listening."

I nodded, and swallowed to wet my dry throat with barely a few drops of saliva that I could manage. "Sasha," I called, "we're moving."

If Sasha heard me, he gave no indication. But a moment later, Reece kicked hard at Calavastrix's side, and earned himself the slightest opening to escape. Sasha roared a word, and the wind struck the behemoth and drove him a few yards across the ground, along with a handful of Templars and even two of the wolven.

The night in the field was bright—a full moon, a clear sky, everything was bathed in enough light that it was mostly visible.

Once we passed the tree line, that changed entirely. Pitch black fell around us like a curtain. As if in answer to the unspoken panic I suddenly felt, soft fur brushed my fingers, and one of the wolven paused there long enough for me to get the message. I held on to a handful of fur loosely, as he led us through the darkness, weaving around trees to get toward the fence that cut through the pines.

Behind us, there was a crash, another dragon's roar, and then the ground shook as something large lumbered into the woods.

The wolven pressed close around us, herding us away from the danger. The gunfire quieted as, I imagined, the dragons entered for the forest and were no longer easy targets to spot.

We worked our way back until we were at the fence. There, Tarin felt around for a post. "Here," he breathed. "Climb over. Keep heading north. One of the wolven will go with you."

A part of me definitely wanted to run. And keep running, and never stop until I was far away from monsters and teeth and claws and magic that could call down lightning. But the thought of leaving Tarin there—I could tell he was in no condition to go any further. "I'm not leaving," I said. "You're a mess. I can't leave you here. We're going or staying together, but not apart. Not ever."

"He's coming," Tarin husked. He coughed, and then gave a sharp, pained groan. "If he hasn't left yet, it's because he doesn't intend to give up. You have to go, Sasha can't…"

I found his face in the darkness, pressed my hand to his cheek. "Sasha can't what?"

"It doesn't matter now," he said. "Please, Lucas, just go, be safe, take our child and—"

One of the wolven snapped, and slammed into me just as a tree crashed down over the fence. I panicked. I couldn't see anything, but I could feel heat nearby. I pressed against a tree that I nearly ran headlong into, and tried to peer through the darkness for Tarin but didn't even know which direction I had moved except that it was away from the fence.

A second later, another tree cracked and fell, and moonlight broke through the canopy.

Calavastrix was smaller, but still somehow just as frightening. He held Sasha pinned by his wings, on his stomach. With a roar, he slammed his head down into Sasha's as the pale dragon tried to twist his head around. The crack was deafening, and Sasha's head dropped.

I didn't see Reece. What had happened? Calavastrix's eyes turned toward me, flaring with lambent orange light. Fire flickered from between his teeth.

He moved toward me, and one of the wolven launched itself at him, snapping for his neck. He swatted the animal away, and it struck something outside the moonlight with a pained yelp. The rest of them mustered in front of me, but he didn't even take his eyes off me as he swept them aside. His great claw reached for me.

And then, Tarin was in front of me. He held a hand up. "You... can't... have him," he gasped. "He carries my child. By law, he—"

Calavastrix snorted, the hot air bathing us both and staggering Tarin back a step. "You plundered my kingdom, cripple," he snarled. "And I can sense the boy's nature. You have not claimed him. Perhaps you could not? Stand aside, and return what is mine by ancient right."

"No," I shouted over Tarin's shoulder. I pulled at him, tried to get him out of the way before Calavastrix killed him. "I'm no one's property. Not his, not *yours*. I'm not going to be anyone's fucking omega factory, I would rather die."

The dragon's head tilted slightly, turning one blazing eye on me. "Is that so?" he wondered. "Come with me willingly, little omega, and I will treat you like a prince. You will live your life in luxury unimaginable. Yes, you will make children, more omegas, but you will bear my young as well. I will show you pleasures beyond your comprehension, and all your life you will want for nothing. Your family, those you choose—I can shower them all with wealth that will last for generations to come. This one cannot give you what I can."

"I don't want anything you have to give," I shouted, though my voice shook and betrayed how much fear warred with defiance in my stomach. "You have no right to me."

"My people *created* you," he snarled. "All of you belong to us."

"I belong to Tarin if I belong to anyone," I shot back. "He is the one that I choose. He is *mine*. You never will be."

Calavastrix drew his head back, and parted his jaws in what I thought was something like a smile. "This one?" he asked. "This one... is already dead."

He spoke a word.

White lit up the forest and threatened to burn my eyes out. I hit the tree behind me. The smell of ozone scraped at the inside of my nostrils, and I coughed and sputtered as I dropped to me knees.

My hands fell on a hot body. I didn't need to be able to see to know who it was.

"Tarin?" I gasped. A cry ripped from me. I couldn't see anything of Calavastrix through the light blindness except the dull glow of his burning eyes, but I howled at him and in a rage I didn't know I was capable of, I tried to scream him to death.

It didn't work, and when I ran out of breath, heat washed over me just before something massive closed around me. He lifted me up, and took me away from Tarin.

He held me in front of his great eye. "As I was saying, little one," he rumbled. "You are *mine*. But if you do not want the life of a prince—then the life of a slave it will be."

Chapter 33 - Tarin

I couldn't hear. I couldn't see. Even my sense of smell, weak as it was in a human body, was deadened, as if every nerve had simply been fried out of me. I tried to move, but my muscles wouldn't respond, and while I felt a pressure on me that I knew were Lucas' hands, I couldn't feel them on my skin. All I could do was *be*, and all I could be was *helpless*.

I had lost him. My mate. In the end, I couldn't protect him. How I ever thought that I could was beyond me. Prideful. That was how I had lost my scales to begin with, and pride had chased me my entire life. It was even pride, to some degree, that moved me to tell Reece about the new Templars, about Matthew—I wanted to be the hero of dragonkind, I suppose. I thought that if I did something like that, something that utterly changed the course of our futures then maybe, just maybe, I would be rewarded.

Here I was again, suffering the same fate, only so much worse. Struck down for standing up for someone. For loving someone. For protecting what was important. I held on to the thought of Lucas, and tried to will Sasha to action. He saw it now. He had to, if he was conscious. This was what we had talked about. I felt magic stirring, and prayed to the Great Fire and the Ancestors that it was him, working his magic, saving Lucas from his fate.

Except... no. The magic wasn't around me. There was a shiver of it, deep in my bones. Not something that was coming together. Something unraveling. Frayed threads, as burned and raw as my nerves, snapped and peeled back. My fire kindled, rose, pushed through the ephemeral fabric of my binding as parts of it weakened. It burned through me, the only thing I could feel, and carried with it one thought—*my mate and my child needed me.*

It rose up like a torrent. I gave myself over to the burn, let it consume me, let it turn my body to char even as I reached for my scales and felt the sudden freedom of the shape between shapes. Sensation flowed back into me, filling my mind with the sharp clarity of pine, and ozone, and the sounds of breathing animals, and the thudding of giant hearts. The crunch of needles and limbs from some distance away where Calavastrix carried off my mate.

I surged up, half formed, and by the time I oriented myself to the ground, I landed on it with claws that I flexed deep into the earth, tearing through soil, and rock, and roots. The darkness paled, my dragon eyes soaking in the light, and training on the elder dragon.

I roared after him. "Calavastrix the Storm," my voice shook needles and branches from trees. "You will not take my mate from me. Face me!"

Calavastrix stopped, and craned his neck around. "Well, well. I should have gutted you instead. A problem easily amended."

He put Lucas down, and spoke a word. Before Lucas could run, he dropped to the earth and lay motionless, eyes wide. I snarled, and bristled the spines along my back, flaring the spikes at the end of my tail that I very much wanted to bury in Calavastrix's eyes.

But the truth of the moment was that I was no match for him. Brute force was pointless. Lucas' plan had been the right one, and it still was. Beyond the tree line, there were still

Templars hunting, peering, regrouping. Wolven still stalked the forest, looking for their opening. Tristan and Victor were through the trees, where Reece was very slowly trying to stand, still in his scales. Sasha was stirring.

"Look at where you are," I told Calavastrix. "Templars behind you, no doubt bringing others. Three dragons, wounded or not. Our allies, whose reach extends as far as your own territory. Leave now, and you can take your dignity with you. You can appeal to the other Elders if you wish, and leave our fate to the Ancients."

"While you claim one of the few omegas on the earth?" Calavastrix snarled. "I'm no fool. You haven't claimed him because you couldn't. Now you hope to buy time to make him yours." He took a menacing step toward me, and away from Lucas. "I have no need of the others to pass judgment on you, Estarinix. You are an outcast, among outcasts. Your violation of my territory has only one sentence. I will gladly carry it out, and when I take your mate, I will remind him of your fate every time I mount him and pour my seed into his belly."

He took another step. His head lowered, baring his horns. His claw twitched as his jaws parted and magic gathered around him.

I dropped my forelimbs to the earth and raised my hindquarters. My tail whipped over my head and the knot of spikes at the end crashed down onto Calavastrix's head. He dropped, dazed, before the word he planned to speak left his teeth.

"Sasha!" I roared. "Hold him!"

Sasha managed to push himself up, and turned sluggishly but with determination to leap across the divide between them, over the fallen trees, and throw himself onto Calavastrix's back. He dug his claws into the dragon's neck, and clamped his jaws down around one wing.

I didn't need to defeat him. Only take away his objective, and fast. I leapt up and over them, shifting my form smaller in the air so that I could snap my wings open and glide down to the ground by Lucas.

Calavastrix's magic was strong, but he was distracted. I hissed at his spell, spitting words of release, and though it was weak from being dormant so long, my magic snagged on his and worked it apart until Lucas twitched once, violently, and gasped for air as he began to crawl back from the two struggling dragons. He stared up at me, eyes wide when he finally stopped, and narrowed them.

"Tarin?" He breathed. "Tarin, you—you're..."

"Free," I said. I looked toward the tree line, where footsteps moved tentatively into the thick carpet of needles. The Templars had gathered their courage and were moving in. "There's no time. I wanted to do this the right way, and I promise that we will, later."

He frowned up at me. "I don't... do what?"

I swept my wing up and over him, and curled my claws to encircle him. "It will all be okay," I promised. And I spoke the spell. I called my magic, and pressed it into him, seeking out the echo of the old magic that had made his ancestors, until it responded to my call.

Lucas gasped. His eyes fluttered, and he reached for my claw to steady himself. "Tarin...?"

In a moment, it was done.

Behind me, Calavastrix roared fury.

New sensations exploded in my mind, filling me with a visceral awareness of Lucas' presence before me. Like an extension of my own being, I could sense the pounding of his heart, his confusion, and a thread of nervous elation as he realized something change inside himself. Quickly following was a gnawing worry. Something had been taken away. He knew it. I promised silently to give it back if I was able, but for now...

"Calavastrix," I bellowed. "Templars. Hear me. Lucas Warren is mine. I claim him as my mate. Leave with your lives, or die here now."

In answer, Calavastrix snarled and snapped, but ultimately settled until Sasha crawled off of him and prowled backward, ready to reengage.

Reece lumbered through the trees, shrugging aside one of the pines to face the elder down from his flank.

Toward the tree line, the Templars had paused.

"There are thirty wolven in this forest," I lied. "They will tear you to pieces at a word."

From somewhere in the forest, a giant bear produced a booming roar, echoed by another. "And two ursin," I continued. "Know this. They stand guard on this territory and around it. Every Templar that so much as breathes the air in Comfort, Texas, will find themselves on the business end of every tooth and claw for fifty miles. You have your choice to make. Foolish pride, or your life?"

One by one, cautiously, the armored killers—only around eight of them now—crept backward, away from the woods.

"I've left you one in the barn," I called after them as they began their retreat.

"That only leaves you, Calavastrix," Reece growled. "There is nothing to gain here now. No omega for you to enslave. If you wish to continue this fight, we will do so. But you have lost. Take your petition to the Ancients if you must. This territory is claimed, and you are not welcome in it."

Calavastrix eyed each of us in turn, then the multitudes of wolven and the two ursin that came lumbering into the wreckage of the forest.

In the distance, sirens wailed. Every dragon and wolven swiveled toward them.

Calavastrix gave no final word. He snapped once, turned a baleful eye on me with a promise that I would see him again, and then turned and stalked through the woods, shimmering as he cloaked himself in glamour. A moment later, the crack of wings sounded once, twice, and a third time before he was in the skies and gone.

All gathered stood frozen for a time, listening to be certain. When it seemed that the elder dragon was truly gone, Reece let out a great sigh, and his form misted away as he took to his skin again. Whatever damage Calavastrix had done, it followed him. He sagged when he was in his skin. "Black Paw pack," he called to the wolven, "we will have company soon. You should not be here when they arrive. Go."

One of the wolves, a large, black lupine, yipped once, and the rest of the pack scattered, dashing north and east toward the border and their own territory. The bears shivered, shaking out their fur as they changed until they were naked and crouched. "Jumping fences isn't easy at that size," Tristan said. He gave us a nod, and then trotted off toward the fence with his brother.

Sasha changed next, and with a great sigh I followed him.

The change helped with some of the injuries, but when Lucas pulled me carefully to him, it was clear that they were not all healed.

"It's done," I said, pressing my lips to his. "It's done. Mate. My mate."

"Don't talk yet," Lucas whispered. "Just… we need to get you to the house. Come on."

I could see in his eyes that he knew what I'd done. Knew that it wasn't the way it was supposed to be. Nonetheless, he held my gaze.

"If there had been another way—" I started.

Lucas only pressed his lips to mine again to quiet me, breathing hard against my lips, his heart still racing, before he pulled away and nodded once. "I know," he said. "I know, Tarin. It's okay. I trust you."

Chapter 34 - Lucas

The police arrived in force. Calls had been made, reporting all sorts of complaints including but not limited to semi-automatic gunfire, monsters, and even aliens. Reece explained that some wild kids had come through, making noise, riding four-wheelers and shooting guns. When he confronted them, they ran off. When he mentioned him and his *husband* having just recently bought the ranch, the officers seemed to think that a check-in was good enough. They took a look at the torn-up earth outside, and, well... dragon claws weren't anywhere on their radar.

When they had finally gone, all of us gave a collective sigh of relief. Reece fell into the couch, wincing at his wounded leg. Sasha took one of the chairs, one hand tending a shoulder that had been damaged in his struggle with Calavastrix.

My mate was worse off than the two of them. He could barely move, and turning his waist even a little pulled at his ribs until he was red in the face. "I'll heal," he assured me when I suggested that we take him to a hospital. "It will be fast. A few weeks at the most while my magic replenishes itself. I'll shift for a little while at night. Don't worry about me."

I couldn't help it, and told him as much when we took up Yuri and Mercy's room that night—he couldn't have made it up the ladder to the loft and was too exhausted to safely shift into something small. "It's like..."

Finding the words was a struggle. I'd been poking at the new feeling since Calavastrix and the others left us. There was a hard knot of feelings in my brain, distinct from me, like... some kind of tumor, almost. It wasn't the union, the sense of oneness and connection that Matt had described. That, Tarin explained, was because of how he'd done it.

"There are two ways to claim a mate," he said quietly, his cheeks red, his eyes downcast. "The way we tried first, and... this way. By force. If I hadn't done it then—"

"I know," I told him. "And you couldn't very well rip my clothes off and fuck me in the middle of all of that. I get it. I just wanted what Matt has. Which is silly, I know. The way he made it sound, though; that closeness, and connection."

"We can still have that," he said. "I think. It's the same magic, the same connection. It's just one-way like this. When I'm better, and can do it properly without puncturing a lung... I promise. I'll make it right."

"I believe you." I curled up by his thigh and rest my head in his lap. He stroked my hair with his fingers, still damp from the shower where I'd given him a careful, gentle kind of bath to clear off the grime and blood. His wounds were closed, and while his skin was a rosy, fresh pink there were only a few patches that showed any signs of burns from the lightning strike. "So it was Calavastrix that set you free in the end, I suppose."

"I'm not sure," he admitted. "Maybe it was the lightning. Maybe it was being on the cusp of death. Maybe it was some condition of the binding that was met—I'd have to ask the

Ancients who bound me to be sure. I don't think it matters to me, though. You're all that matters. You and our child. Our family."

I smiled at that, and pawed at his thigh, gently. "Our family," I echoed. "It sounds nice. How long do you think we have? Before it all comes back around?"

"Calavastrix won't take it lying down," he muttered. "But it takes time to gather the elders, and longer for the Ancients to weigh in. If we can continue to build the community here, establish ourselves as a legitimate… something. Colony? Tribe? Then they may not have a choice but to recognize us. And if, by some miracle, we could actually hunt down this Ancient outcast and get him on our side, well—that would certainly help. Dragons respect nothing more than age and tradition. Even if he is an outcast, if he's still alive, his antiquity alone can only help us."

None of that quite made sense, but I was willing to take his word for it. Worrying about the future was pointless for now. There was plenty in the present to keep me occupied. "This… one-way claiming," I said softly, "what does it mean for us? I mean, how we… work, I guess. How is it different? Why are Sasha and Reece so upset about it?"

"It has an element of compulsion to it," he said. "But I would never abuse that; it's not something I want, I swear. You don't have to worry."

I sat up, and pursed my lips, looking him over. "Compulsion," I muttered. "Like… how do you mean?"

"When a dragon claims a mate in this manner," he said, "we call it a 'thrall'. The thrall is bound to the will of the dragon. You can only have one mate, but you can have many thralls. It is no longer a practice. A thrall cannot refuse a command by his, or—in antiquity—*her* dragon."

"Really," I said skeptically, raising an eyebrow. "So if you told me to do something… I would have to do it?"

"You would not be able to resist," he agreed. "I'll be very careful how I speak to you until I'm recovered."

I drummed my fingers on the bed, still not quite satisfied. "Can you do it now? Just once? I mean, so that I know what it feels like."

He looked horrified. "I wouldn't violate your will like that, Lucas."

"You're not," I reasoned. "I mean, if I'm saying I want you to, then, you know… it's my will too. By proxy."

He groaned softly, shaking his head. Even that seemed to hurt him.

"Come on," I told him. "Anything. One little thing."

Tarin's lips thinned. He sighed, and looked at my lips. "If you insist," he murmured. "Then… kiss me, Lucas."

My body moved on its own, though it felt somehow natural. I didn't resist, didn't want to resist. I leaned into him, careful not to put weight on him—so, whatever the compulsion was it didn't make me take the shortest route to a problem, I guessed—and pressed my mouth to his gently, taking his lips into mine. There was a faint, coppery taste there where he must have been bleeding. Whatever revulsion I might have had was shorted out by the flush of warmth that washed through me. Our eyes closed, and the kiss lingered, and in a moment I was hard and wished that being with him wouldn't put him in agony.

I don't know if the order was fulfilled or if I just needed air, but I pulled away after a time, and bit my lip as I narrowed my eyes at him. "I can't really tell if that was you or not. I mean—even if I wasn't compelled, I would have kissed you anyway."

"I could tell you to hop on one leg if you prefer," he said, smiling weakly. His eyes trailed over me, and found my hard cock standing up, bobbing as if in a light breeze. "You're so beautiful, Lucas. You don't know how much I wish I could claim you properly, right now."

I looked down at my erection, bit my lip, and toyed with it languidly as he watched. "So... when you say any command," I murmured. "How far does that go? I mean... is it just conscious actions, or...?"

His eyes lingered on my hand where I stroked myself with light fingers, only teasing myself to keep it hard, and only because I loved the way his lips parted, how his breath came audibly a little faster. I regretted it when he winced from breathing too deeply, and took my hand away.

"Ah," he breathed, "I'm not really sure to what extent it works."

"So," I mused, shifting so that I was next to him, our thighs pressed together, "if you were to... tell me to come for you... would I...?"

Tarin cut his eyes sideways at me, careful not to turn his head too far. He licked his lips, raising an eyebrow. "It's all as new to me as it is to you," he said. "Would you like that, though?"

I shrugged a shoulder. "Sort of novel. You can try. If you want, I mean. I don't mind..."

A knot of anticipation formed in my stomach as he nudged his shoulder against mine, clearly hesitating and, I thought, embarrassed. Why, I couldn't guess. I understood, of course, how he felt about the arrangement. But I didn't see why, if we were both willing, it couldn't be fun as well.

Turned around, so that I could lie down with my head near his feet, I reached for his hand. I put it on my cock, and closed his fingers around it. He gave a weak, tortured laugh. "This is unfair."

"I'm happy to get you off very gently," I told him. "If you think you can take it. My conquering hero does deserve a reward."

"Having you with me is all the reward I need," he said. "You know that I would never—"

"Tarin," I laughed, "I love you. I trust you. If it really makes you that uncomfortable—"

He gave my cock a squeeze. "Come for me, Lucas."

At first it was nothing. A bit of a thrill that I thought was just from hearing him say the words, reminding me of *other* times when he'd said them. But that thrill grew into a tremble, and it nestled down between my legs, found the root of my cock and seemed to vibrate there. I gasped at the sensation, and then arched my back as currents of pleasure converged around the length of my dick, tingled over my skin and finally released in a gush of cum that spattered over my chest. My cock twitched in Tarin's hand twice more as my head swam with the unexpected rush of it. When it was over, I laughed, marveling at the absurdity of the event. I looked down at my dribbling cock, tingling with the ghost of a release that my body gave up to Tarin in exchange for just four words. The ultimate submission.

Then I squirmed as Tarin's hand slipped up, slick with my cum, and swirled around the head of my cock. It wasn't as sensitive as it was when we took the long way around, but it still made me shake. He only teased me a little. "Well," he said. "There's your answer, I suppose. Was it good?"

"Not as good as when you do it the hard way," I answered. "But… different."

He swiped some of the spilled fluid off my stomach, and brought his fingers to his lips to suck them clean. "You taste just as good either way. But I think I agree—I like the long way. Come—ah, that is, would you come up here? I'd like to hold you."

I couldn't help smiling as I sat up, and helped him move down so that he could lie flat. I helped him until he was comfortable, and then nestled into his arm, careful to avoid putting pressure on his ribs. "What happens now?"

"Now," he said, his fingers tickling my side with slow, light caresses, "we build a house, and sow the fields, and raise goats and sheep and… live life for a while. While we can. Is that all right? It's not the glory of Camelot Legal by any stretch, I realize, but—"

"It's good," I told him. I kissed the side of his chest, wishing that my kisses could heal him faster. "It's perfect."

"I think it just might be," he agreed.

Chapter 35 - Tarin

Four weeks.

It took almost a month to recover from my injuries. Each night, I shifted for a few hours just to get away from the pain of my human body. During the day, Lucas cared for me, washed me gently in the shower, and insisted that I not put undue stress on myself. Mercy applied salves and compresses that supposedly helped promote bone health. "In humans, anyway," she admitted. "Dragons… I'm not so sure about. But they do smell nice, so it can't really hurt, right?"

Reece and Sasha helped us move into the new house. It was decided that we should take it, since we were now officially claimed, or at least, one of us was. We started making plans with Sasha for the second bedroom the day after we were settled. Lucas insisted on helping, both in the design and in the building process.

Once we had our bed moved in, we did give sex a try—but it proved to be too taxing to finish. Though I assured Lucas that I was happy to please him, he insisted on swearing off his own pleasure until I was well. After a week, though, he begged to show off for me.

It became something of a game that he turned out to thoroughly enjoy. Through the compulsion, though with his permission, I could command him to perform for me, stroking himself slowly, teasing his own cockhead the way I loved to do even though it drove him to the edge of madness—but unable to come until I allowed it. I was uneasy with it at first, but Lucas begged me, and I could not deny him.

The night that I finally was able to stretch without the pain of knives stabbing at my lungs, however, I was more than happy to see the game over.

We let the others have dinner to themselves.

"Let's try this again," I murmured in his ear, hard for him and nearly insane from craving him. "I have missed being inside you. Dreamed about it. Been struck dumb thinking about it, about being able to give you what you want, Lucas."

I spread my kisses from his lips, across his cheek and down his neck. As I did I urged him back, first against the bed and then down onto it. I laid his body out and trailed my lips and tongue over his chest, teasing the hard little nub of nipple between my teeth, tasting his smooth, soft skin as if I could sample every inch of it and never be sated. I nipped at his side, just above his hip, and he squirmed under me, giggling with quiet delight.

When he was breathing faster and gasping louder, I tugged his pants down along with his briefs, and shucked them from his legs. I cast them aside and stood a moment to survey him, to savor the sight of him. He reached between his legs to stroke himself languidly as I watched. I bit my lip, and he dipped a finger lower, beneath the taut mound of his balls to tease at his opening. His eyes invited me, and I threw off my own clothing before I climbed onto the bed between his thighs.

He was impatient for me. He wiggled his hips as I pulled his thighs up and positioned my knees under them. Like an animal in heat, he rutted against my swollen cock, trying to get me inside even before there was any possibility of entering him without pain. I grinned down at him and helped, teasing his hole with the head of my dick until he was whining with need for it.

"I'm ready," Lucas begged. "And I mean that—the hormone thing is making me fucking crazy, so... get in there, big guy. Let's do this."

I chuckled softly as I trailed my fingertips over the length of his cock, teasing the wrinkle of sensitive skin where he'd been cut as a babe. Lucas' eyebrows pinched, and he bucked his hips for more. "Tarin, *please*..."

From the tip of my cock, I milked a fat drop of precum and scooped it up with my finger. I reached between the cleft of his cheeks and spread it slowly over his hole, growling softly as he arched his back and mewled pleasure. He relaxed for me almost immediately, the muscle loosening as I dipped into him, wiggling against the inner ring until that too opened for me. Eager as I was to claim him properly, the sight of him in ecstasy was too beautiful to waste. "Sing for me, Lucas," I whispered, and worked my finger deeper until I found that secret gland inside him and stroked it slow and firm.

His hands clawed at the bed, balling up bunches of sheets into his fists as he wailed, his hips swiveling on their own as I worked the spot, teasingly gentle one moment and punishingly sharp the next. His skin flushed pink, and sweat broke out over his chest as he danced a slow, aching rhythm to my playing. ?" he breathed. "Fuck, Tarin... don't stop... make me... make me come for you..."

We had all the time we needed and more. I ran my free hand over his stomach, down over his cock with feather lightness so that it jumped to meet my touch, over his balls and down his thighs. All the while, his gland grew firmer under my assault, swelling gradually with each stroke until finally Lucas let out a strangled cry that anyone could have mistaken for a cry of fear. His body vibrated as the gland hardened, and with a final stroke his cock stood up, strained, and finally began to dribble cloudy fluid as he bucked.

"Shit," he groaned as he looked into my eyes, "shit... Tarin... fuck me... fuck..."

I held his eyes as I tracked the pulsing of his gland, applying pressure each time it throbbed, until the fluid on his stomach was a small pool, and his eyes rolled with the prolonged orgasm that kept him writhing for a long minute.

When his body simply couldn't continue, I gave him a final few teasing, gentle prods before pulling out of him. "Now we're ready," I murmured.

He licked his lips, groaning softly as he nodded. I swept my hand over his stomach, gathering what he had spilled, and used it to slick my cock. I spread some over his hole and worked it in to be sure, and added a gob of spit to the mix. When I finally angled myself to enter him, he sucked in a breath and held it as I rocked my hips forward. The head of my dick slipped in easily and a shiver ran along my spine as he closed around me, enveloping me in slippery warmth.

By inches, I eased past his entrance, and rested my hands on his stomach. His rose to meet them, holding tight as I invaded. His stomach rose and fell, his fingers clutched at mine, and when I finally sank into him to the hilt of my cock, he pulled at my arms until I leaned forward and rested my weight on him, his legs wrapped around my waist.

His lips found mine. Electric tingles passed between us, and I drew myself out of him slowly until only the head remained, then shared his breath in a sigh as I thrust back in.

"Fill me," he muttered against my lower lip. "Fill me up and make me yours, Tarin. I need it. God, you feel so good inside…"

Lucas' body moved with mine, rocking slightly as I took him slowly, filling him up with patient thrusts as he kissed me, begged for me, whispered soft prayers and curses. Heat filled me, igniting fire at the root of my cock that steadily grew each time I sank into him, pressure building until my knot began to swell. I forced it past his ring the first time, and began to pull out again but he dug his heels into my ass and pulled me back. "Inside," he breathed. "Inside, please… give me your knot, Tarin, I want it so bad. I want you, baby. My love, my mate… come with me. Claim me. Please, make me yours, Tarin…"

I needed no more encouragement. If I had wanted to hold back now, I couldn't. His hole squeezed me, held me, his body milking away any control I had left until I felt the exquisite agony of my knot filling him and bucked once more into him as every nerve lit up with release and I pumped my seed deep into him.

At the same moment, my fire rose and my body half-shifted automatically in preparation for the claiming. Lucas turned his head, exposing his neck and shoulder to me, and I bit down urgently on the tender flesh where his neck and shoulder met.

This time, heat flowed from me into him. He clawed at my shoulders, crushed me tight to him, and then cried out as his cock twitched between us, spilling more heat as I poured into him, body and soul. The stiff, hard-edged feel of him in my mind softened, opened, and his pleasure broke over the border between us as I claimed him at last. Wonder and joy flooded him, poured into me, and was answered. We passed the emotions back and forth in a feedback loop until he began to sob against my shoulder, and my own eyes burned with tears.

"Mine," I breathed into his ear. "You are mine, Lucas Warren—and I am yours."

"Thank you," he whispered.

We stayed like that, tied together and drowning in a sea of emotion, for the rest of the night, whispering sweet things between short bouts of sleep and sudden renewals of pleasure, just me and my mate. My Lucas. My love.

Mine, at last.

Chapter 36 - Lucas

By late spring, seeds were planted. Spitfire Ranch, after a great deal of paperwork and grant writing, was officially a real business. A farm with fields, sheep, and goats. And employees. I took on the paperwork both because I was familiar and because it was a soothing distraction from pregnancy. Within a few weeks of the formal 'launch' of the Spitfire Ranch, I became the official business manager.

Hiring human ranch hands was a point of contention at first. However, the wolven preferred to keep to their own territory and while Tristan and Victor agreed to stick around for extra security and two pairs of very strong hands, they weren't enough. After Reece and I went back and forth about it a few times, he agreed that we not only needed more people—but that having humans on the ranch would help deter incursions by the Templars. At first, it was easy enough having them around. After a while, though, when Matt and I started to show, it began to get more complicated. Even with a new fence put up behind the main house, Matt and I barely ever ventured outside, to ensure that none of the human employees caught on.

All of that strategizing and organizing managed to keep me busy and distracted for several months, at least during the day. At night, it was a different story.

"I'm enormous," I complained to Tarin, staring at myself in the mirror in our place. "Look at me. How is there even room?"

At eight months along, my belly was swollen like a prize watermelon, the skin taut and smooth, my navel inverted. Each day now, it seemed like I would burst.

Tarin snorted softly as he came up behind me and nuzzled at my neck. "You're beautiful, mate. And you smell delicious."

His soft growl tickled against the back of my neck. "Anything you need? How are your feet? Your back? Are you hungry at all?"

I chuckled at that. Dragon fathers, it seemed, turned into puppies as their mates swelled. It was a source of endless amusement between Matthew and I. He insisted that when he and Reece were alone, the normally grim, aggressive dragon became practically servile. "I'm okay at the moment," I answered, smiling at him in the mirror. "Just ready to have this baby and for my body to go back to normal. Matthew skimped on the details. I think you can carry the next one."

"Next one?" Tarin mused. "So we aren't done, hm?"

I shrugged. "We'll see."

"Come, sit—let me rub your feet." He tugged me toward the sofa.

There was no sense in fighting him. Tarin grew anxious and moody when I didn't let him tend my every need, even when it wasn't necessarily a need. Still, once I propped my feet on his knees and let him get to work, I didn't regret it. His thumbs hunted down tension in my arches that I had gotten used to since the morning.

"How's the search going?" I asked. "I haven't been there for the meetings with Hank since a few months ago."

Tarin grimaced. "We are pouring money into it. I've got my dragonmarked currently in China chasing down an old legend. We're up to three outcasts now searching remote places as well. I'm not optimistic, but Hank seems to be happy that we're doing the work."

"Good," I muttered, groaning as he found a spot so painful it felt good again. "I regret that I doubted your instincts, this is wonderful."

"Let that be a lesson," Tarin murmured. He coughed quietly. "Also, Mercy informed me in... detail... that *internal* massage can make the birthing process easier."

A sly smile spread over his lips as I grinned at that. "God bless that wonderful woman. When you're done down there..."

There are a lot of things I can say about Tarin—among them is that he has fingers of pure gold. By the time I was panting and spent on the bed, several hours later, I suspected that if Mercy was right about that, well... giving birth was going to be a *breeze*.

***

When it came time, four months later, a month after Matthew and Reece's son, Ronin, was born, it happened in the dead of night.

"Fuck me hard and sideways," I gasped, sitting up from a deep sleep. A rolling ache had forced me from my dreams, striking every muscle in my hips and spreading in a powerful, terrible wave all the way through my stomach and down through my back. Tarin shot up at the same moment, and I could feel the echo of my pain in his body. "Baby's coming. Shit, fuck... that's a fucking... holy god of Moses, get Mercy. Go, Tarin, go *now*, go get our fucking—*son of a...*"

Half-dressed, bleary-eyed but waking up fast, Tarin dashed from the bedroom as I waved him out. I could hear him stubbing toes and spitting curses on his way out of the house.

Minutes later, as I tried to remember everything Mercy told me about breathing correctly and the value of getting on my feet to walk around, the two of them returned, laden with bowls of water, clean towels, and swaddling cloth. Tarin was wide-eyed, panicked as he set the bowl down. "He's in a great deal of pain," he said. "Is that normal?"

Mercy eyed him sideways as she guided me to the middle of the room. "Yes," she said, "that's very normal for childbirth. Come sit over here, and try to stay calm."

Tarin was well beyond any ability to be 'calm'. His eyes shifted, and scales ghosted over his skin. He was barely in control of himself. But he did squat down next to me while Mercy laid cloths in the bowl and draped others over her knee.

"Yuri and Matt are on the way," she told me. "Just keep breathing for me, and focus on the pressure inside. In and out. In and out, that's good."

Despite Matt's descriptions and his assurances that my body was made for this, by the time he and Yuri made it, I was ready to accuse of him of lying to me. I'd never experienced pain like that before, and at every contraction Matt and Mercy both had to remind me that it was normal, that I wasn't dying, that the baby would be fine.

It took hours of screaming, and cussing, and swearing off dragon dick for the rest of my life even as Tarin held me in his arms and told me how good I was doing. *Tarin* wasn't squeezing an infant out of his body. "Stop saying that," I begged him. "I can't... I can't get the baby out... I need a hospital, and *drugs*."

"No, you don't," Mercy assured me, her soothing tone tempered with a steady, no-nonsense sort of confidence. "We're almost there. Breathe and push, Lucas, we're all here for you. You're so close. Ready?"

"No," I shouted, but I did breathe and I did push.

It took hours. Agonizing hours. But then... it was over. Pain that should have stayed with me was replaced by a swell of relief that turned every part of my body to mush as I melted back into Tarin's arms. He gave a shout of joy when it happened, when the baby was finally with us, as Mercy, Yuri, and Matt cheered us on.

The three of them cleaned me up and then tended the room once Tarin carried me and the baby to bed. "Congratulations," Mercy told the baby as she and the others prepared to leave us. "You made it. These are your daddies. Lucas and Tarin. You are gonna love them, kiddo."

Bright brown eyes, tinged through with yellow, blinked sleepily up at us. A little mouth opened wide, closed, and little limbs wiggled and reached instinctively. "Our son," Tarin said, his voice strained. "That's our son. We made that."

"We did," I crooned, laughing quietly as I nuzzled our son close. "It took a fucking year and it was awful, and I am certain my ass is never going to be the same again. But it was all worth it, little one. Every second of it. Look at you."

"Did you settle on a name?" Mercy asked.

I looked up at Tarin, smiling. We had decided only a few nights before, after months of picking and discarding and changing minds. He held out a finger to our son, and his little fingers closed around it, squeezing as if he knew that Tarin was here for him.

"Hero," I said. "His name is Hero."

It was a hope, and a promise. It was the trust between Tarin and I, that we could do this right, and that we had brought something good into the world. It was a battle fought, and won.

And there would be more. I knew. More conflicts, more danger. More obstacles between us and a secure future that we could trust.

But we would win those, as well.

Together.

Printed in Great Britain
by Amazon